FRAGILE
CHAOS

AMBER R. DUELL

FRAGILE CHAOS
© 2017 Amber R. Duell
www.amberrduell.com

www.radiantcrownpublishing.com

Duell, Amber R.
Fragile Chaos / by Amber R. Duell 1st ed.

Available as an eBook with exclusive content
ISBN-13: 978-1-946024-00-8 (Trade Paperback)
Library of Congress Control Number: 2017934549

Editing by Leah T. Brown
Maps by Tiphaine Leard
Cover design by White Rabbit Book Design
Book design by Inkstain Design Studio

Printed in the United States of America
First Edition: July 2017
10 9 8 7 6 5 4 3 2 1

FOR DAN,
I see you. I'll cover you. I respect you. Thanks for rolling the dice with me.

ASGYA

SHADOW
COVE

GULL ISLAND

PLE
VAR

KISK

HUVARIA

ONE

THEO

The musky hint of smoke follows me through the ruined Kisken city, over twisted metal and jutting pipes. The once-bustling tourist destination is hard to navigate without moonlight, but there isn't time to be careful. Not tonight. The handle of the sledgehammer digs into my shoulder as I find the edge of town and follow a line of olive trees toward the cracked highway.

With a deep breath, cold ocean air fills my lungs. War is a captivating, magnetic disorder. And it's mine. Only the God of War can decide when and how it ends, and right now I'm perfectly happy to let it rage on despite what my brother wants. He may be older, and the King of the Gods, but this is my decision.

"Theodric?"

My muscles tighten at the sound of my sister's voice—especially *this* sister—but I don't break my stride. "What are you doing here, Astra?"

She catches up to me in steel gray fatigues, her honey hair braided and tucked under a black beret. A round, blue pin with a red triangle at its center is stuck through the stiff wool. "Working," she replies.

"Right." I raise an eyebrow and scan the uniform. It suits her, despite her small frame, but it's nothing the Goddess of Love would ever think of wearing normally. Not with pride, anyway. "When did you enlist in the Asgyan army?"

She tugs at the wide, buttoned cuffs and crinkles her nose. "Most of the men and women deployed on this forsaken island have families waiting at home. If I have to wear this thing to bring a few of them peace of mind, I will."

Of course she will. She loves mortals as much as they love her, even if no one believes we exist anymore. Love is the one true universal obsession. It's said to overcome even death. Something to be longed for and placed on a pedestal. Something to live and breathe, fight and die for. But I prefer the cold, hard revenge that encompasses my heart. It's made of stronger stuff. It's reliable.

We walk in silence past barren fruit trees and thorny brush until we reach a rusted guardrail. I step over it while Astra scrambles to keep up with my long stride. Raw sewage assaults my nostrils. An icy breeze nips at the back of my neck and sends debris skating over the parched ground. The overpass isn't much farther; the pillars black shadows in the distance.

"Where are you going?" Astra asks.

I shift the hammer to my other shoulder. "Don't worry about it."

She folds her arms across her chest. "It doesn't mean you're weak if you listen to Ebris, you know. This island has been a battleground for over a year now, and we're all tired. The troops on both sides are at the end of their rope, and Kiskens are on the verge of extinction." She motions toward the flattened city behind us. "I know you don't like being told what to do, but he's right. This war is too much. It needs to stop."

"Ebris might like to think he owns me, but he doesn't," I snap. "He doesn't own *this*."

"That's not—"

"If he wants to stop the war, he should talk to Drea. She created the famine that turned Asgya into a wasteland. If she had offered them any hope, they wouldn't have turned to Volkana for help." I focus on my destination to avoid my sister's stare. It's common knowledge the Volks take any opportunity to infiltrate another country, but no one expected the Asgyans to drag the Kiskens into it. Not even me. "I'm only playing the hand I was dealt."

"Don't be a child," Astra says with an edge.

"A child? You're nineteen. Don't act like you know better than I do when you only have two years on me."

"Two *mortal* years."

A breath heaves from my lungs. Two years is still two years, even if time moves differently in our realm. "I don't interfere with Ebris' business or yours. I don't deserve this," I say.

Astra scoffs. "Ebris respects you; we all do. You're our brother and we love you but—"

I grind my feet into the pavement. None of my siblings respect me. They think I'm too young, too angry, too reckless to understand the consequences of war, but they're wrong. Understanding and caring are two different things. Lesser evils are still evil and hard choices are still hard, but someone has to make them. I turn to face her.

"Astra, go back."

"If you would only be open minded," she says in a rush. "I know you remember the Ostran War."

I stand rigid. Heat coils through my body, a spring ready to snap. I remember *everything* about that war. Including what it cost me. "That was a long time ago," I say through my teeth.

"It was a *mistake*," she says. "Look what you're reduced to. Before Ebris stripped your power, you could've fixed this with a flick of your hand."

The hammer drops to the ground with a low thud. My chest pitches under the pressure to control my breathing, to control myself. "It only became a mistake when everyone else tried to control the situation. I knew what I was doing then and I know what I'm doing now. Don't turn this into another disaster." I take a deep breath through my nose. It's no use. They have less faith in me than modern mortals. I can prove myself again and again, battle after battle, but they'll never trust me.

"I'm going to block the highway," I deadpan.

She tilts her head, her eyes narrow, and I know she's not going anywhere. "Why?"

"Why?" My laugh is bitter. As much as I want to brush my brother off completely, it would be foolish. It has to at least look like I'm trying. "Ebris wants Kisk to have a fighting chance, doesn't he?"

I skirt around a boulder, dragging the metal tool behind me, and arrive at the overpass. Abandoned vehicles line the desolate road, pushed aside by enemy tanks to clear a path. Pieces of concrete dot the ground from the half-fallen street above while wires and strips of guardrail hang precariously over our heads. Cracks run up the wide cement post holding the pavement in place, one section crumbling from impact. It won't take much to finish knocking it down. Not much, but all that I have.

"How will more destruction help?" Astra asks.

"Because." I heft the hammer. "Once the highway is blocked, the convoy heading this way will be forced onto the coastal route."

She blinks.

"Do you know who camps there?" I ask.

"Should I?" she asks flatly.

No. And that's exactly why she has no business sticking her nose in this.

"Kisken militia." I swing. The impact of metal on concrete rocks my body. "I sent word to them earlier." I swing again, and bits of debris fly back into my face. "If they're resourceful enough, their sad little band of fighters will have real weapons instead of knives and shovels by morning."

Astra shakes her head. "That's—"

"Whatever *you* do in a war zone, it doesn't involve strategizing. Go home," I shout over my shoulder.

"I'll wait." She backs away, her black military boots crunching against bits of rubble on the pavement. "We can go back together."

I hold my breath, fighting to ignore my sister's gaze on my back. The odds that she's here at the same time I am are small. Kisk is one tiny part of an entire world, and she doesn't like to witness the atrocities of war unless she has to. No, Astra didn't come here for work. She came to pressure me to stop the war like Ebris did earlier today. Like I'm sure my other three siblings will in the near future.

They don't understand. Of course they don't; I'm nothing like them. I

13

can't grow crops or help two people find each other. The sea is predictable in its unpredictable nature. And even death is accepted as part of life. But every fiber of my being is woven from the rage of mortals. Threads of petty jealousy, intense greed, and misplaced righteousness knotted together, snarling in a violent ball that is warfare. I need war the same way my siblings need air, and they're trying to suffocate me.

Anger boils under my skin, and I hit the post a third time. Then a fourth and a fifth. Each impact shudders through my tense muscles. I swing until my arms ache, until I'm panting from exhaustion. Until steel support rods groan under the weight of the overpass. I drop the sledgehammer and bolt before it buries me. Today has been hard enough without having to climb my way out from beneath two tons of cement.

It happens slowly at first. The weakened part of the pillar bends. Then larger pieces of pavement slam down with a deafening boom. The ground vibrates beneath my feet as a dust cloud swallows everything in its path. When it settles, the same gray-white powder that coats the cars covers me as well, but the job is done. No one will get around the jumbled mess.

"Do you feel better now?" Astra calls from the tree line.

I push the sleeves of my sweater to my elbows and silently retrace my steps through the city. Astra walks beside me like a ghost.

♦

Flames lick at the starless sky, the pops and crackles of a bonfire lost in a soft chorus of voices. From a distance, the two groups standing around the blaze are nothing but dark silhouettes. I throw up my mental shields, diverting their eyes. Astra does the same. If they look in our direction, their gaze will subconsciously skip over us as if we aren't there at all. There's no reason to create panic by letting them see an enemy solider strut through camp with an outsider. Especially if they heard the road collapse.

And there's no way they didn't hear it. Didn't feel it. That part of the highway is only a ten-minute walk, but no one runs. No one screams. They stand, somber, around their fire like it's just another evening. One more noise going bump in the night.

Waves crash against the rocky cliff below as Astra and I round the bottom of the hill. My temple looms above, black stone cutting into the darkness. In a few dozen steps, I'll be inside those walls, flashing back to my own realm.

I follow Astra up the first few stones set into the grassy incline before a silvery voice from below makes me falter. I shouldn't turn, shouldn't waste precious time on curiosity, but I do.

A girl in an oversized khaki jacket is sitting at the edge of the firelight's glow. Shadows flicker over her tan skin, dancing in time to the flames. She can't be more than sixteen. "Last roll," she says.

"Theodric?" Astra whispers. "What's wrong?"

I hold my hand up to silence her. There's no answer to give. I don't understand why this girl's voice caught my attention nor why it's holding it. The war shows on the girl's dirt-smeared clothes and the snarled mass of black hair knotted at the back of her head. I can't look away. There's something about the careful way her chestnut eyes dart across the city center, like she knows something she shouldn't.

15

"What is it?" Astra asks.

A gaunt man sitting across from the girl nods once. They both raise their hands and a pair of iron dice fall, clinking against a sheet of rippled aluminum. A few bounces later, the dice come to rest between them. There's a moment of stillness before the girl grabs the loaf of bread and faded blue and yellow windbreaker from the edge of their makeshift table.

"Wait," the man croaks. His hand covers hers.

"It was best two out of three," she says evenly. "A fair game."

His knuckles protrude as he strengthens his grip. "A rematch then."

"I'm sorry." She pries at his fingers, but he clamps down on her with his other hand. "Let go."

"Go ahead without me," I say to Astra, and before I realize it, I'm standing beside the man and the girl without my shields. "She said let go."

The man jumps and the girl uses the distraction to twist her hands free. She turns and looks at me. Whatever response I was expecting from her, it wasn't this harsh glare. I stare back until the man pushes up from the piece of fallen wall he was using as a chair.

"Wait. Take this." She rips the bread in two and holds the smaller end out to him. He snatches it from her, barring yellow teeth, and trudges away, stumbling on the uneven ground. She tugs the collar of her jacket tight around her chest and shakes her head. Then her eyes snap back across the table to me. "I didn't need your help."

She shoves the half-loaf into a messenger bag on her lap followed by the windbreaker. *She didn't need my help?* That man would've fought her and, frail as he looked, he would have won. He's too desperate not to. But I'm too

16

tired from fighting about the war with my siblings all day to argue again with someone else, so I bite my tongue.

Snatching up one of the iron dice, I roll it between my fingers. *Fate Dice.* An odd choice for someone who doesn't believe in the gods. She doesn't. I don't have to ask. The believers—all fourteen of them—prowl the temple in woven black robes. This set of dice is high quality, though—heavy, with intricately carved symbols on each of the six sides, one for each god, and intertwining vines along the edges. They belonged to someone with money. Perhaps someone who died in the bombings, their things left to be plundered by a young girl in a khaki coat.

"Care for another round?" I ask.

"Not tonight." She holds out her hand for the die. "I already got what I came for."

"No stakes." I take the recently vacated seat across from her, and a thrill runs up my spine. I grind my teeth against the need to talk to her. There's no time for distraction while I'm working. During times of peace, it's easy enough to waste days away with a bit of mortal fun but not now. Never now. I have to remain neutral. "For fun."

"No."

A laugh flies from my mouth. At least one of us has some sense. "Please?" I tilt my head.

She fidgets uncomfortably, eying my hand. "They don't like strangers here. You should leave."

I glance at the two groups around the fire: One of bedraggled Kisken survivors, perhaps twenty total, with filthy, threadbare clothes. The other, four

17

men from the temple. Each stays as close to the fire and as far from each other as possible.

"And you?" I ask. "How do you feel about strangers?"

Her stare cuts through me like a hot knife. "You're not Kisken."

It's an accusation, not a question. My skin is almost as bronze as hers, my hair just as black, and if it weren't for my blue eyes, I could easily pass as a fellow islander. "Not fully, no." *I'm everything and I'm nothing—the original race that all others stem from.* "I'm not here to hurt anyone, if it makes you feel better."

She rolls her eyes. "Forgive me if I don't trust someone skulking around in the middle of the night after what I heard a few minutes ago."

She's referring to the overpass collapsing, but it isn't fear I see in her expression. It's unwavering certainty. Of what, I'm not sure. I toss the die up and catch it midair. "I'm not skulking. Three rolls. Each round I win, I get to ask a question."

She inches forward on her seat and clears her throat. "And if I win?"

A grin breaks free of my control. "Win once and you can ask me something. Twice and I'll go away."

She glances at the fire over my shoulder before pinching her lips together. "Fine."

I ignore the expanding sensation in my chest. There's no reason to play a game with this girl and every reason to walk away. Instead, I ask, "Ready?"

She nods and we drop our dice. Hers lands on a crown—*king*—and mine on a black dot—*death*. My win. But I pause. I had no specific question in mind when I suggested this. It was merely a way to hear her speak again. To learn something about her, maybe a clue about why she caught my attention. What she likes. What she hates. Although, I'm fairly certain the answer to the latter

18

is *me* at the moment.

"I don't know anything useful," she warns.

"I'm not a spy." I pull my winning die back before she can get any ideas of quitting early. "What's your name?"

Her shoulders rise and fall with each slow breath. "Why?" she asks, her expression pensive.

"Why not?"

After another moment of silence, she sighs. "Cassia."

"Cassia." Like the flower, delicate and graceful. It almost suits her, but she seems tougher, able to weather harsher conditions. With a smile, I hold my palm out in the Kisken greeting and wait for her to touch it with her fingertips. "I'm Theo."

She scans the area again, ignoring my gesture. "I didn't ask your name."

"That man didn't ask to split the bread, either." I pull back and rub my hand on my jeans.

Cassia picks up her die and gives it a small flick with her fingers. "Love," she says when it lands on an infinity symbol. "You lose."

"I haven't rolled yet." I drop the die but I had to hope for the same or a wave—*water*—to roll again. It stops on a flower—*life*. My loss. "Your question?"

"There's nothing I want to know." She swipes up her die and shakes it in her fist. "Again."

Both iron pieces drop just as an argument breaks out near the fire. A low rumble of voices, unclear but distinctly unhappy, fill the air. The flames smolder in Cassia's eyes as her gaze darts between two points behind me. Her chin jerks toward the table, and she snatches the dice with stiff movements.

19

"Your win." Her voice is light but the unevenness gives her away.

"Why do you fear them?" I ask without thought.

Her breath hitches, and I feel a small pang of regret. She doesn't owe me her secrets. Not for winning in a game of chance. Before I can change the question, a shrill scream shatters the night. Jumping from the rubble, my hand falls to the hip my broadsword usually hangs from. I left it home tonight, expecting nothing a sledgehammer couldn't fix.

A middle-aged survivor claws at the face of a man in black while two others pull the attacking woman away. She screeches again, lunging forward, but they keep their grip on her arms. The rest of the group closes in.

Blood runs from the man's scratches as other believers drag him, shouting a string of obscenities colorful enough to raise my eyebrows, toward the stairs where Astra still stands. We lock eyes for a brief moment, before she darts toward the temple to avoid being run over. I fight against a shiver. Tensions run high in hard times, but it feels like more than a common squabble. Heavier.

"What was that about?" I ask.

But when I turn, Cassia is gone. I squint into the darkness but it's still as death. Needles of disappointment scrape through me. I shake the sensation off. It's better not to get involved anyway.

That doesn't stop me from glancing over my shoulder again before I rush up the hill behind the zealots.

TWO

CASSIA

A halo of orange hugs the sun as it rises over the coastline, painting the sky pink. I watch the world usher in a new day perched on rusty monkey bars in the old park playground. It won't be much different than the last, but in the first quiet hours of morning it's easy to pretend there's no war. That my parents aren't dead and my brother, Oren, wasn't hanged for treason. For a moment, I can forget how alone I am.

I don't blame the Kiskens for refusing to let me stay with them. Their loved ones are dead and their homes reduced to dust because of Oren, but I was only fourteen at the time. Fifteen when the bombs dropped over a year ago. It isn't fair to make me shoulder his mistakes. But that's the thing, nothing's fair.

Zipping my jacket against the chill, I slip between the metal bars onto solid ground. The others will still be tucked away in the remaining wing of the mall, sleeping soundly out of the elements. I have roughly thirty minutes to drop supplies and run. They know I'm the one leaving the scavenged items— clothes, shoes, photo albums. It doesn't make them like me, but it's not like I have anything better to do with my days. And, although I shouldn't, I *do* feel a little guilty.

I grab my messenger bag from where it hangs on the handle of the slide and make my way toward the old city center. The cracked fountain at the bottom of the hill is full of black ash, wisps of smoke still rising from tiny red embers. Vendors used to set up stands for tourists here, so there wasn't much to destroy when the bombs hit. But the cobblestones are uneven now. The path to the cliff's edge where visitors went for the ocean view is gone, but it's still the closest thing we have to normal.

I slip the bag off my shoulder and kneel, pulling out yesterday's spoils. I would've left the ripped blanket and pair of socks last night after I won the bread if my opponent hadn't tried to cheat me. And if Theo hadn't delayed me.

Theo.

My head snaps to the aluminum table at the edge of the center, and I frown. Strangers don't pass through, and they certainly don't do it in the middle of the night. Not for any good reason, anyway. Not when the north, south, and east are crawling with troops that will shoot first and ask questions later. The only thing west is the ocean.

Theo couldn't be much older than me, but he was gorgeous. I don't know who he's fighting for or where he comes from, but I'll give him that much. The sharp angles of his face, the slight stubble on his cheeks, the cords of muscle running through his forearms. *That smile.* I've never seen eyes so blue before.

22

Maybe he's one of the zealots, transferring from a foreign temple. Rumor has it they stockpile everything during times of peace in their fortress atop the hill—food, soap, razors, shampoo— to entice people to convert during wars. Theo was well-fed and smelled sharply of steel instead of rotting onions, so it would make sense.

Except I've never seen the zealots recruiting. They hide in their temple, pretending they're untouchable while the rest of us pay for our disbelief. Last night was the first I've seen of them in months.

I set the things down beside the fountain with a sigh. The air shifts. An eerie stilling. The hair on the back of my neck rises as I stand. Before I can turn, a dark sack is thrown over my head. My heart slams against my chest and, for a moment, I forget how to move. Then my father's self-defense lessons come rushing back. I twist my head to the side, bend my knees, and haul the attacker over my body. He lands with a grunt and I run, ripping the sack off as I go. Voices rise up behind me. They're close and getting closer.

My joints ache with fear. I pump my arms, refusing to give into the urge to freeze. If I stop...I can't stop. Two men in black are almost on my heels.

Zealots.

The glance back throws me off balance, and I trip into thick debris. I grab a coiled pipe to stop from face-planting, but my hip crashes into a steel frame. Pain rolls over me like a wave. I swallow hard and shove to my feet.

A wide arm hooks my waist, lifting me off the ground. I scream until my throat burns. No one will come though, no matter how much I cry for help. I swing my legs back. My heel cracks against a shin, and my captor staggers.

"Hold her." A man with jagged scratch marks on his face limps over to us.

A silver handgun gleams in his hand, and my heart lurches. "I don't want to use this, but I will," he says.

I spit in his face, and his smug look disappears. "What do you want?" I growl.

"This isn't about me, Cassia. It's about Kisk." He jerks the gun and a second man comes from behind to grab one of my arms. Together, the two men drag me toward the base of the hill. "Quickly. We can't lose the dawn."

My pulse races. There's only one reason I can think of to take someone like me to the temple. Sacrifice is illegal, but chickens and goats still came up missing from farms across the country before the war. There's no livestock left now, but there's also no police or government officials to hold anyone responsible for murder.

And no one will miss me.

No. I can't think like that.

I slam into the man holding my right arm, but, even though he staggers, his grip stays strong. We start up the grassy hill and I know it's now or never. Kicking out, I slam the soles of my sneakers against an uneven stone step and press back, locking my knees.

"Calm down," the gunman says. "We're offering you a way to earn a place among your countrymen again."

As a dead girl.

No one holds a grudge against the deceased—not unless your last name is Stavros. Then they'll curse you all the way to the grave and toss your family onto the street.

My sneakers slip, morning dew still coating the ground, and I scramble to regain control of my legs. If I can kick one of their knees out, he'll have to let go to stop us all from tumbling backward.

"It's a long way down," the man adds as if he's reading my mind.

He's right. We're too far up the hill to end the fall uninjured, but broken and bruised is better than corpse. I'm more sorry than anyone can know that my brother brought us into this war, but I won't die for it. I twist sideways and sink my teeth into the man's upper arm. He screams and a fist lands on my jaw. My vision blurs and a deep throbbing pain takes over.

"What are you doing? She's not to be harmed."

"She bit me," the man snarls.

"Listen." I fight to drag in a breath. "You don't have to do this."

"The whole city agrees it's for the best," the gunman says.

The whole city?

It doesn't make sense that the other Kiskens would agree to anything the zealots proposed. They may hate me but they think the believers are certifiable. Obviously, they're right. Sane people don't haul people off to slaughter. I stretch my jaw side to side and relax into them. All I need is one second with their guard down. One fleeting moment of distraction, and I'll make a break for it.

The hill flattens at the top. A round three-story stone building towers over us with two levels of roofs and five turrets evenly spaced around the perimeter. My breath catches when I notice the only windows are long narrow slits I would be lucky to fit an arm through, let alone my whole body.

A pair of massive wooden doors groan open, the only entrance I see, and the men rush forward, dropping me in a dim inner chamber. Dusty red banners hang from the ceiling, following each solid stone wall to the floor. An altar is directly across the main chamber with a matching red cloth adorned with a black shield. A polished sword lies across the surface. I stay on my knees to hide how badly my legs are shaking and scan the rest of the room for an escape route.

There's a pit in the center of the floor. A circular opening, big enough for a large man to fit in with ease, seems to lead straight to the center of the universe. Bile rises in my throat. A mythology textbook in school painted a vivid picture of what happens there.

Not to me.

"Cassia, welcome." A round woman with gray streaked hair shuffles forward in a flowing black robe. A small silver shield is pinned to her left shoulder. "I'm glad you decided to join us today."

A man slithers up beside her, his face deep-set with wrinkles, and takes the gun from the man with the marred face. I'll need to get it before I escape. If I can get him alone, it shouldn't be hard. He's too old to put up much of a fight. Then I'll have to find an exit without raising any alarms. I'll only get one chance; I can't rush it.

"*Decided* is a strong word," I say.

The woman's laugh bounces off the high-domed ceiling. "We won't keep you long. This is High Priest Ciro and I'm Nessa, the Temple Mother."

"Yeah. Great." It doesn't matter who they are, only that they can shoot me. "What do you want?"

"We thought you might like the chance to help Kisk." Ciro motions a young boy with a wooden cup forward. "If you make tributes to the gods, perhaps they'll listen."

"Me?" I rub a hand over the ache in my chest. They nod. *Exit, exit, exit.*

26

I don't remember seeing another door from the outside, but I never paid attention before today. What kind of temple devoted to a war god wouldn't have the foresight to make an emergency escape? It seems like a lesson in War 101: *In case of a siege, have multiple ways out.* "I don't even believe in your gods. This is the first time I've even been near this place. Why would they listen to anything I say?"

"You will believe. It's impossible to give tribute and not feel their power." Ciro takes the cup from the boy and holds it out to me. "Drink this."

I blink, looking between him and Nessa. They can't be serious. Yet, deep down I know they are. This is their life, as outdated as it is. Everything they do is to keep Theodric happy, and right now their God of War is angry with the island.

Incense wafts down from a hanging metal bowl, a line of thin white smoke snaking through the temple. I struggle to inhale. "I'll pass, thanks," I say around a cough.

"It purifies you for the tributes," Nessa says. "You need to drink it."

I cross my arms. If these tributes really do end in sacrifice, I'm not going to be an accessory to my own murder. "I'm not thirsty."

Ciro raises the gun to my chest and my mouth runs dry. "This doesn't have to be difficult."

My stomach lurches as the sandalwood smoke continues to saturate the cool, musty air. Saliva fills my mouth but I won't throw up. They don't get to see me weak. "I'm sure your War God would rather hear from one of his believers."

With a snap of his fingers, Ciro signals the men back to my side. "Last chance."

"I'm not drinking that." There's more attitude in my voice than I intend. Definitely more than is smart under the circumstances.

The men shove down on my shoulders and press against my heels with their feet until my legs begin to slide out from under me. I reach out to grab them for balance, but they brush my hands away. Finally, I slip. My head slams hard against the stone and the room spins. Stars twinkle in front of my eyes. By the time things right themselves, Nessa is straddling my chest.

Sweat rolls down my temples and tremors wrack my body. *I have to get out of here* now.

"She bites," one of the men warns.

"Come on, dear," Nessa says, ignoring him. I slam my lips shut and try to buck her off, but she's too heavy. The hands holding me down are too tight. Nessa snaps her fingers. "The funnel."

The same boy that brought the cup rushes over with a blue plastic cone. A long clear tube curls from the end. I thrash under Nessa's weight. My body tingles with adrenaline as I push and pull against them. The sound of Ciro pulling the hammer back on his gun grates in my ears. I freeze.

"Open," the woman says.

I shake my head and she pinches my nose. The seconds tick on until my lungs scream for oxygen. Instead of gasping for it like I want, I crack my lips while keeping my jaw tight, but it's all the opening she needs.

The tube rams inside my mouth and slams against my molars. I fling my head sideways, but a pair of sweaty palms squeeze against my ears. A bitter liquid floods my mouth. I gag. Nessa yanks the tubing away and holds my jaw shut with the heel of her hand. I try to block the drink from slipping down my throat, but it sneaks around my tongue, pooling at the back of my mouth. Eventually, I have no choice but to swallow.

"That wasn't so hard, was it?" Nessa stands and the men haul me back to my feet.

"Screw you," I breathe.

"Do the tributes and this can all end," Ciro says.

I straighten my back. "I won't."

"You will." Ciro gives me a little push toward the first of five stone arches.

I plant my feet. "Touch me again and I'll cut your hands off."

"With what?" he asks. "Now, go. We're on a schedule."

I inch forward while keeping the weapon in sight. Inside the rounded alcove, Nessa waits at a small altar with an elaborately scrolled silver box. Something warm and round is pressed into my hand from behind, but I'm only partially aware.

"This is the altar of Ebris," she begins. "All you have to do is say the words: *Ebris, King of Gods, please accept this tribute.* Then leave the coin in the chest."

I glare at the box as static begins to crackle and pop in my head. "That's it?"

She nods. "Go ahead."

I sigh, my body prickling with heat, and repeat the words. Then I set the coin on a bed of blue velvet before shutting the lid. There's no otherworldly sensation. No gusts of wind or clap of thunder. It's too easy. Years ago a man saved a little boy from drowning in the town pool. His front stoop was littered with flowers, candles, and casserole dishes for a month. These are gods they're talking about; the zealots will need more than this if they want to gain favor.

There's just as much non-reaction when I plant a peach pit in a pot of soil for Drea, Goddess of Life. When I rinse my hands in water for Brisa, Goddess of the Sea, I'm shocked to find I can't feel the water. I see it gliding over my

29

fingers but I can't *feel* it. I tilt my head and examine the beads of water clinging to my knuckles. My pulse loses its rhythm. I want to panic, but my mind won't let me. I pinch myself until blood wells beneath my nails. *Nothing.* I try to wiggle my toes in my sneakers, hoping to feel the rough fabric of my socks, but I can't tell if I'm succeeding.

"What did you give me?" I ask.

"The robana bean is a traditional purifier for the gods." Nessa smiles, silently guiding me to the fourth alcove.

White-hot anger fizzles in my gut, but it won't help; the zombie drug will make sure of that. It's already latched onto my control. If I don't find a way out now, I never will. But I *can't* leave. Not now. Not without help. I'll never make it down the hill alone. If I do, what then? I won't be able to move without someone telling me to once it's in full effect.

Try.

The word feels far away. My teeth click together, the only thing telling me I'm shaking, and Nessa hands me a book of matches. A fuzzy part of my brain screams, *Fire! Set the place ablaze. Escape. Run.*

Run.

"Light the candle," she says.

My fingers shake as I try to strike the match. The flimsy stick snaps, and I fumble to free another from the inside flap. Nessa finally takes pity and strikes the flint herself, setting it carefully between my fingers. I mumble the same mantra I said at the first three altars. "Astra, Goddess of Love, please accept this tribute." The words are mine. I hear my voice speaking them, but I don't feel my lips moving.

"Good." She takes the matches and ushers me back into the main chamber. Ciro waits with a wide smile, the gun still in his hand, and I blanch. "One more and then you can have a bath."

A bath will be nice.

My insides smolder. No. It won't be nice. It will be bad. Very bad. I have to run. Run...somewhere. Because...There's a reason. I'm sure of it.

Under the final archway, a tall, smooth bowl sits on the altar with a needle-like blade beside it. "Stab it," Nessa instructs.

"Stab..." My breath rasps. I lean forward to peer in the bowl. A long brown rat sits on its haunches, staring back. I've never killed anything bigger than a spider. There are some big spiders in Kisk, but still. Definitely never anything cute and fuzzy. Never anything that could look as terrified as this rodent does with its beady eyes and puffed out whiskers.

Nessa takes a deep breath. "Do you think we gave her too much?" she whispers to Ciro. He whispers back, but I don't understand. "I'll help. Start with the words."

"Le...Leander, God of Death." My tongue fills my mouth and I scowl at the creature. *What am I doing?* "Please ac...accept this tribute."

The ivory handle of the blade finds my palm. Nessa's fingers blend perfectly around mine. I can't tell where my hand ends and hers begins. There's no time to think before the tiny sword plunges mercilessly down at the brown rat. A high-pitched squeal echoes through the small room and the poor thing twitches. Its sides move with rapid, worried breaths for another moment before it falls limp.

My knees buckle but Ciro is there. The gun is gone, probably tucked safely away somewhere beneath the black robes. He carries me from the final alcove and down a flight of stairs behind Theodric's altar. I watch the doors disappear on the other side of the temple.

The doors. They were important before. I can't remember why.

Fluorescent bulbs hang bare on the ceiling of a yellow room at the bottom of the steps. An oval pool, filled to the brim with milky white liquid, is set into the ground.

Not a pool. A smile curls on my lips. *A bath.*

Ciro sets me in a wicker chair beside a rolling trolley covered in assorted bottles. "I'll wait outside."

Nessa descends upon me, pulling at my clothes and cutting the rubber band from my snarled hair. I let her even though I never would've allowed anyone to see me naked thirty minutes ago. When she eases me into the bath, it's worth it. The scent of jasmine makes my eyelids flutter shut. I giggle as a cup of water splashes over my head. Stiff fingers rub circles against my scalp before more water flows over me. She washes my hair three times before scrubbing my body with a rough sponge.

Pull her in. Hold her under.

I fight a yawn. Why shouldn't I be here? It's rather nice. There's a *bath.* And the tributes have been painless.

Not for the rat.

"Out you come," Nessa says.

She hoists me up, patting me dry much too soon, and produces a white wrap dress. The gauze-like material slips over my shoulders and cinches shut with a wide ribbon. I glance down at the elbow length sleeves and examine the intricate white embroidery there. "Pretty," I say.

"Hold still." Her fingers work through my wet hair, twisting it into a low, tight bun. Bobby pins scrape the nape of my neck, but all I feel is slight pressure. "There. Done."

She leads me from the room and Ciro nods. He helps me climb the stairs myself this time. There are a lot of them. It didn't feel like this many on the way down. "You should put in an elevator," I mumble.

The main room is full of men and women in black. More than I expect. A dozen, at least. I thought only a handful lived here. My head lolls to the side. "I think you made a mistake," I whisper into Ciro's ear. "My dress is the wrong color."

"It's not a mistake." He pats my shoulder. "Thank you for your sacrifice, Cassia Stavros."

I giggle again. *What is wrong with me? Get out! Go!*

"The next part is simple." He walks toward the altar. "After this, it will all be over."

"Okay." I totter after him.

"Stand here." Ciro lifts me by my upper arms and sets me on my feet in the pit. It's taller than I am by at least two feet.

Pit. The pit.

My brain claws at the fog shrouding my rational thought.

"Theodric." Ciro's voice booms through the cavernous main room. "God of War, please accept this sacrifice for the good of Kisk. Save us from the enemies that plague us. Bring us peace."

The sword from the altar looks heavy in his hand as he looms over the opening. *When did he pick that up?* I stretch onto my toes, trying to connect

33

the dots, but it's too hard to think. *Pit. Sword. Sacrifice.* I shake my head, but it only sends a wave of dizziness crashing over me.

"Wait." My voice is a hoarse whisper.

I reach up, trying to find purchase so I can pull myself up, and Ciro snatches my wrist. His outline is blurry. I catch the flash of the blade a moment before it slices down my forearm in one swift, clean motion.

Blood pours down my elbow and splashes at my feet. *This should hurt.* But it doesn't. I stare, transfixed, at the crimson river.

This should definitely, absolutely hurt.

Then blackness creeps into my vision, swallowing me into nothingness.

THREE

THEO

Usually I relish the aroma of old paper mixing with the sharper scent of metal that emanates from the wall of weapons. Swords and shields, guns and grenades, all arranged on either side of the solid French doors leading from the war room to the rest of the mansion. Books and maps are scattered throughout the rest of the room. They hang from walls, cover tables, and line shelves. My personal sanctuary—the place every war ever waged began and ended.

But today I find no solace here. The prayers of the Kisken high priest buzz through my head, a soft, incessant whisper, making it impossible to concentrate on anything else. It's my fault. Ciro hasn't been this pious in months. I thought he had finally given up begging for help, and I became careless maintaining the mental block.

I lay on the padded bench beneath a tall, arched window with my eyes shut and concentrate on stacking the imaginary wall higher. Each brick dulls his murmurs. Every layer of mortar brings me closer to sanity. The last thing I want to listen to all day is *Theodric, hear our prayers* over and over. And over. Not when I have to deal with the result of the blocked highway, whatever it may be. Once I've reclaimed my privacy, I'll check the briefs from my spies to see who ended up with the weapons. But so help me, if the Kiskens couldn't manage one small convoy...

"Theodric?" I groan at the sound of my adviser's voice and lace my fingers over my abdomen. Boots thud in the entryway, almost a run, before the door to the war room slams open. "Theodric," he says between heavy breaths.

"Not now, Goran." I sigh and squint at the ceiling. "Just leave the reports on the desk."

"Yes, *now.*" The blond general looms over me with hard brown eyes. Red splotches coat his pale cheeks. "We have a problem."

"What?" I glower at him. "Did the road block fail? I can't handle another visit from Ebris right now."

"There's a new sacrifice in the temple," he blurts.

I sit up and grab the reports from his hand. Ciro mentioned one earlier, but I hoped he hadn't gone through with it. There isn't much more I can do for Kisk without soldiers. The only government sanctioned ones left on the island are from Asgya or Volkana, and all they're interested in is killing each other. "Does he seem useful? Do you have any idea what they want in exchange?" Goran remains quiet while I flip open the first folder and skim the pages. He's never silent. "What is it?"

"It's..." He pauses.

I exhale, my agitation growing the further I get into the report. "Asgya commissioned a new fleet with nonexistent funds, and a rebellion is stirring. Volkana is clustering forces on their eastern border, and this priest won't stop today. I don't have the patience for this. Take him to the Wall if you think it's manageable, and I'll factor in the sacrifice when we strategize this afternoon." I swing my feet to the ground, standing, and toss the reports on the desk beside a rolled canvas.

When I turn to Goran, he's wringing his hands, too nervous to speak. He's been with me long enough to know what that means. "There's more," I say.

"It's a girl," he answers in a hushed voice.

I stand still as stone. It takes a moment to register, but when it does, rage explodes through my body, sending heat racing across my skin. The legs of the desk scrape the floor as I push away from it. The words barrel through me, stealing the air from my lungs. "Will they never learn?" I shout.

I have never, since the beginning of time, accepted a female sacrifice. The mortals always believe their offering will be more appealing than the last—prettier, sweeter, stronger. That I'll change my mind this once, and they'll be saved. Swaying one battle in exchange for another manservant is one thing; with my power limited I need them. But no woman is worth giving up control of a war. An *entire* war.

"Kisk?" I ask. None of the other high priests have been bothering me with sacrificial mutterings. Or any mutterings at all, for that matter.

"By the looks of her," Goran says.

I grab my leather scabbard from where it leans in the corner and strap the broadsword to my hip. The scroll work is minimal—a simple lattice running

37

along one side, making the hilt of the sword with its ribbed center and ruby end the focal point. Dispatching a bride to the Netherworld with it is usually nothing more than a simple inconvenience; a quick walk to the temple and it's over in a matter of minutes. With Ebris breathing down my neck, it's a disaster. I'll hear about it when he finds out exactly how desperate the Kiskens are. But, regardless, the girl has to meet the same fate as the others. I can't afford to do anything else.

"Are you sure?" Goran asks.

"Each time you ask that, and each time I have the same reply," I say in a low, steady voice. Colored glass pieces tremble on the war table, shifting positions, falling, when I brush against the curved base on my way out. "I don't need to be obliged to anyone. You know this."

He hurries after me. "Of course I do, but maybe we could find something else to do with her. You aren't technically accepting if…"

If I don't take her as my bride. A loophole I've always known but never bothered to use to my advantage. These girls come here for one reason: to save their country. They aren't likely to accept my decision to remain neutral. To do what's best for the war as a whole. It would mean their death was for nothing; that their loved ones would still perish.

"I don't need her wandering about distracting me, either," I say.

"If you insist," he grumbles.

"You don't have to like it, Goran." He follows me across the tan marble flooring of the entryway. Past granite statues of men in different suits of armor and dark paneled walls. "I keep you around for your military expertise, not your opinion on would-be brides."

"You don't listen to me in either arena," Goran says. I scowl at him over my shoulder, but he simply shrugs. "It's true. I don't know why you bother asking."

"I *didn't* ask." I open the front door, scrolls of wrought iron trapped between glass, and step into the morning sun. "And just because I don't agree with you, doesn't mean I don't listen."

Servants scatter from the courtyard, rushing back to the safety of the surrounding wall, as I storm down the stoop. I continue across the gravel, crossing under a stone archway. The roof of the temple skims the horizon. My steps are steady along the dirt path leading down the hill. With a simple swing of my sword, I can go back to blocking the priest and planning my next move.

Goran sprints to keep up. "I feel I should add that she wasn't a willing sacrifice."

"Why?" I crack my thumbs inside my fists and try to stuff the shock back down. "Do you think it will save her? Or do you think I should punish Kisk for the insult?"

"Punish Kisk?" he repeats in a dull voice. "I'm not sure it's possible without annihilating the entire race."

I grunt. If left alone, Kiskens could repopulate within a few generations. The refugees would need to return, though. But, considering the level of destruction, they won't. There's nothing to save and no immediate opportunities to rebuild. The island will belong to whoever wins the war. Rejecting the girl's sacrifice, letting her continue to the Netherworld, is punishment enough.

Goran darts ahead of me and pushes the temple doors inward. Light spills into the main chamber and, unlike most sacrifices that call out for help, this one is screaming her lungs out. No words, just a piercing shriek, high enough to make me wince.

"Was she doing this when you were here earlier?" I ask, rubbing my ears.

"It might be *because* I was here," he half-shouts over the noise. "When I was collecting the reports, she started going off about being drugged and murdered. I left without engaging her but perhaps that wasn't the best course of action."

I cringe. The sacrificial rite must begin at dawn and take no longer than an hour—she's been in the pit for awhile now. I lead the way into the main chamber and wave a hand in the girl's direction. "Pull her out. Let's get this over with."

Goran gives me a long glare before kneeling by the circular pit. When the girl falls quiet, my ears continue to ring. Loud, gasping breaths spill from the opening. The tips of her fingers dance along the edge. They're tinged red, the nails ripped and torn. How long has she been clawing at the smooth walls?

"It's okay." Goran smiles. "You don't have to worry. I'll help you out."

Her fingers snap back into the darkness.

"Give me your hand," Goran says in an encouraging voice.

Silence wrings through the temple, almost as deafening as the screams. Ciro's prayers buzz in the back of my mind, and the threads of my patience begin to fray. I step forward to yank her up myself when she speaks.

"Are you one of the zealots?" she asks.

Zealots. Such an ugly term for the true followers. I inhale and Goran glances over his shoulder with a cocked eyebrow.

"I'm not," he says. He tugs the sleeve of his sweater up to get a better grip. "Let's get you out of there."

I glare at the domed ceiling, at the long piece of sculpted iron hanging down from its center like a javelin, and wait. Goran doesn't always have to be so nice to them. Simply bring the girl up so I can remove her head, and she'll be in a better place. But I keep my mouth shut. It makes Goran complain less and makes the girl easier to deal with. With him, they come out of the pit without a fight and are gone without suspecting a thing. Mostly. Before, when I pulled them out myself, they knew as soon as they saw the sword, and their screams put this girl's to shame.

A tan hand wraps around Goran's pasty wrist. He braces himself against the altar opposite the pit. With one swift tug, a young, dark-haired girl lands face first on the temple floor. She leaps up, the white sacrificial gown floating around her bare feet, and bolts for the open door.

"Wait." Goran catches her hand. This temple is a mirror of the one in Kisk. She must not realize the ritual is finished, that she's here instead of her own island. "This isn't what you think."

"Wh—"

"Enough." I straighten my shoulders and they both freeze.

In one fluid motion, I pull the blade from its scabbard and swing toward her bare neck. She sees it coming, but I'm moving too fast for her to get out of the way. Then, at the last moment, my gaze flickers to her face, to the chestnut eyes, wide with terror. My arm stills, the edge of the sword resting against her flesh. A line of blood glides down her smooth skin, seeping into her neckline.

"Cassia?"

She stares at me, unblinking. Then a flash of recognition lights her expression and she gasps. "Theo?"

The grungy girl from last night has been transformed into a pious sacrifice.

41

The white dress is snug, highlighting her curves, unlike her bulky jacket. She's thinner than I thought. Smaller. Her hair, once a snarled mess, is neatly brushed back into a tight bun, and she glows with the after effects of a good scrub. The scent of jasmine wafts from her body and my jaw tightens. Each moment we stare at each other, the air grows thicker with unspoken accusations.

"You weren't with the believers," I grind out. "Did you find the Gods overnight?"

She doesn't move. Doesn't speak. Barely draws breath. She watches me with a wild expression as she begins to tremble. My grip tightens on the bronze hilt. I've never known any of them before. Never been curious. I shouldn't be now. I need to finish this before it's too late, and continue this war on my own terms. There's no room for distraction, no matter who the pretty face belongs to. She's nothing to me. I've barely thought of her since returning.

And yet, I have thought of her.

Briefly.

Twice. Once before falling asleep and again when I woke up, before the prayers took over.

My sword clatters to the floor, a chorus of clangs echoing off the walls. I run a hand through my hair and turn away. Heat rises in my tightening chest. I have to do it. I can't let her stay.

I *can*.

I shouldn't.

A sharp, metallic scrape rings against stone behind me. "No," Goran shouts.

I spin on my heel to see Cassia hefting my sword with two hands. Or trying to. The tip never leaves the ground. Goran reaches her first and pries it from her stiff fingers.

"I'm not dying today," she says in a shaky voice. "I'm not."

I take the sword from Goran and point it at her chest. "Technically, you're already dead."

She winces. "I'm not dying *twice* today."

My nostrils flare. She's one more in a long line of girls. A mortal. She would've died in a handful of decades anyway. Maybe sooner given the war.

"Theodric?" Goran's voice is laced with worry and shock.

I know if I look at him and see even a trace of victory I'll change my mind, so I focus on the floor instead. "Take her to the house." The words burn their way from my throat.

Cassia gapes at the gleaming blade as I step close to Goran. I slip the onyx ring off my middle finger and press the band into his palm, giving him a piece of what little power I still have. "Go down there. I want to know everything about her before the end of the day," I whisper. "And watch your back."

Goran opens his mouth to speak but shuts it in favor of a single nod.

I leave them, retracing my steps to the mansion in a blind fury.

This can't be a coincidence. Granted, Kisk doesn't have many options for a sacrifice, but the one girl I showed any interest in? The believers didn't know me. They couldn't recognize me. Not that they were paying any attention to us. Astra said she couldn't hear what they were talking about before the woman attacked, but I have a sneaking suspicion it was this. Sacrificing Cassia. Somehow they were put up to this.

Ebris.

He can't get me to stop the war by asking nicely, so he's decided to play dirty. The high priest wouldn't dare send an unwilling sacrifice unless he was

43

influenced to. Desperate or not, it's a slap in Drea's face to steal a life, and the Kiskens can't afford to offend her right now. Not when she could cut the heart from the island and let it die a slow, agonizing death.

A servant stands in the courtyard, raking footprints from the fine, black gravel. He freezes as I rush forward, the rake paused mid-swipe. "Move," I say without slowing. He darts to the side and scrambles away from the house. I don't see if he disappears into the outer wall; I'm already inside, slamming the door to the war room.

I toss the broadsword onto the long table covered in maps and grip the back of a wooden chair. A thin strip of blood shines along its edge. The more I try to calm my rapid breaths, the harder my lungs fight to inhale. *What did I do?* I shove the chair aside and snatch a paperweight from the desk, hurling it at the bookshelves.

The glass ball explodes in a shower of tiny, glittering black shards. I pant as it scatters over the floor. *What* didn't *I do?* Whatever game Ebris is playing, he's playing it well. And I'm playing right into it. I should march back to the temple and finish Cassia before it's too late. Before she gets anywhere near the Wall or steps foot in this house.

But, it's already too late. I panicked when I recognized her. I shouldn't have but I did. Now the thought of killing her paralyzes me. Death is too permanent to leave unanswered questions. I need to know why I hesitated, but, sacrifice or not, I will maintain control over this war. I have to.

FOUR

CASSIA

I burrow beneath a heavy blanket that reeks of dust and mildew. A hard lump in the mattress digs into my side. I roll onto my back, my head pounding. I blink heavy eyelids as a groan slips from my mouth. Strands of cobwebs sweep down from an elaborate rib-vault ceiling, making a design of their own. I blink again and memories from yesterday crash over me. The zealots. The drugs. The murder. My hand flies to the left side of my neck where the cut Theo gave me still stings.

But Theo shouldn't exist because gods don't exist. They're fairy tales created thousands of years ago by people desperate for something to believe in.

I jump out of bed and my stomach churns so violently, I grab the uneven mattress for support. *The wine.* I had too much of it in the temple yesterday after the whole near-second-murder. The Asgyan—*What is his name?*—thought he was being kind as he spoke comforting words and offered something to calm me down.

I didn't want to calm down. I wanted to scream and hit something, anything, including him. But I also wanted to forget what happened. So, when he poured a glass of ruby liquid, I snatched the entire bottle from him instead. The alcohol was more pungent than I expected, but it didn't stop me from guzzling far more than I should have. Apparently I'm a lightweight because I don't remember much after that.

So where am I?

Hazy sunlight sneaks in around wooden shutters. I push myself upright, crossing the cool floor. One of the slats is broken. When I peek outside, all I see is a sky so blue it can't possibly be real.

Panic thunders through me until I can't see straight. Maybe I *am* dead and this is some sort of warped afterlife. It seems more realistic than gods. My fingers slide up the slatted window coverings until I locate rounded knobs through the hazy gray of the room. They don't budge as I tug. The musty air is hot. So hot. The dark hues of the room close in on me. I clench my teeth to hold back a cry and throw my weight into the shutters. Pressure builds behind my eyes, but I ignore it. I haven't cried since my parents died and I'm not going to start now.

A bulb flicks on overhead and I spin around with a yelp. My knee slams against one of the massive bedposts. I stumble back to the wall and breathe through the blazing pain as the Asgyan from the temple smiles in the doorway. Emotions flash in and out too fast for me to grasp a single one. Anger, fear, denial. Humiliation at what I may have done after blacking out. Hatred

46

for what his country has done to mine, both now and for all the years they controlled Kisk as a colony, stuffing their way of life down our throats. But I block each thought as it sails to the front of my mind. He can't be blamed for what his country did eight hundred years ago any more than I can be blamed for what my brother did. Plus, between him and Theo, he seems like my best chance at getting out of here in one piece.

"We do have electricity," he says. "Unless you're trying to air the room out, in which case you'll likely need a crowbar."

I rub the soft spot beside my bruised kneecap. "What?"

"A crowbar," he repeats. "The windows haven't been opened in ages."

"Do you happen to have one?" *So I can beat you over the head with it.*

He smiles again, one side of his mouth lifting to reveal a dimple. "Not on me."

"Shame." I rub my nose with the back of my hand and take in the details of the eight-sided room for the first time. Half the space is taken up with stacked furniture: tables, chairs, dressers, a desk, other things I can't make out, all pressed against one side of the bed. The rib-vaults are intricate; one line runs into another which loops around another in one seemingly endless line. The floor is rough, untreated wood, and gold wallpaper curls away from the wall. "Hey, um…"

"General Goran Marinos, Resident Adviser to the God of War." He gives a slight mock bow. "But Goran is fine."

"Right." I hesitate. If I could remember more about yesterday, this might be slightly less awkward. "Is there a reason you stuck me in storage?"

"We don't keep rooms ready for guests. This was the best I could do on short notice." He scans the room. "I'm sorry."

47

"So Theo wasn't hoping I'd be crushed to death in my sleep and save himself the trouble?"

"No." Goran steps closer, a glint of amusement playing on his refined features. "You can't die here."

I straighten, forgetting my aching knee, and stare at him. "Of course I can die. Theo was about to kill me yesterday."

"You can't," he says. I open my mouth to call him a liar but he keeps talking. "You belong to the War God now. Only he can decide your fate."

He says it with such a straight face that my breath sticks. "Let's get one thing straight, I don't belong to anyone."

"The gods are ancient. So are their customs and laws. Try not to be offended. Instead, think of it as an honor to be in the high esteem of one of your creators," he says patiently.

"An honor? High esteem?" A laugh spills from my gut, angry and erratic. "You're serious? He doesn't look very ancient to me. And maybe it's time they rewrite the laws."

Goran folds his arms across his chest. I catch a glimpse of criss-crossing scars on his knuckles. "Time is slower here. He's both ancient and the equivalent of a seventeen-year-old."

I laugh again. He can't mean that—that would imply Theo was waging wars since childhood. When Goran doesn't join me, I push away from the wall. The laughter gives way to a yawning chasm in the pit of my stomach. "Great. I get to live as the property of a psychopathic, mass-murdering deity. No, thanks."

"You don't get to change your mind," he says quietly.

"You're suggesting this was a choice I made?" My heart threatens to beat through my chest. "It's no wonder people stopped believing in all this cruel, barbaric nonsense."

"The Gods have never been cruel, Cassia. Strict but not cruel. People want to do right by them, or they used to." He clears his throat. "Listen, I've never had to have this conversation before. I'm obviously doing it wrong."

"You mean the welcome-to-eternal-servitude speech?" I grumble.

He takes a deep breath. "I understand the truth is new and confusing. While I can't pretend to know how you're feeling, I *can* try to make things easier for you. Theodric isn't as bad as he seems, but there are a lot of dynamics at play right now. You complicate his situation. But, between you and I, I'm laying a good portion of hope at your feet."

"Mistake number one," I say. There's no reason someone like me, with no war experience, should give him hope for anything.

"Perhaps." He smiles again, his spirits renewed. "If you can stop being angry for two minutes, maybe you'll find a bit of hope yourself."

"Hope for what? You just told me I'm a prisoner."

"You're not a—" He releases a sharp breath. "Forget I said you belong to Theodric, all right? Think of yourself as a...special house guest."

"House guests can leave," I say from between my teeth.

"You're welcome to explore anywhere you'd like. My suggestion is to stay out of the Wall, but I'm not your keeper."

No, you're not. But a spark of curiosity keeps me from saying so. "Why?"

"Why what?"

"Should I stay out of the Wall?"

He blinks slowly. "There are roughly three hundred men living there. And, while they were honorable enough to have sacrificed themselves to Theodric, I can't speak to each man's character."

Curiosity squashed. "What am I supposed to do then? Scrub floors? Polish boots? Because I promise my cleaning skills are sub-par."

He cocks his head and stares at me. "You don't know anything about how sacrifices work?"

"No. Well, maybe." I scowl as I try to remember everything I learned in mythology class. The painting of a two-headed buffalo with a thirst for blood is hard to forget. Blood was mentioned a lot, actually. But if everything they taught was true, Theo would be flying around on a chariot made from the swords of fallen soldiers. "I didn't pay much attention," I admit.

"Of course not," he says, more to himself than me.

"I didn't know I'd be in this situation," I snap. Besides, other things were more important than school at the time. My brother was arrested a week before classes began, and the trial lasted throughout the year. If we hadn't been bombed to smithereens, I would've repeated all my classes. "So, you're right," I add. "Of course not. Why would I pay attention to stupid stories when I needed to concentrate on things that actually mattered?"

He holds his hands up. "You're being difficult on purpose."

I walk across the room and poke him in the chest. "Screw you."

"Calm down."

"Don't patronize me," I growl. A flush of anger sweeps through me, but I'm directing it at the wrong person. Theo did this. He singled me out last night. He's the reason I'm here. *Then why did he look so surprised in the temple?*

I shake the thought away. "Where is he?"

"Who?"

I put my hands on my hips and dig my fingers into the gauzy fabric. "Don't play stupid. You know who I'm talking about."

"Theodric is busy preparing for—"

"I'll find him myself." I squeeze by Goran into a hall with green wallpaper and clear blown-glass wall sconces. My breath echoes in my ears as I barrel down two floors on a spiral staircase of black wrought iron. Once I reach a grand entryway with dark wooden paneling and a tan marble floor, I pause to catch my bearings. There are only four interior doors, two across from me and one behind. The last is directly across from the front door. Hallways branch off on either side. Time seems to slow as I realize how long this could take on my own.

"Theo!" I call.

Goran sprints after me. "What are you doing?" he asks in a hoarse whisper.

"What does it look like?" I ask. "I'm getting answers."

"You're not doing yourself any favors."

"Theo!" My voice echoes through the entryway. "We need to talk," I call. Goran pleads silently for me to stop, his eyes wide and glistening. I look away. "Theo!"

Footsteps thunder down the same steps I just came down. A pair of black boots come into view. I shuffle back as Theo rounds the staircase wearing jeans and a gray T-shirt. I don't know how I failed to notice how different he was in Kisk—maybe I did but didn't understand what I was seeing. It's more than his ridiculously good looks that make him intimidating. It's the overpowering way he carries himself. The untouchable arrogance and supernatural superiority. It wraps around me like vines, squeezing. My courage folds in on itself and, at the sight of the sword swinging from his hip, evaporates.

I lock my knees to keep myself standing and clasp my hands behind my back. He can't see how badly they shake or know how badly I want to vomit if I'm going to gain any sort of advantage.

"What is this?" he growls at Goran.

Goran steps between us. "She—"

"I don't need anyone to speak for me." I smack the back of my hand against Goran's chest and push him out of the way. "What am I doing here, Theo?"

Tiny crinkles form between his brows as he squints. "I've been asking myself the same thing." When I don't say anything, he adds, "If you want to leave, I can finish what I started in the temple. It would be a quick death."

My nerves spark and, before I can stop myself, I slap him. I gasp and clamp a hand over my mouth. I've never hit anyone before. This probably isn't the best time to start nor is he the best person to start with. However much I don't want to be here, I don't want to be *dead* dead more.

His hands flex, balling into fists, and the rest of his body grows eerily still. I need to apologize but can't remember how to speak. My chest heaves with each breath as we stare each other down.

"Theodric?" Goran's voice is strained, his movements jerky in my peripheral vision.

Whatever held Theo back snaps and he advances. Each step he takes, I take one back, until my lower back smacks into a wooden credenza. The rich scent of soap and cool metal reaches my nose as he towers over me. I hold my breath, refusing to look any higher than his wide shoulders. No part of me

52

wants to see the look on his face, and I can't let him see the fear on mine.

"Never touch me again," he breathes.

"Says the guy that tried to decapitate me." I bite my tongue to hold back a groan. *What's wrong with me? Stop talking.*

His shoulders rise with a deep breath. "If I wanted you dead, you would be. Stay out of my sight unless you want me to rethink the decision."

I take a shaky breath. "You'll never have to see me again if you send me back."

An angry laugh slips from his lips. "If only I could."

"You're a god. You can do whatever you want."

The air grows heavy, weighing me down from every direction. I don't move and neither does Theo. My anger at him, at the zealots, my brother, at being murdered and waking up here, simmers when I look up to see my fury matched in his expression.

"Tell me, Cassia." My name is nothing more than a hiss against his tongue. "What do you hope to accomplish here?"

"Unwilling sacrifice," Goran says quietly behind him.

I shoot Theo a sarcastic smile. "What he said."

He leans closer, his nose an inch from mine, and flares his nostrils. "Yes, but now that you're here, what would you have me do? It's your right as a sacrifice, isn't it?"

Is it? The reason I was killed hasn't crossed my mind—*why* doesn't matter. I loved Kisk once; it was home. I had a family and friends and a life; I tried not to blame the others for hating me, because they lost the same things I had. I even held onto hope that after the war, when things got better, I could find a way to fit in. But Nessa said the entire city agreed to the sacrifice. They turned on me when I did nothing to them. I suppose they thought the person that got Kisk into the war should get them out. Too bad that someone swung from a noose over a year ago. An old sliver of resentment splinters open. Vengeance leeks out, swirling and twisting around me until that's all that fills me.

"Nothing," I whisper. "I'd have you do nothing."

His pupils dilate. He stays close, his gaze traveling over my face, and my pulse slows. My fingers relax at my sides and I exhale slowly. The crisp metallic scent of Theo is still there. His jaw is set and his body is held tight, but I'm not afraid. Well, not *as* afraid. Maybe he'll kill me, but I doubt it. I don't know why, given the way he's staring at me, but there's a change in the gap between us. A calming in the static.

When Goran fakes a cough, Theo steps back and mumbles to his adviser before disappearing around a corner at the back of the mansion.

"I did try to warn you," Goran says with flushed cheeks.

I glare at him. "I'm still alive."

"Lucky for you," he says. "Follow me. We'll get you something to eat."

With Theo gone, a chill sets into my bones and my stomach rolls with nerves. "I'm not hungry."

Goran looks at me with newfound pity. "You should try to eat something. It will help."

"It won't."

I storm past him to the third floor and back into my cluttered room. Slamming the door behind me, I jump onto the massive bed and curl up under the musty covers. One word. *Nothing.* That's all it took to allow the wolves to keep gnawing on the bones of their prey. Kisk will disappear, swallowed up by the war's victor, and I let it happen. The truth of it scares me. This isn't me. This isn't the person I was brought up to be.

But that was before. This is now.

When the tears I was sure would come don't, I sit up and concentrate on the steady thump, thump, thump of my heart. The room seems clearer despite the grime-coated light on the ceiling. The sense of calm that took me when Theo studied my face returns, stronger than before, and I pull it close.

Just because Kisk won't benefit from my death doesn't mean I can't. Life doesn't have to be bad here. It won't be any less lonely and, on the plus side, there's no threat of war. A threat of Theo, maybe, but I can handle one person. It shouldn't be hard to avoid him in a house this big. And one day, when I've been here long enough, maybe we can even be friends.

The door creaks open and I draw a fast breath. Specks of dust rise to dance with the shift of air and Goran peeks inside.

"Are you all right?" he asks.

"Never better," I mumble.

He pushes into the room carrying a silver tray with bacon, eggs, and something bright yellow that resembles oatmeal. "Don't worry, I'll leave you alone. But you'll want this. We may not have to eat, but it takes our bodies awhile to realize that. One transition at a time is enough."

My stomach growls as the smell hits my nose. I offer him a small smile. "Thanks."

He hurries to set the tray on the foot of the bed like he's afraid I'll change my mind. "There's a bathroom on the second floor if you want to wash up. Third door down. Theo spends most of his time in the war room these days, so don't worry about running into him if you want to look around. There are woods behind the Wall with a nice brook if you enjoy the outdoors."

"Goran?"

He steps back and scratches his chin. "Yes?"

I study him. He's older than I am, mid-twenties maybe, but as awkward as any of the boys I used to know. I wonder how long he's been here and how old he was when he arrived. *Will I be frozen in time like I am now?* Exhaustion tugs at my center and I don't have the energy to ask. "I don't know how to do this."

"We'll fumble our way through it. Carefully," he adds. "I'd rather not have to clean you off the floor."

I jolt.

"Sorry, bad joke." He takes a deep breath and backs toward the door with his hands raised. "Like I was saying, feel free to explore anywhere you'd like, but would you mind holding off until I come back?"

Not a prisoner, huh? "Why?"

Goran fidgets with his sleeves. "We're expecting a visitor. It's best if he doesn't know you're here yet."

"Why?" I ask again.

"Trust me, it is." He steps into the hall and looks to the left. "No matter what you hear, don't leave this room."

I raise my eyebrows. "What exactly am I going to hear?"

"I don't know. Theodric isn't in the best mood."

No kidding. "Fine." I grab a thick strip of bacon from the plate, the grease hot between my fingers. "But in exchange, I want something else to wear."

He flashes me a quick smile. "I'll see what I can do."

Two hours later, after I've counted every round medallion on the wallpaper, masculine voices slice through the stillness of the mansion. A door slams at the front of the house and I press my ear to the wall. Only silence rings back. I rock onto my heels. So much for hearing anything interesting.

Then muffled shouts begin.

My eyes flick to the dull silver doorknob. Whatever is going on is none of my business. I should stay put like Goran said, and try to get comfortable. But there are a lot of things I *should* have done in my life—learned how to build a fire, told my parents I loved them more often, stayed far away from the temple. I'm fairly certain eavesdropping on a god doesn't fall into that category.

I chew my bottom lip, and slip into the hallway anyway. Goran underestimates me if he thinks, after seventeen months spent avoiding an array of enemies, I haven't gained some degree of stealth.

Then again, the zealots caught me without much trouble.

I wince at the memory of being dragged up the hill. At the weight of being held down, and the bitter taste of the robana bean. But this is different. This time I know the danger lurking around me.

The iron steps are cool beneath my feet as I slink to the first floor. With a quick glance around the entryway, I hitch my skirt above my knees, and sprint toward the back of the mansion where the commotion is. A statue of an armored horse is tucked around the corner. I squeeze behind it to gain my bearings, the stirrup pressing into my stomach.

A door is cracked a few feet away, allowing the shouts to escape unchecked. Their voices are clear, but the language, however, is not. The sound is ancient and crude, almost as if they're grinding rocks with their teeth.

I creep closer. Theo stands behind a wide table. A man with the same nose and blue eyes leans his knuckles on the polished wood across from him. He's handsome in a different way than Theo—less rugged and more untouchable. A threatening fierceness lies within him, brimming, ready to boil over.

Theo speaks again, and I catch a name at the end of his gritty sentence: *Ebris*. King of the Gods. I draw in a deep breath, and release it slowly.

Ebris' reply is almost a growl, and Theo stiffens. Before he can respond, the desk splinters beneath his brother's fingers. The series of cracks sets my hair on end. I flatten my back against the wall, willing myself to disappear. Ebris hadn't moved a muscle. The desk was simply in one piece, and then it wasn't.

"We understand," Goran says from inside.

Silence fills the room, a rubber band stretched to its breaking point. I was wrong to think there was no chance of war here; another kind of battle is brewing before me. I can't be caught spying on them. Being on one god's bad side is one too many.

I race back to the stairs, and make it to the second floor before footsteps echo below. I double my efforts, taking the steps two at a time, using the railing to help propel myself forward. The front door bangs shut, and my body jerks to a halt on the third floor landing.

"He's lucky I didn't run him through," Theo snarls.

"How do you plan to appease him this time?" Goran asks.

Somehow, the idea of Theo appeasing anyone is laughable, but I still hold my breath in anticipation of his answer.

"After that?" Theo is quiet for a beat. "I'm done appeasing my brother."

"What?"

There's a short pause before Theo says, "Find me a new table."

"Theodric, don't walk away," Goran calls. "Please. We have to do *something*."

But there's no reply. After a moment, hard-soled boots clap against the stairs. My pulse leaps into overdrive, and I throw myself into the bedroom. The door shuts with a soft click. I run my hands over my hair and dress, smoothing everything into place, but there's no time to regain control of my breathing before the knock comes. Even expecting it, the gentle tap sends me straight into the air.

"Our visitor is gone. You can come out whenever you'd like," Goran says from the hall.

"Okay." I clear my throat. "Thanks."

My gaze fixates on the shadows of his boots beneath the door, waiting for them to shift, and him to come inside. Instead, they disappear, and my body sags in relief.

I fall back on the bed, kicking up a cloud of dust. I shield my nose and mouth from the floating particles, and try not to cough. If I'm stuck here, I may as well make this place somewhat habitable. It's better than chancing a run-in with Theo before he calms down.

Besides, it appears I have all the time in the world. Waiting a few days to search for a way out of this place won't make much difference.

FIVE

THEO

Three days.

Three days since Cassia told me not to do anything for Kisk.

Three days since Ebris threw his latest round of threats at me.

And, three days since I decided there might be something to *nothing.*

"It will work out," I say from a high-backed chair. "We only need to ignore things long enough for Ebris to realize I'm not stoking the flames in the west but keeping the fire under control."

Goran pinches the skin at his throat as he stalks across the war room. He turns at the sofa and retraces his steps to the tapestries hanging along the far wall. Gold and silver threads weave through the deep red fabric depicting battles waged long before things fell apart. Before I was forced to wage wars in the crudest manner possible.

I grind my teeth and run a finger over the map in front of me. The edges are torn, lines faded. Tiny pin holes dot the paper where I plucked it clean last night. A hasty decision I'm sure to regret later when I need to know numbers and positions of soldiers.

"It will work out," Goran repeats, eying the stack of unopened reports on the edge of the desk. "So you have a plan to fix this when the war dominos out of control?"

There's no plan because there's no way to know how far things will go before Ebris breaks down and admits he's wrong. No way to know what the mortals will do when left unsupervised. They're more than capable of causing destruction without divine intervention. "It won't," I say, although it might. "Stop pacing."

He ignores me. "This is a dangerous game, Theodric."

I shrug. He isn't wrong. This is a game I never wanted to play, but now that I'm on the board, I have to make my moves.

"And you lied to Ebris about Cassia."

My eye twitches. "I did not."

"Letting him believe something that isn't true is the same thing as a lie." His laugh holds no humor as he gnaws on the pad of the thumb. "You know he'll see it that way."

"He doesn't need to know she's here. I haven't accepted her in the way I need to for Kisk to be saved."

Goran lets out a long, shaky breath. "You can't hide her forever."

"I don't intend to." Each sibling received tribute during the ritual—they know what day she arrived. When she doesn't show up in the Netherworld,

Leander will mention it to Ebris. Another week, maybe, then I'll hear about it. It's enough time to decide what to do with her.

"You're going to end up in the Between," Goran says.

I stiffen at the mention of the dark abyss. The endless nothing that threatens to suspend the Gods between realms. None of us have spent time there, but we've all come close. The threat is usually enough to put us in check, but I'm tired of cowering. Tired of being the only one with limitations. I know I'm testing boundaries that shouldn't be tested, but my brother, despite his cruel streak, does care about his family. Even if he tends to forget that at times.

"Don't worry. It'll be fine," I say.

Goran glares at me as he makes his way back across the room. "Unless he finds out Cassia's brother is a Kisken traitor."

"Colonel Stavros is nothing more than a scapegoat. If the Volks hadn't discovered his plan to help Asgya, he would've been hailed a hero. Ebris can view it as a reprieve for her. A kindness for all she's endured since her family was branded villains."

That's not what will happen though. Ebris will insist I accept my obligation to the island. Accepted is accepted, he will say. But the rules are very clear regarding this situation. A bride is only officially a bride after consummation, and I will never let that happen. I exhale and slump in my chair. Loophole or not, I should have killed Cassia when I had the chance.

But I couldn't.

She's an angry, disrespectful distraction I can't afford, but she doesn't want to force my hand. She cared enough to rip a loaf of bread in half for someone who hates her, only to tell me not to help them a day later. She's a walking contradiction. I can't help being curious. It's a mistake to allow my feelings to get in the way, but the same thing that drew my attention at the bonfire is stilling my sword now.

Goran stops on the other side of the desk and sets his fingertips on the folders. "If you're not going to read the reports, let me. I won't tell you what they say unless absolutely necessary."

"No." I bat his hand away. "I won't have any of the blame falling on you if things go wrong. Someone will need to take care of things here."

"I can't manage three hundred men, plus the hundreds you have scattered all over the world, while keeping any semblance of peace," he says in a gritty voice.

I force my lips into a tight smile. "Peace isn't exactly one of my goals."

Goran tugs at his hair. "Are you listening to yourself? I can't handle a war by myself, either."

"You're overreacting." I swipe the files into one of the desk drawers before standing. Out of sight, out of mind. "Why don't you take the day off and go somewhere—somewhere *east*. Keep away from the war." I toss him my ring. "If you happen to hear anything, it can't be helped."

"This—"

"Go." I wave a hand in his direction and take a deep breath. "Have some fun. Relax."

"As you say," he grumbles.

When Goran leaves the room, I cross to the window to make sure he heads for the temple. He means well and I know he's right. *I know.* But sometimes I think he doesn't truly understand how much I hate pitting myself against my siblings to maintain control. Deep down he may, but he continues clinging to his values. His portrait of rights and wrongs, colored in black, white, and every shade of gray. His ability to advise what's right, then, when I disagree, advise what's necessary, makes him valuable. It can also make him extremely irritating.

My shoulders relax when he passes through the arch in the Wall. *One more day.* What can happen if I turn a blind eye for another twenty-four hours? Forty-eight tops. It won't be more than a week before Ebris sees the truth.

A flash of white flutters in front of the turret beside my window. I twist my head a moment too late and it lands out of sight, kicking a small puff of gravel dust into the air. Two men rush from the Wall and I grip the windowsill.

She wouldn't... Would she?

I bolt from the room and up the staircase to the third floor with a knot in my stomach. If Cassia's room is empty, I'll know the answer. I don't need to see the carnage of her attempted suicide. I take a deep breath and force my feet to advance toward the open door at the end of the hall. My steps echo through the dusty corridor and I concentrate on the harsh jingle of boot buckles until I reach her room.

A low creak sounds from inside followed by a crash that vibrates the planked floor. I sprint over the threshold and my shoulders slump. She's here. Alive. Wearing the awful gauze dress with a deep red stain at the collar. She kneels on a mountain of forgotten furniture, her arms braced against the ceiling. She skews her lips and blows at a piece of hair hanging in her face. While assessing the pile beneath her, she eases off her knees and onto her toes. The pile creaks again.

"What are you doing?" I ask.

She stumbles and grabs the leg of a table for support. "Theo," she breathes.

Her gaze darts down to the sword at my hip. "You scared me."

"*I* scared *you*?" I step over the wooden debris of whatever fell a moment ago. An old trunk, maybe. It's in a dozen splintered pieces now. "I thought you jumped out the window. Now I find you trying to bury yourself in an avalanche of junk."

She frowns. "Why did you think I jumped out the window?"

The table she stands on wobbles and my chest tightens. "Come down from there. You're going to hurt yourself." I lift my arms to catch her.

"Most likely." She continues to glare at my hip. "But I have a better chance of staying in one piece up here than I do down there."

Stupid, foolish girl. I drop my hands and work the buckle at my waist. The scabbard falls away. I step back, leaning it against the wall, and raise my hands away from my sides. "Satisfied?"

Her nod is tight, resigned. She doesn't look at me when I offer my hands but she carefully sets her palms against mine. The table slides back and I yank her toward me before she can go with it. She collides against my chest. My breathing hitches. Each place her body touches mine feels as if it's exploding. I push her away, stepping back at the same time, and drag in a breath. I roll my shoulders against the discomfort raging through me.

"What were you thinking?" I snap.

"I was thinking I don't want to sleep in a storage closet anymore," she snaps back. "I couldn't pull anything from the bottom without the whole pile falling on top of me."

I glance down at the ruined trunk. "That could've been you."

She crossed her arms, her eyebrows lifted. A splash of pink rises in her cheeks. "What do you care?"

"You can't die here. Not unless I kill you myself." The words fall from my mouth before I can stop them. She'll heal but it won't be painless. For her or me, because it will be my fault if she tries to hurt herself. Maybe for keeping her here, maybe for not keeping her here the right way. This entire situation is over my head. I know I'm not doing it right—I'm just not sure how I'm doing it wrong.

"Then why would it matter?" She nods to the open window, a spark of curiosity on her face.

I glare at her as she brushes the dust from her hands. My stomach clenches at the sight of the cut on her neck. It would have healed by now if it had come from anyone but me. "You can still get hurt," I say. "And it's my job to protect my sacrifices."

Her eye twitches. "Goran already told me, but if I *had* jumped out the window...?"

"Are you considering it?"

She grunts and crosses the room without turning her back to me. The breeze catches strands of hair that escaped a loose braid as she leans out the open window. "I was airing the comforter out. It must have fallen," she says, looking down at the courtyard. "I'll bring it back in once I figure out where it went."

"The men took it," I say. The room is uncomfortably warm now. Stifling. "I'll have them wash it before they bring it back."

"Thanks." She takes a deep breath before leaning back inside. "So, are we expecting an attack?"

I blink at the change of subject. "Who would attack us?"

"Why else would you carry a sword around all the time?"

Her expression says she knows another reason—to finish what I started in the temple—but she doesn't suggest it. "I always have it nearby." It's next to useless in this day and age but it's an old friend. The only sword I've ever carried. "I'm not here to hurt you," I add.

Cassia fiddles with the tie on her dress. "Why *are* you here?"

Good question. She's alive and that's all I wanted to know. She's on solid ground again, so whatever duty I have to keep her safe is fulfilled. I should leave but my knees seem locked in place. I *want* to want to leave but my heart thuds, heavy, at the thought.

"When I'm gone, are you going to climb back up there?" I ask.

She scowls at her crooked perch. "It's not safe."

"It wasn't safe the first time you did it." I roll the sleeves of my dress shirt past the elbows. "What were you planning on doing with it all?"

She shifts. "Dragging it into the hallway for now."

I lift an eyebrow.

"What?" she asks defensively. "It's not like anyone else uses this floor. The rest of the rooms make this one look bare."

True but irrelevant. "Fine. I'll have the men take it from the hall this afternoon. They'll probably be able to put some of it to use."

"Are you offering to help?" Her voice rises and she stands straighter. She's…I could be wrong but I think she's irritated.

"Some of this weighs more than you do." And I have nothing better to do now that I'm ignoring the war.

I grab the legs of the table she was standing on and pull it from atop the pile. I guide it through the door and push it up against the wall at the end of the hall, near the back stairs. When I return to the room, she stares at me with heavy skepticism. Heat rises into my cheeks, and I twist away so I don't have to see her expression. It's too skeptical, too curious. Too *seeing*.

"What?" I ask when I can't take the silence anymore.

"Nothing." She pauses. "There's no chance you could, I don't know, poof it away?"

My body jerks and I latch onto the door frame. "I'm a god, not a magician."

She maneuvers around the bed and yanks at the back of a slatted chair. It's caught on something further under the pile. "Worth asking," she mumbles. She rocks the chair back and forth until the aged wood snaps. "Whoops."

I sigh and grab an oval frame from the heap.

◆

We work in silence. Pushing, pulling, lifting, dropping. I could have done it alone but, for a mortal, she carries her weight without complaint. A sheen of sweat coats her face, pieces of hair clinging to the moisture, and her breaths are heavy. I wait for her to ask for a break, but the question never comes. By the time we reach the final piece, we've found an easy rhythm.

Together we turn the desk upside down and set it on top of two nightstands outside the door. The hall is nearly impassable, but when we turn back to the now-empty room it's doubled in size.

A smile flits over Cassia's lips. "Finally." She flops face-first on the bare mattress and sighs. Shifting, she reaches beneath her stomach and pulls out a crowbar. It drops to the floor with a hard thunk. "Sorry about the shutters, by the way." Her voice is muffled by the bed. "It was Goran's idea."

I hadn't noticed the chips of wood scattered beneath the sill before. Some of the pieces are still big enough to tell they were once slats. Holes mar the window frame where nails held the hinges in place and the latch that seals the diamond-paned glass together is missing.

Cassia sits up and brushes the hair from her face. She glances at me, then turns to look out at the blue sky. "Hey, Theo?"

I slip my hands into my pockets. "What?"

Her hands ball into fists on her lap but she quickly straightens her fingers and sits up straighter. "Why didn't you kill me in the temple?" she whispers. "I know you regret it."

A sharp pain lances through me. Not because she's wrong—I do regret it. All of it. I never should have stopped to play Fate with her in Kisk, let alone looked at her in the temple as I went in for the kill. But I did. *Why?* It's better to keep the faces of each sacrifice blank. Not to see them as girls, but nameless problems to be dealt with.

"I don't know." I bend down and grab my sword from the floor. The hilt is familiar against my palm as I hold it in front of me. This is what I know. War. Not women. "I don't know," I say again, quieter.

"I'm glad you didn't," she says.

I meet her gaze, nerves prickling. "You haven't changed your mind about Kisk?"

"No." She blinks slowly. "They don't deserve it. Besides, it wasn't really home anymore. Not since…not since we were brought into the war."

Not since her brother brought them into the war, she means. Not since he was convicted and her parents were lost in the bombings. She doesn't say any of that. Whether it's because she doesn't want me to know or it's too painful to talk about, I can't be sure. I strap the scabbard back in place. "I'll have the men come up later for the furniture. Don't try to help."

She gives me a two-fingered Kisken salute, placing her index and middle finger vertically by her eye and moving them straight out. *I see you*, it says. *I'll cover you. I respect you.* But the sloppy way she moves her hand, the eye roll she tries to stop in time, tells me how much she doesn't mean it. Not that I would have thought she did if it were done in perfect form. She isn't one of my men. She isn't a soldier meant to follow my orders—she's a bride. I should be saluting her.

"Goran's gone for the day." I shift my weight between my feet. I'm stalling. "I'll be around if you need anything else."

She gives me the smallest of smiles. "Thanks."

I back out of her room and hurry to the safety of the war room. To where things make sense. Weapons and strategies and armor surround me. *Armor.* I need to find mine. To build it around me like I built a wall to block out the high priest. I can't let Cassia get to me. She's here because someone wants her here. Because she'll force me to listen to Ebris if I accept her sacrifice. The sacrifice she didn't want to make.

I lean over my desk and stifle the frustrated scream building in my gut.

Pull yourself together.

Focus.

She's a pawn. A new piece in a game she doesn't know exists. I can't forget that no matter how much I may want to. I've come too far to fall into this trap.

SIX

CASSIA

For a place where eating is optional, there's enough food in the kitchen to feed a small army. Unfortunately, most of it is prepackaged junk I don't recognize in languages I can't read, but there's a bag of apples and honey in the refrigerator. I flip the squeeze bottle over. The golden goop is crystallized at the bottom. I sigh and turn back to the cupboards as my stomach gurgles.

Shifting through boxes of crackers, I gasp. A lone bag of sage flavored chips are hidden behind a box of pasta. This flavor went out of circulation a few years before the war. But they can't be that bad; the bag is still sealed.

I rip it open and plop down on the floor, my back against the white wood of the island, with a book I hijacked under my arm. *Book* might not be the right word. It looks like a book—leather binding, golden edged pages, a deep red ribbon running down the middle. The entire library was full of identical spines. Scratchy handwriting fills the pages. Numbers of soldiers, lists of weaponry, terrain. Names of generals and countries and battles. It seems Theo has kept a thorough record of every war since the beginning of time.

But somewhere in all those volumes there could be a notation of something else: a sacrifice. Specifically, one that got out of here without dying. It sounds impossible. I can't un-die but I can't stop the voice in the back of my mind asking *is it*? I wouldn't have said any of this was possible eleven days ago. If there's even the slightest chance Theo can put me back somewhere far away from Kisk and the war, I need to find out.

The thin pages crinkle as I turn them. "So many numbers," I mumble around a mouthful of chips.

"Numbers are important," Goran says above me.

I jump, slamming the book closed. A blond head hovers over the edge of the marble counter top. I force the half chewed food down and exhale through my mouth. At least it's not Theo. I haven't seen him since he helped me move things last week, and I'm not sure where things stand with us. I can only assume he's over wanting to kill me. Unless he's trying to lull me into a false sense of security. A semi-lit kitchen without a clear path to an exit doesn't seem like the best place to find out. "Hi, Goran."

He rounds the island with a cocked eyebrow. "Did you take that from the archives?"

"I don't know what you're talking about." I smile as I slide the tome under my thighs.

He leans forward with his hands behind his back. "You're welcome to read them, but I don't imagine you'll be very entertained."

Lucky for me, I'm not looking for entertainment. I'll plod through as much algebra as I need to until I find mention of the other girls who came before me. I rattle the bag of chips at him. "Want some?"

"No." He wrinkles his nose and steps back. "They smell like death."

I put another in my mouth and chew slowly while I stare up at him.

"There's someone here to meet you," he says. "I thought you'd like advanced warning."

"What?" Bits of food fly from my mouth and I slap a hand over my lips. Who could possibly want to meet me? *Me.*

Goran laughs. "I think you'll like them."

"Them?" He said someone. Singular. And coming from the same man to tell me Theo wasn't that bad, I don't know if I believe him.

"Really, Theodric." A feminine voice floats in from the hallway. "I don't see why you're making such a big deal out of this. It's not like I haven't seen her before. You had to know this day was coming."

My blood pressure spikes. I wipe greasy fingers on my dress and stuff the book into a bottom cupboard before scrambling to my feet. I shoot Goran a scowl and he winks. "Who is that?" I ask in a hushed whisper.

Before he can answer, a woman in a short, green tulle dress practically skips into the kitchen. A sheet of long honey-brown hair slips over her shoulder as she turns toward me. The chips churn in my stomach. With the same long, sculpted nose as Theo and matching blue eyes, I don't have to ask who she is. A goddess. It doesn't matter which one because all three would strike equal terror in me.

"My goodness." Her smile is like coming home. "Look at you. I never thought I'd see the day."

I fidget while she looks me up and down. She's appraising me, I think, but not unkindly. It still makes my skin crawl. The counter feels like a barrier, offering a small bit of protection. A variety of snarky comments rush to my tongue but I swallow them. While I may not be able to stop myself around Theo, I can't piss off all the gods and expect any kind of support in the future. So, instead, I let heat rush to my cheeks as I stand there, fuming in silence.

Theo leans against the doorframe behind her with his arms crossed. "See?" he says. "She's fine."

"Fine?" The goddess casts a glance over her shoulder. "No wonder Goran contacted me. It's been almost a fortnight and she's still in the sacrificial gown. I know you've never kept a bride before but at least—"

"Whoa. Bride?" Panic seizes me, squeezing tight. The blood that was pooling in my face seconds ago drains to my feet. "No, no, no. You must be confusing me with someone else."

She blinks, her lashes almost brushing her high cheekbones. "I'm not sure I understand. Is she not...?"

"Leave it alone," Theo growls.

"But what—" She cuts herself off as understanding creeps across her face. "She doesn't know?"

"I said leave it alone, Astra." Theo straightens, the veins in his neck visible from across the room.

I snap my mouth shut, unease tightening my throat, and lay my palms on the counter. *Astra.* As the Goddess of Love, she should know nothing exists between Theo and I. I look to Goran for backup but he's studying a knob on the oven. "There must be a mistake," I squeeze out. Mythology lessons trickle through the cracks in my resolve. Bigger rewards are expected when women are sacrificed to the men, and men to the women, because they were meant to mean more to the god. "I'm not a..." I can't finish the statement. Partly because my mouth is suddenly parched and partly because it would be a lie. That's exactly why the zealots sent me here. I can't believe it hadn't dawned on me earlier.

Before I realize she's moved, Astra has her arms around me. My body prickles against her intense heat as one hand smoothes over my hair. The scent of roses envelopes me. This can't be right. Theo tried to kill me, not marry me. Not that I want him to. I really, really don't.

"There, there," Astra whispers in a soft voice. "Forgive me. I wasn't aware of the circumstances of your," she pulls back enough to glance at Theo, "visit."

Visit. It sounds so temporary.

"Are you finished?" Theo snaps.

Astra brushes the hair from my face before stepping back. "Don't start with me, Theodric. I'll leave when I'm good and ready."

His chest puffs. Our eyes meet for a brief moment and I shudder. "Things are fine the way they are. Don't mess up my household the way you're trying to mess up my war," he says.

"You don't need my help to do either. You're quite capable on your own." She snaps her fingers and a young girl steps around Theo with a black dress bag. "I heard Goran promised you something new to wear."

I nod. Goran keeps his head down, looking in every direction except Theo's.

"I brought you this," Astra says. The girl, no older than fourteen with a mass of red curls, places the bag in my arms. "I wasn't sure what you'd like so I took your clothing in Kisk into consideration. Not that it was your usual wardrobe, of course, but, well…"

"In Kisk?" I ask in a shaky voice.

She smiles, apples forming in her tan cheeks. "I was with Theodric the night you met."

"Funny." I grip the bag. "I don't remember seeing you." *And I would.* She gives off the same vibrations Theo does. Maybe more.

She clasps her hands in front of her. "I need to have a few private words with my brother, but I'm so glad we officially met."

She hugs me again, a light embrace, then breezes out of the kitchen with the young girl at her heels. She takes her heat with her and a small part of me wants to follow. Theo stays in place, watching me with a hard expression. I clutch the clothes Astra gave me so hard my fingers threaten to cramp.

"That wasn't so bad," Goran pipes.

Theo flares his nostrils. "She isn't gone yet," he says before fleeing. Goran rushes after him and I'm left alone, my head spinning.

And I thought servitude was a bad deal.

No wonder Goran looked at me like I was crazy when I asked him about scrubbing floors. Theo certainly isn't treating me like a wife, though. He isn't treating me like anything at all, which is exactly what I want. It gives me more freedom to snoop around for answers. Theo wasn't terrible the other day, but marriage is out of the question. *Absolutely.*

On the way back to my room, I stop in the second-floor bathroom to take a quick shower. Chucking the horrible white dress in the trash, I pull on a pair of jeans, a pink T-shirt, and a gray knit sweater, followed by a pair of matching flats. It's the best I've felt in ages. When I step into the hall again, there's a bounce in my step.

I hug the book tight to my chest as I make for the staircase. It was stupid to read it in the kitchen—I was bound to run into someone. I'll have to be more discrete if I don't want Theo or Goran to catch on. Goran's smart; he might already know. Why else would I be reading this thing? I don't know anything about nautical miles or ammunition. It's not that I'm doing anything wrong, but I can't honestly say I trust either of them. Not really. It's better to keep things close to the chest.

A man in a white T-shirt rounds the corner, and I jerk back a second before we collide. The book falls to the floor with a thud. "Sorry." I scramble to grab it before he sees. "I didn't see you there."

"Cassia, right?" he asks.

Black tattoos cover his bronze skin, circling his arms in ancient bands. *Kisken* bands. One identifies where he's from, another which family he's part of. Skills he earned, battles he fought. Some may be for family members lost or children born. I don't recognize most of them. Once Asgya planted roots on our island, the tradition was repressed under foreign rule. The only two I can identify are for reaching his fifteenth birthday and marriage. He must be one of the men from the Wall but he's the first one I've seen up close. They're like ghosts, swooping in unnoticed before disappearing again.

"Who are you?" I ask.

"Cy." He blinks once before snatching my wrist and yanking me through the nearest door. I open my mouth to scream, but he slams a calloused hand over it before I can make a sound. He scans the small parlor with hooded eyes. "I'm not going to hurt you. When I take my hand away, don't scream."

Yeah, right. Theo may not like me, but if I scream he'll come. *Probably.* At least, Goran will. *Likely will.* I don't think either of them will like me being assaulted. I do *belong to the God of War* after all.

"Please," he adds. "We have to talk."

The earnestness of his voice calms the fight brewing in my muscles. When he raises his brows in silent question, there isn't danger written there but doubt. An internal fight of his own. I nod once and he steps away, exhaling slowly.

"All right, Cy." I speak slowly, like he's an animal ready to pounce, and rub at my cheeks where his hand pressed. There's a clear shot to the door if I need it. "What do we need to talk about?"

"You weren't a willing sacrifice." It's both a statement and a question.

"No."

He rubs his hands over his face and groans. "Gods above."

Unease skitters across my back. I don't like anything about this. "I'm leaving."

"I didn't think Astra was telling the truth," he says in a rush. "When she came home... I never imagined he would..."

I shuffle back a step. "*He* who? What are you talking about?"

"I shouldn't say. You should know—" He cuts himself off and searches my face. "Things in this world aren't always what they appear and almost never what you want them to be."

My palms sweat and I eye the door handle. "What are you talking about?"

"Be careful."

The warning strikes new fear into my soul. Not a fear of Theo or swords, but one of drowning. Of being sucked under by a riptide of the unknown, minute details filling my lungs until there's no room left for oxygen. I'm treading water so deep I can't imagine its depths.

Cy moves to leave but I step in front of him, hysteria rising to the surface. And with it, the same sense of fight-or-die I've lived with since the bombings. "Hold on. You can't drag me in here, string together a bunch of cryptic nonsense, and then walk away. Did you hear something in the Wall? Are the men planning an attack? Are they mad I'm here?"

"What?" His brow lowers. "Why would Theodric's men care if you're here? And you're clearly insane if you think they would ever move against him."

"I'm insane?" I snap. "I don't even know who you are. Why should I listen to anything you have to say?"

"I'm Astra's husband but you certainly don't have to listen to me. I did my part by warning you. The ball is in your court." He jerks to move around me and pauses. "If you mention this conversation to anyone, I'll deny it until my last breath." Then he slips out of the room.

I stand there for a second, letting his words sink in—his lack of words—before I leap into the hallway after him. "What did you warn me about?" I ask, but he's gone.

I rap my fingers on the side of my thigh, the book hanging from my other hand. If I go after him, I risk running into Theo. Judging by the way Cy dragged me in here, we shouldn't be seen talking. But if I don't, I'll never understand his warning. Or maybe I will, but not until it's too late. A small, frustrated sound escapes my throat and I barrel down the stairs.

Cy is halfway across the main entryway when I catch up to him. Theo's hard voice travels from the front room but I ignore it. If I get answers fast enough, I can be hiding in my room again before he's done talking to Astra. I grab Cy's wrist and pull him to a stop.

"What are you doing?" he hisses.

I raise my eyebrows. "We didn't finish our conversation."

"We did."

"Really?" I ask. "Because I have no idea what happened up there."

"I told you. Be careful."

I pull in a deep breath. "But why?"

He yanks free from my grip. "Ebris will use you against Theodric to end the war. Theodric knows that, which makes you a threat to him."

Was that what their fight was about? Me? Goran said it was best Ebris didn't know I was here yet, but that doesn't mean he didn't find out on his own. I narrow my eyes at Cy. "I don't care what Theo does," I tell him.

"You should." His eyes zip over the paneled walls. "Others do."

Maybe I should, but I don't. "I get it. You're Kisken too. You want to save our island."

"Please." He lets out a disgusted huff. "The country I loved is gone. It has been for a long time now."

"I don't understand."

"Your—"

"There you are." Astra steps out of the front room and slides up next to Cy. She snakes an embrace around his waist. "I wondered where you went."

He sets a stiff arm around her shoulders and gives me a pointed look. "I was giving Cassia some advice about settling in."

"That's good of you. I know it can be hard on some."

Unspoken words hang in the air between us. *Some like me.* The girl who didn't believe in the Gods and knows nothing about how any of this works. At least she didn't give voice to what we're all thinking.

"She'll be okay," Cy says.

"If there's ever anything you need, let me know." Astra lets go of Cy to hug me a final time, speaking into my hair. "We have to cut things short today, but I do hope to see you again."

"I'd like that," I say truthfully. Just because I cause friction between Ebris and Theo doesn't mean I can't have an ally here. Especially one that gives me access to Cy, so I can pry the rest of that sentence from his lips.

"We'll plan something soon." She kisses my cheek and heads for the front door. "Take good care of her, Theodric."

Theo stands in the doorway with his hands in fists. "Why are you still here?"

She tuts as Cy steps outside, joining the red-headed girl in the courtyard. "Before I forget," she calls to me. "What's your favorite color?"

I swallow hard as Theo's gaze lands on me. "Blue."

Astra smiles before turning away, leaving me alone with Theo—the bear she poked with a pointy stick. *Very alone.* I look around for Goran, but the one time I actually need him, he's nowhere in sight.

"So...that was your sister?" I cringe at the question but I didn't know how else to break the thick silence. And it had to be broken. Turning and running in the opposite direction is cowardly, although probably the smarter choice.

"The most irritating of them, yes." His chest rises and falls with heavy breaths. "But not the most opinionated, by far."

I'm not sure if he's trying to make a joke or a complaint, but either is an effort toward conversation. It's still important he doesn't want to lop my head off while I'm stuck here, so I force a smile. "My brother was full of opinions too."

Theo inhales sharply and brushes past me. My grip tightens on the leather binding. There has to be an answer somewhere in these books. If not in this one, maybe another.

SEVEN

THEO

Cassia stands in the middle of the brook, jeans rolled to her knees, with a white bucket by her feet. The soft sound of water brushing against stone is punctuated by the plunk of rocks as she attempts to skip them downstream. My insides quake and I pause behind the safety of the trees. It's not too late to turn back. I don't care how much time Astra needs to redecorate the third floor bedroom, nor do I care if it's a surprise. If my sister wants her occupied, she should do it herself. I can't spend five minutes with the girl, let alone an entire afternoon.

Besides, fixing the room gives the wrong impression. It implies Cassia is staying. Two weeks is a far cry from forever, and I haven't made any decisions yet. Once Ebris comes to his senses, I can get back to work. Avoiding her and the war at the same time has been nothing short of torture. I can't sit, can't read, can't sleep. I've snapped at Goran more in the last few days than I have in the last year. I should stop waiting for Ebris but I can't. That's what he wants me to do. I would be handing him a small victory.

I clench my jaw against that train of thought and focus again on Cassia, growing discomfort in my chest. Each time she's around, words fail. Everything I've thought of to narrow down possibilities for my curiosity disappear behind a cloud of resentment. This has to be Ebris' doing, but that only makes it worse. If she were here of her own accord, I wouldn't worry about misstepping in my brother's favor. If only I could ignore her as well as she's been ignoring me.

"I can feel you watching me, Goran," she calls. I freeze, afraid to move and give away my position, but she doesn't turn around. "Yes, I'm still here. No, I haven't drowned yet. I'm not giving up until one of these stupid rocks skip, so you can go back to your war mongering. I know the way back."

I grit my teeth. It's tempting to leave, but each second I stand here, the less I find I'm able. She reaches into the bucket for another stone and wings it. The motion sends her hair curling around her torso, skimming the inside of her elbow. I cringe against the desire to find out how soft it is. The rock sinks beneath the surface and her head hangs in defeat.

"If you think you can do better, by all means…"

A swell of amusement pushes at my agitation, and I swat long, sweeping branches with small oval leaves from my path. The mossy ground gives under my boots as I approach the bank and crouch beside the water. Cassia rubs her thumb over another stone, her fingers moving against the speckled surface. The water is cool as I dip my hand in and grab a smooth, round rock from the bed. With a quick flick of my wrist, it hops along the surface six times before disappearing.

"Show off," she mumbles.

"It's all in the wrist," I say.

She spins around so fast she slips, catching herself on a large tree root jutting from the bank. Water splashes up her jeans. She rights herself and brushes her hands across her bare arms. "Theo." She takes a deep breath and sloshes her way through the water. "I didn't think you ever left the house."

"No?" I cross my arms. "We met in Kisk."

Her cheeks glow. "That was different."

She's right—that was work—and I can't remember the last time I was in my own woods. There's been no reason to come here since Drea stopped supplying game. She claimed I was using the entire world as my personal hunting grounds so there was no need to hunt here as well. It was an uncharacteristically bitter moment but she could have taken it all. The trees. The grass. This place could have been turned into a wasteland so I keep my mouth shut.

"Jumping realms is normal but taking a walk isn't?" I ask.

She slips wet feet into her shoes, grabs her grey sweater from the base of a wide tree, and steps back to put more space between us. "I have no idea what's normal for a god."

"No," I say. "Seeing as you've only recently come to believe we exist."

She sighs. "Are you ever going to let that go?"

I look away. She won't be here long enough for me to forget her disbelief. Not that it matters. My power doesn't come from prayer; it comes from within. Or, it would if Ebris hadn't ripped it away. I roll the ring on my middle finger with the pad of my thumb. "What are you doing out here?"

"Nothing." She leans over, rolling her pant legs back down. "I needed a break."

I raise an eyebrow. "From what?"

"What are *you* doing out here?" she asks, almost too quickly. "Spying on me?"

Heat sweeps up my back. I should have turned around when I had the chance; I can't do this.

"I'm kidding," she says.

Her eyes skim along my cheek. The muscles in my jaw jump. "Would you like to walk with me?" I ask, the words stiff.

She chews on the inside of her lip. Her gaze flickers to my hip and the sword hanging from it. My fingers twitch. Of course she doesn't. What reason have I given that she should want to spend time with me? She must dread the thought as much as I do.

Finally, as I'm about to turn, she gives a quiet *hmm* of consent.

I stuff my hands in my pockets, away from the hilt of my sword, but her face remains tight. I try not to let it bother me. To be understanding. I did try to use it against her. *Only once.* It won't do any good if her guard is up, though; I need to see some of that girl I saw in Kisk. Some of that spark that caught my attention after knocking down the overpass. The stern, no-nonsense girl that gave away her bread. The cautious one who disappeared the second my back was turned.

A kernel lodges itself in my chest. That's the same girl I'm with now, only her wariness is centered solely on me instead of split amongst an entire group of Kiskens. I clear my throat and start upstream. It doesn't matter who she is as long as I can narrow down why I care. If I know, Ebris will never be able to put me in this situation again.

"Have you seen the waterfall?" I ask, forcing a little cheer into my voice.

The next twenty minutes are torture. Cassia's presence tingles at my back, tense and high-strung. She's ready to run if I make any sudden movements, and my brain rushes desperately over a thousand things to break the silence. To ease her fears. Each thought vanishes as quickly as it comes, finally being replaced by the soft whisper of the falls. It grows into a steady roar as we near the edge of the woods.

I slow and Cassia steps up to walk at my side instead of behind. Her concentration drifts over wide tree trunks and swoops up the full branches, as if she's expecting an ambush. As if I would need to lure her into one. When the forest ends abruptly, giving way to hills covered in dense grass, her steps falter.

Water cascades, white and graceful, over the peak of a cliff high above our heads. It rushes into a wide pool at the lowest point of the valley where it feeds the brook. In the distance, mountains link together in shadow. The edge of my realm. On the other side is the Between, connecting this place to my siblings' like the hub of a wheel.

She says something, but the falls drown out her voice and she inches closer to ask again. "Where does the water come from?"

I shrug one shoulder and tear my mind away from the darkness. "Brisa."

Cassia scowls and bites her bottom lip. I can tell it's not enough of an answer for her. It wouldn't be for someone who has no faith and knows nothing about how the Gods work. I'm a poor example, but the others are nearly limitless within their abilities. The water is there simply because my sister wills it.

"It's amazing," she says after a moment.

I rub at the knot in my stomach. "Yes."

Mist lights on the hair covering her shoulders and droplets cling to her eyelashes. It kisses her skin. I wonder what it would be like to touch her cheek as gently as that. To feel her yet not. The thought spurs my pulse into a marathon.

"What's on the other side of the cliff?" she asks.

"Nothing." I try to look away from her but can't. We've never been this close. At least not consciously and not without anger driving us to it. A small divot marks the corner of her jaw, the mere hint of a scar. "Brisa's kingdom lies in that direction, but the only way there is through the temple," I add.

"I bet the view from the top is amazing," she says.

"Probably, but there's no way to get up there."

She studies it a moment longer before saying, "There's a waterfall back home." Her focus on the cliff dulls and she rubs at her chest. "It's on the other side of the island though, so I only saw it once and it wasn't anywhere near this size."

I nod, unsure where she's going with this.

"What's your favorite part about Kisk?" she asks carefully.

I shift my weight between my feet. "Are you regretting your choice not to save your country?" I ask sharply.

Her laugh is low, unamused. "No. I'm just curious."

I pause but her expression remains neutral, like my answer doesn't matter. Like she's simply trying to find common ground and maybe she is. "Tabowi fruit," I answer.

"Tabowi fruit?" Her voice rises and falls with each syllable, and she looks up at me with disbelieving eyes. "Out of everything you could pick, that's it?"

"I could say the good-natured people, the crystal clear beaches, or the inviting culture, but it wouldn't be the truth. Those things may endear Kisk to my siblings, but not me. Your military has never been the strongest, preferring instead to rely on easily-broken alliances. It's location between Asgya and Volkana makes it an easy target." I take a quick breath. "So that's my answer."

"But still." She looks away. An unspoken thought shutters itself behind thick doors. "If you're going with food, there are much more exciting things to pick."

"Sorry to disappoint you." A smile tugs at my lips. Then, because I can't stop myself, I keep talking. "There was this place awhile ago that served it in something similar to a modern day crepe. It was worth the trip alone."

She scrunches her nose. "Tabowi crepes?"

"It was thinner than a crepe, and I'm fairly certain it contained more sugar than fruit."

"Well, in that case." She smiles and a soft laugh floats in the air between us. It mixes with the rushing water to create its own music. The sound suspends me, shutting down my senses. When my hand rises to brush a strand of wet hair behind her ear, we both freeze. Reality slams down as fast as my arm does.

"What were you doing in Kisk that night?" Her voice is quiet. Strained.

"Working." I draw a sharp breath. "You never answered my question," I say before I can think better of it. "You disappeared after I won the last round of Fate."

Pain lances her features. "You mean, why was I afraid of the others? I think that's obvious now."

Of course. Everyone thinks her brother is a traitor, and it was only a matter of time before the survivors took their anger out on her. *Really* took it out on her, not merely kept her on the outskirts. "But you didn't know their plans that night."

"How would I know? If I had, I never would've gone near the temple." She wipes her forehead with the sleeve of her sweater. "I feel naïve for ever believing things would get better after the war."

Not as naïve as I was for stopping to talk to her. Maybe if I kept walking, she wouldn't be here. "I was helping the Kiskens the night we met. Getting them weapons."

She shrugs. "They aren't my problem anymore. The zealots made sure of that when they murdered me."

I wince. "It was a sacrifice, not a murder. They knew you would be safe."

"Safe?" She laughs bitterly. "Either way, I'm dead."

"Not yet." I scratch at the back of my neck. *She should be. She almost was.* "Not until Leander helps you cross through the arch in the Netherworld. The believers weren't wrong; you're safe here." *For now.* I swat the thought away. As long as she's here, she's safe. But eventually she'll have to leave. It will be better for both of us if she crosses the arch and finds her family.

"You told me yourself I was already dead." She sighs, resigned. "It was one of the first things you said to me after Goran pulled me from the pit." When I'm quiet too long, she adds, "It's not fair."

I can't help collateral damage; it's impossible. Campaigns requires months, sometimes years, of preparation. Pieces need to be moved and align with the right situation. It revolves around things my siblings are in charge of: the death of a king without the gift of an heir, a loved one being stolen away, trade routes over calmer waters. It's a waiting game I've played a million times. If Cassia's brother hadn't done his part, she would still be alive but the West would remain stagnate. I'm not only creating war, but instigating change.

"War isn't meant to be fair," I say quietly.

"Not when one man is running everything." She turns to face me, her chin held high. "What's the point? Do you know the outcome before the war starts?"

I curl my fingers into a fist, fill my lungs, and exhale. It had to come sooner or later. The questions. The demands. Everyone makes them. "You don't understand," I say in a hard voice.

"You're right. I don't." She glares. "Explain it."

"I don't have to explain anything to you," I snap. "Nothing is ever black and white, Cassia. Every country thinks they're doing the right thing—that they're fighting as heroes instead of villains. You don't know the layers of deceit involved."

"Please." She bites off the word. "Invading another country is never a good thing."

"Isn't it?" I lean closer and bury my hands deeper into my pockets. "There are a dozen reasons I can think of right now that would justify it. It's my job to remain neutral; I need to understand the motives from all sides."

"What could possibly be justifiable about Asgya invading Kisk? We were allies."

"Layers and layers of deceit," I say slowly, enunciating each word. "But I thought it didn't matter."

Her face turns stony, her fire dying, trampled by new thoughts. Finally, she whispers, "It doesn't."

The silence pounds in my ears. This is why I shouldn't have agreed to keep her away from the house. Nearly everything she says is a challenge. She's so confident about each word that comes out of her mouth. It's infuriating. My body itches to end her, my muscles aching to swing the sword, but my brain is in revolt. *No,* it screams. *Wait. Stop. Don't.*

"Sorry." Her voice is so quiet I almost miss it. "It's none of my business."

No, it's not.

"I forgot the bucket," she says.

She turns and her sweater brushes my bare skin. Before I realize I'm moving, I've grabbed her hand. Heat explodes at the connection. It travels up my arm and my breath hitches. We're locked in that moment for what seems like forever before I find the strength to break the connection.

This isn't right.

Low bramble catches my jeans as I storm back into the woods alone. I'm too afraid of what will come out of my mouth if I open it. I ball the fabric of my shirt in a fist over my diaphragm. I'm no closer to understanding what's between us, but, for the briefest of seconds, I didn't care.

EIGHT

CASSIA

Splotchy black ink blurs on yellowing paper. Light filters into the freshly painted bedroom—a calming Wedgewood blue—through sheer curtains as the sun inches its way into the sky. I drag heavy limbs onto a mattress so soft it feels as if I'm floating, and lug the book I've been reading along with me, my retinas burning. It was tucked under a pile of decorative throw pillows when I got back from the waterfall fiasco at dusk. An anonymous note between the pages read, *For a more insightful read,* and then exhaustion gave way to curiosity.

That was nine hours ago.

I should have slammed the thing shut and tossed it into a fire as soon as I read *Ostran War* inside the cover. Everyone knows that war—it forever changed the face of the East. My stomach churns as I skim over numbers reaching into the hundreds of thousands. So far, it doesn't seem different than the other volumes I've gone over in the archives. Larger numbers, but equally dry and tedious. I keep going though, waiting for something to catch my attention. *Anything.*

I shift into the dusky rose duvet and rub my eyes. The words fade in and out of focus, my brain registering every other line. "Arrows." My voice is hoarse. "Bows." My head bobs and I jerk myself awake. "Catapults."

I fight a yawn. Without military training I could be wrong, but the war seems to be petering out. The countries allied against Ostra have more weapons and more men, but I'm only halfway through the tome. I have to keep going, though; it was left here for a reason. There has to be something…Something…

A steady knock tugs me from deep sleep. I fight against it, landing somewhere in the hazy place between reality and dreams. The knock comes again, and the breeze from the open window carries a hint of fresh paint too real to pretend it's my imagination. I choke on a gasp as I land solidly in the present and spring off the bed onto a thick beige carpet. My head throbs with the last remnants of sleep. Three more knocks rattle the door. I shake the sleepiness away. "Yes?" I call. I snatch the open book off the bed and shove it under the pillows.

There was a long pause. "It's me."

Theo?

I cringe. I knew I should have kept my mouth shut yesterday. It doesn't matter if Theo planned the war that ruined my life. It's his job; he didn't set out to destroy me personally. I'm not sure about my brother; maybe he set Oren up to become a traitor, maybe he didn't. I can't ask without telling him how connected my family is to the war, and the last thing I should do is give him a reason to doubt me. At least not until I find a Plan B for his Plan A.

It takes a minute before I'm able to move toward the door. When I do, my feet are lead, weighed down with uncertainty. Theo stands outside my room, his pupils dilated, one hand behind his back and the other clutching something to his chest. I take my obligatory glance at his hip and, for a second, I forget to breathe. There's no sword. I stare at the blank space beside his thigh a moment too long and Theo shifts in the doorway.

"I left it in the war room."

I blink. "Oh."

"I got you something," he says in a gruff voice. "Goran says you like reading, and I thought…"

A black, hardcover book with a blazing foil sun lands in the crook of my elbow before I can lift my arms to take it. *The Gods: A Complete Collection of Tales.* Electricity zips up my spine. This is either a kind gesture or a passive-aggressive slap in the face. If it weren't for the missing sword and his obvious discomfort, I would know the answer.

"Do you like the room?" he asks.

"It's great." I turn to follow his gaze around the room. Everything from the simple iron chandelier to the antiqued furniture is strangely perfect. Not to mention the wardrobe full of clothes. "You didn't have to."

His eyebrows rise and fall in sarcastic agreement. "Astra didn't exactly ask my opinion."

Of course not; he would've said no. Some of the weight settles back on my shoulders. "I suppose I should thank her then. Any idea when she'll be back?"

A muscle jumps in his jaw. "Sooner than I want her to."

The sooner the better. And with Cy, so I can corner him the way he cornered me. Only this time it will go my way. An aching heat seeps into my muscles the longer we stand there. I eye the bedroom, the hall, anything but him. We can't pretend like the other doesn't exist when we're three feet apart. I sigh. "Well—"

"About yesterday." Theo squeezes whatever is in his palm and looks down the hallway. "I may have overreacted."

My lips part as I inhale. That's the closest I'll come to an apology from him and much more than I expected. Silence stretches between us until the shock ebbs away. A flush creeps across his cheeks, and I realize I'm staring. "It's fine," I say. "I should have minded my own business."

His Adam's Apple bobs and he extends his fist. "Here."

For a moment, I consider slamming the door shut so I don't have to deal with the fallout of whatever is in his hand, but something stops me. The hope I had after our confrontation in the entryway flutters, trying desperately to resurrect itself. The possibility of living together but separate without all the tension might be a pipe dream, but I don't want to wonder *what if*. Especially if I don't find anything useful in the archives.

I reach out my hand and my muscles tighten against the movement. Two heavy dice land in my palm, hot with his body heat. I'm torn between dropping them to the floor and clutching them tight. I can still trace the exact line over my temple where he moved my hair yesterday, and my fingers remember the steady grip of his before he left me at the waterfall.

I blink rapidly. "Fate?"

"I thought we could have a rematch." He rubs at the slight stubble on his cheek "Winner gets answers again."

I must be imaging things—I swear he asked me to play Fate. Again. Only this time, it's different. I'm not simply a random mortal that caught his eye; he can't get up and disappear without a second thought. I suppose I was the one that disappeared that night, but it's what he would've done. It's what they all did when they won what they wanted from me. What possible outcome could he want? What questions does he want answered?

"All right," I say carefully.

He turns on his heel and is halfway to the stairs before I remember I'm supposed to be following him.

Two chairs grate against the sitting room floor as Theo pulls them closer to the coffee table. I wince away from it even though it isn't that loud. Theo lowers himself onto the first, his back to me, and leans forward to rest his elbows on his knees. His shirt stretches against his muscles, showing each taught line. I hesitate near the door and try to look anywhere but the perfect rise of his shoulder blades. He turns his head to the side enough that I see his hair fall forward, skimming his eyebrows.

"What's wrong?" he asks when I don't join him.

"Nothing." I move slowly into the room and perch on the edge of the second seat. I make a silent plea for Goran to come running through the open door with urgent news. Or maybe I'm hoping that he doesn't. "Three rolls?" I ask.

"Until we run out of questions." Theo's hand unfurls between us, but I cling to both dice. "Unless you have something else planned for the day."

Flustered, my hand darts out and drops one of the die into his waiting palm. "Playing for answers didn't end very well last time. Maybe we should play for something else."

An uneasy smirk lifts one corner of his mouth. "I'm sure you have questions to ask this time."

"I had questions in Kisk; I just didn't ask them," I admit. I will this time. After what Cy told me, I'm not sure I can believe anything he says, but it won't stop me from hearing his answers. "What happens if I ask something you don't want to answer?"

He takes a slow, thoughtful breath. "We all have our secrets, don't we?"

"Some more than others." I think back to the pages I read before I fell asleep, racing to pull something of importance from them.

Theo holds himself rigid, his thumb picking at the vined edges of the die. "Cassia." The last time he said my name it was with venom, but now it's almost as if he's savoring it. He cracks his wrist. "It would be nice not to hate each other," he says.

I suck in a breath, ready to be the voice of reason. I can't possibly not hate him because he tried to kill me, and he can't possibly not hate me because I'm a threat to his lifestyle. But I already don't hate him, and he looks like maybe he doesn't want to hate me anymore either.

"I want to believe you mean that," I say.

He inhales as if he's about to speak, but drops the iron piece instead. *War.* I hesitate before letting mine fall beside his. *Death.*

He looks up at me through his lashes with an unreadable look. "Go ahead."

I bite my lip. I have a million important questions, but it doesn't feel right to lead with them out the gate. Maybe if we warm up to them, I'll have better odds of getting an answer. "What do you do when you're not planning wars?" I ask.

"I'm always planning wars." He shrugs one shoulder. "I plan thousands of scenarios and wait for one of them to fit the circumstances."

My stomach twists. *What scenario did Kisk fit into?* I'm not sure I want to know.

"You?" He picks up his die but doesn't throw it. "What did you like to do…before?"

Before my life fell apart? I pick up my piece and consider dropping it without answering. I don't know why he wanted to play this game, but it's not to learn about my hobbies. If he wanted to do that, he could have come out and asked. Besides, it's not his turn, but in the spirit of playing nice—even if it's a ruse—I say, "Scavenger hunts."

His brows rise. "Scavenger hunts?"

"There was a club at school. We had to figure out clues, puzzles, and things like that to find a prize." There's a dull pang in my chest remembering it, and I take my second roll before he can ask more.

King. His follows. *Love.*

My loss.

"Tell me about your family," he says.

My throat constricts. Does he know about Oren? Is he trying to get me to admit to something? I won't. He already doesn't want me here, and harboring the sister of a traitor wouldn't exactly be keeping with his so-called neutral stance. "That's not a question."

"Okay." His nostrils flare. "Where is your family?"

"Why are you asking something you know the answer to?" I shift uncomfortably on the edge of the chair. He studies my face, his expression curious. *Careful.* This could be a trap. "My parents were killed in the bombings," I say. "My brother is dead too."

He blinks once. "Not in the bombings?"

"Before." I fight against the vortex that threatens to suck me into that chasm of sorrow I escaped over a year ago. I snatch my die and let it fall again. *King.*

Water. He rolls again. *Life.*

My leg bounces as I consider my options. "Why did you give Goran your ring in the temple?"

"It…" Theo spins the band around his finger. "This is what's left of my power. Without it, all I can do is travel back and forth between your realm and my own."

"And with it?"

His lips curl into a sneer, but it seems directed at some faraway place instead of me. "With it, Goran can travel too."

I'm nowhere near brave enough to clarify, but something tells me he knows what I meant. I can't help wondering if it would work the same way with me. Cy's warning is still fresh in my mind, contradicting Theo's promise of safety yesterday. But stealing from a god won't do me any good. Even if I could get the ring and make it home, Theo probably wouldn't have any trouble finding me.

"Yesterday you said I was safe here." I pause. The words flow out before I can change my mind. "Did you mean it?"

Theo sits up, his expression tight, and grips his knees. "I haven't threatened you again."

A breath falls from my lips in the form of a laugh. I try to keep my voice light as I say, "Once was enough."

"Is this about the men? Goran spoke to them after you arrived. They won't bother you."

"They take off running at the mere sight of me," I grumble. It's incredibly irritating, actually. Having someone else to talk to would be a nice change of pace. I'm beginning to feel like a leper.

"I'm not sure I understand where this is coming from," he says.

Cy. It's coming from Cy. "Can I *trust* you?"

His eyes fall in increments from my eyes, to my nose, my lips, my chin, the pink scar on my neck, then back up. "You'll believe what you want, no matter what my answer is."

"Nevermind. Forget I asked." I reach for the die to throw again, praying I lose, but his hand pins mine to the table. While his touch is gentle, it sends shock waves crashing over my body.

"Did someone do something?" he asks.

I don't know. That's the problem. I don't know anything. "No."

The muscles in his jaw twitch. I school my expression into what I hope is indifference, but my heart hammers so hard I swear he can feel each beat. When he eases pressure from my hand, he doesn't take his fingers away. Instead, they linger there, lifting slightly so they graze my knuckles, then trail toward my nails before falling away.

The lack of contact is jarring, and I whip my hand back. It must be the lack of sleep, because there's no way I'm disappointed. Touching hands isn't a big deal. People do it all the time in greeting or helping someone up. It happens every day for a million different reasons. Theo did it yesterday too. That was less provoked than this, but the spike of adrenaline is so much more powerful today.

"Theo—"

"We'll play again another time," he says in a rush.

He doesn't look at me before he rushes out the door. I clutch my hand to my chest and rub the skin until the entire back of my hand burns from the friction. My head spins. I flop against the back of the chair and roll the Fate die between my fingers.

Later, sitting in the same chair Theo left me in, I glare over the top of the mythology book to the pair of dice on the table. The ghost of him lingers across from me.

I force my attention back to the glossy pages. The book is full of stories about creation, heroes, and fantastical beasts. The two-headed buffalo is in here in all his glory, but apparently Drea killed it after she realized what a mistake it was. Even after coming here, most of this seems laughable. Human men that sprouted wings. Stardust sprinkled in the eyes of seers at conception. It all makes for a very dramatic story.

But I'm looking for a specific kind of tale. One I won't be able to find in Theo's library.

My mind catches on *Oskar and the Pearl* in the Table of Contents, and I flip to the page listed. On the left is a picture of a man in a white loin cloth pushing a pearl easily three times his size across the ocean floor. Coral slices his feet, tendrils of red rising up behind him to form a cloud of blood. Dark shadows lurk in the distance—some big, some small, all ominous—but the man's features are focused. Streams of bubbles escape from his nose. He looks straight ahead, ignoring everything around him.

Across from the picture, blue scrolls border a page covered in elegant script.

Once, the Sulyiv Peninsula was beloved by the Goddess of the Sea. The Sulyiv were open and honest, relishing in the gifts Brisa bestowed upon them. They sacrificed to the Goddess once a month in gratitude for the calm nature of their ports. But over the years, the Sulyiv grew proud and began to think themselves masters of the sea. Their sacrifices became fewer until, finally, they came only during the Quinquennial Honorings.

Brisa allowed this for fifty years before revoking her blessing. On the first night of the fifty-first year, a hurricane ravaged their coasts. Only the head of the royal fleet was spared to deliver a message. If the Sulyiv didn't want another storm to come the next night, their emperor would need to sail across the raging waves and sacrifice himself to the Goddess of the Sea.

But the emperor was the proudest of them all. He wouldn't forfeit his life under such an ultimatum, for he thought the hurricanes would disperse as all hurricanes do, and things would return to normal.

On the seventh day, in the midst of the seventh hurricane, the emperor's only son, Oskar, donned his father's robes and rowed the royal barge across raging waters. Brisa kept the ship afloat while Oskar made tributes to her siblings. Once he cut his arm, she sucked him down to the bottom of the sea. Inside Brisa's palace of glass, Oskar removed his father's robes and fell hopelessly in love with the beautiful goddess before him.

Brisa, however, was angered by his deception and refused to end her assault on the peninsula. For another three nights, the country was held in her grip. This angered Ebris, for what was the emperor's son if not the future emperor? He declared Brisa must keep her word and, to atone, push the pearl from the Mother Oyster for as many nights as she broke the covenant.

Oskar, wretched over his dishonesty and enamored with his bride, offered to receive her punishment instead. As Brisa's husband, surely he was her equal. Surely it would be the same. Ebris agreed, and for three days Oskar pushed the pearl from the Mother Oyster across the seabed, braving the horrors of the deep.

When he was finished, Brisa looked upon her weary husband and kissed his brow, healing his wounds.

I blink at the last sentence. That can't possibly be the end, but a new tale about a bird and a boulder begins on the next page. How much of this is true? What happened to Oskar? Did he stay with Brisa or go to the Netherworld? Is he still with her? The most important part is missing.

But, of course, I'm assuming Oskar ever really existed.

With a frustrated sigh, I slam the book shut and start back to my room to scour the account of the Ostran War again. At least I know that's made only of fact. At least it will have an actual ending.

NINE

THEO

A white suspension bridge cuts across the limestone gorge leading to Volkana's capital. Streetlights flicker to life on the other side as night begins to take hold of the city of Ubrar. Below, the deep crevice looks as if it could reach straight into the Netherworld itself. Goran shivers beside me, his breath a cloud lost in the fog rolling down the mountain range behind us.

"I hate this city." I adjust the zipper on my parka. "It's nothing but trouble."

"I could've done this alone. It's probably nothing." Goran shoves his hands in the pockets of his trench coat. A stretchy black hat hides his heritage along with his blond hair, but there's nothing to be done about his pallor. Sending an Asgyan, hidden or not, into the middle of Volkana alone is ignorant at best. I'm the one who should have done this alone, but Goran knows exactly where we need to go.

"A spy goes missing and you think it's nothing?" I ask, giving him a sidelong glance.

"It's only been four days."

It's unusual to go more than two days without word in times of peace. Never in times of war. If Ebris wasn't being so stubborn, I would have a better idea what's going on, but without reading the reports, anything could have happened. It's crucial I don't have blind spots when I dive back into the trenches. If a spy is missing, I need to find him. Besides, it's my responsibility to make sure nothing happens to them. Sacrifices can die here, and there's nothing I can do to bring them back.

"Let's make this fast," I say.

The grated metal bridge clangs beneath our boots. I change my breathing to exhale with every other step and cloak both of us with my shield. We can't hide under it forever. We'll have to talk to Volks at some point if we want information, but at least we can make it into the city without being harassed.

A few bills are tucked in a secret slit in the cuff of my jacket for bribes, but, approaching the edge of Ubrar, I regret not bringing more. Cash is the first language here, Volk the second. Thieves will be severely disappointed if they look in our pockets. I clutch my ring hand close despite not being seen.

Inside the city, Goran leads the way down a narrow sidewalk. Past women in scanty clothing and men with needles in their arms. Two police officers stand brazenly on the corner, drinking from flasks with a tall man in a heavy fur jacket. I try not to look, to avoid the corrupted souls and the problems that follow in their wake. They flock to the outskirts like rats, but the city center isn't free of vermin. They're better at disguising themselves in high-end brothels and opium dens. But a rat with a pretty bow still eats from the garbage. It's surprising Volkana has enough able-minded men left to fight the war.

Finally, Goran stops in front of a four-story stucco building with a clay roof. A crack webs up the corner. "He lives here," he says.

I run a finger over the names beside a silver intercom. "What's his name again?" I ask.

"Timun." Goran leans forward to read the tags and jabs one of the grimy white buttons. A faint buzz rings through the speaker and we wait. And wait. He presses it a second time. A third. A fourth.

"Stop," I say. "He's not here."

I drop the shields hiding us from view and slide my hand down the whole row of buttons. The speaker crackles as the buzzing echoes back at us from every apartment then falls silent again. I back up and glare at the side of the building. Scaling the wall wouldn't be hard—the verandas are perfectly spaced—but I'd rather not chance it with the amount of rust holding the railings together.

A window slams open to my left and an old woman with curlers leans out. "You," she snarls through yellow teeth. "Do you know what time it is?"

"Excu—"

"Hello, ma'am," Goran says in perfect Volk. "We're looking for our friend, Timun, in apartment eight."

"You have some nerve waking me up to look for that flea bag," she snaps.

I pull the first bill from my sleeve and dangle it in front of her. "Where is he?"

"You don't have to bribe *everyone*," Goran whispers. "It draws attention."

"What do you think a crotchety old witch screaming at us on the street does?" I whisper back.

The woman snags the money with a claw-like hand and leans back inside. Her lips pucker. "Drafted." She slams the window down and whips tattered curtains over the glass.

"Drafted?" I turn to Goran. "You're supposed to keep them out of the system."

His face is ghostly pale under the streetlight. "I…I don't know. Maybe…"

My men fought their battles before they sacrificed their lives; they didn't do it to march back into war. Sending them back as spies is bad enough when they came to me expecting eternal paradise. I won't let them become cannon fodder.

"Maybe what?"

"Maybe they're so desperate for men that they're pulling them off the street." Goran's voice wavers. "Or it could be a lie. That woman might not know where Timun is."

"No." The Volks are wild and ruthless but their military is ruled with an iron fist. They wouldn't drag boys off street corners and toss a gun at them. The old woman is telling the truth. She has no reason to lie. I crack my neck as we turn away from the apartment building. "I know what happened." This is the next move in the game. A piece moved across the board. "Ebris is going to pay for this."

Goran draws a breath. "Theodric, don't do anything rash. We don't know—"

I storm past him. I *do* know. Ebris isn't coming to me to fix my mess because if I stay away, he can maneuver things any way he likes. I'm such an idiot not to have seen it before now. "What's the fastest way to The Black Pony from here?"

"Turn left," Goran says with resignation.

The air is thick with the scent of alcohol and sweet perfume as we slip down the alley toward the Volk army's favorite bar. Situated between the garrison and a brothel, it's easy to have a night out on the town and still make it back to the barracks before dawn.

Boisterous laughter ripples over me when we reach the street. Goran slips out of the shadows beside me, hunching into his coat. Two dozen green and brown uniforms blend into the bar front. A few men and women stand at the end of picnic tables covered in white plastic but the majority of them are sitting. Some of them are too drunk to even be doing that and lean onto the table for support. Broken glass and plastic cups litter the cobblestone. One of the bigger men checks me with his shoulder to get to the alley where he urinates on the corner of The Black Pony.

I hate this city.

Goran tugs his hat down and shifts uncomfortably beside me. "What are we doing here?"

"What we came to do," I say. A waitress rounds the table in front of us in a low-cut shirt, apparently oblivious to the chill. She plunks a foaming pint down in front of the youngest solider in the bunch. I take a deep breath and grab the two remaining on the tray at her hip before easing onto the edge of a bench.

"Oye." The waitress kicks at my boot. "Those are bought and paid for."

I tuck a bill in her half-apron and wave her off. Only she doesn't leave. She lets the empty tray dangle from her hand, her red lips parting to read me the riot act, but Goran steps in with apologies and a charismatic smile. I look down the rows of men as he charms her into compliance. I'm not sure what Timun looks like—there are too many sacrifices to memorize all their faces—but I'm confident he would recognize me.

"That's why I said I would take care of this on my own," Goran whispers as he sits down across from me.

I tap a finger against the pint. "I don't have time to be tactful."

"Then you better have time for an argument," he says.

I don't. I won't lower myself to argue with a mortal over a couple drinks. "Do you see him?" I ask.

Goran sips the beer, discreetly trailing over faces. "No."

Soldiers burst out of the bar and saunter toward the building next door where the candied perfume originates. The door remains open behind them until the waitress yanks it shut behind her. It was long enough to see the place is filled to the brim with uniformed Volks.

"So many," I say quietly. "Too many."

Goran lifts a hand to motion to the burly man beside him with thick sideburns and pretends to scratch through his hat to hide it. "Yes."

This isn't a few men flying out to meet a battalion. This *is* a battalion. The only time this many soldiers get to break curfew is right before they go into battle. "They'll attack before the end of the week," I say.

"Theodric," Goran warns.

"We have to go." It isn't safe to talk here, and the conversation can't wait.

This is a new low for Ebris. I could learn to get over him talking the zealots into sacrificing Cassia. If it were any other girl it wouldn't have mattered, so

I take responsibility. But this? The world is changing. My men are limited. Sacred. The most important link I have to the world. I shouldn't have waited so long to check in on things. Now it's vital we scour the stack of reports and learn where the Volks are heading so I can cut them off.

When I push up, my shoulder knocks someone behind me. Glass shatters. Beer splashes my pant leg and a hush falls over the group. A man two tables down stands up with a shout, and motion seems to slow. I know what's coming. Goran eases off the bench with a pointed look. I incline my head in agreement.

Run.

We're outsiders. Strangers. Suspicious. More importantly, we're outnumbered. As much as I'd love to take a little frustration out on them, I have to get Goran out of here. He's no stronger than they are, and I can't be as strong as I am. I already have one missing sacrifice—I can't lose another.

I lunge toward the alley but a blow to the cheek knocks me off course. I stagger sideways. A metallic taste hits the tip of my tongue. I round on the man who hit me. He shakes his hand out as he steps forward. I bend my knee and slam the sole of my boot into his stomach. He wheezes, gripping the table, and the rest of the soldiers leap up in support. They scramble over the benches, knocking tables aside in their rush to get to us first.

Damn.

I bash my elbow backward into someone's throat. Goran reaches the alley, funneling the attackers into single file. I yank the nearest man by the collar and toss him into one of his comrades. A fist flies at me from the left. I swing back, pulling my punch so I don't kill him, and he somersaults over a table.

I dodge more hits, taking a few in the process. I'm almost to Goran when the cry goes up. "Spies! Asgyan spies!"

A flash of blond hair falls in the alley. "Son of a—" I slam the man in front of me into a wall and toss his unconscious body over my shoulder. Two soldiers ahead of me wrestle Goran to the ground. I reach into the tangle of limbs and drag one of them off by the ankle. Soldiers clamber behind us, tripping over their fallen. I launch myself over Goran and snag his upper arm. The soldier leaning over him falls to the ground when I yank him free. We duck around the back of the bar. I slam the shields into place and we run.

Shouts continue to rise up as they search for us, calling for a lockdown of the city. A horn echoes through the night, pulsating through my bones. I push myself harder. Faster. I'm not interested in being stuck on this side of the bridge, shielded or not.

A flare goes up, painting the streets a brilliant red. Men and women peek out of their homes while the filth on the streets retreat into the shadows. We weave through the confusion, dodging cars, then the bridge rattles beneath our heavy footfalls. It isn't until we've reached the temple ruins in the mountains that we stop.

"This never would've happened before." I punch one of the few walls that survived the earthquake years ago. "Never. Those men would've been on their knees the second they raised a finger against us."

"Theodric." Goran rasps for breath.

"I'm going to kill Ebris for this," I growl.

"We don't know this is his doing."

"Of course we do," I shout. My throat burns from it. "This entire war would be finished by now if he hadn't stuck his nose where it didn't belong. *Again*. It's never going to end. My siblings will never trust me, Goran."

"I know," he says in a strained voice.

He's never agreed before. It's always been *don't lose hope* and *eventually*. I let my head fall back. "And now I'm stuck with *her* on top of everything."

"This isn't Cassia's fault."

"I know that," I snap. "Why do you think she's still alive?" There's a long silence, the only sound is my own breath grating in my ears. I take in my adviser with his bloody nose and cut eyebrow, and my throat tightens. This is what Ebris wants. To tear me down to nothing, starting with those closest to me. "Do you think she was coached to tell me she didn't care?"

Goran's eyes pop. "Now you're being paranoid."

"Am I?" It makes sense. I take the slightest interest in a girl and the next day she's in my temple. Maybe she was planted at the bonfire that night. Her anger at the other Kiskens is likely real given the circumstances, but to want the entire island to fade away? Not many mortals are that cruel. And there's the matter of her brother. She has to blame me for that.

"Cassia isn't working with Ebris." Goran's face twitches. "She hasn't tried to change your mind."

She's not trying, but every day I find myself wondering if I should gift Kisk a small victory for her. She's invaded my very being, and I can't get her out. Not even now, after losing Timun and being assaulted. If there was ever an inappropriate time to be worried about a girl, it's this moment.

"She can't know the truth about her brother," I say. If she told me the truth yesterday during Fate, if she told me who her brother was, I would have told her everything. It wasn't my intention when I asked her to play, but I know the words would have come. She had a chance to be honest but she withheld. Now I'm going to keep the information tightly under my belt until the war is over. Longer, if necessary. "I don't want to give her a reason to switch sides," I admit.

"You mean that he was set up?" Goran asks. "Or that he's still alive?"

I let out a long breath. "Both."

He nods.

I swipe a hand through my hair and pick the dried blood off the already healed cut on my lip. "We have to get back. I can't wait for Ebris anymore. It's too dangerous to let things continue unchecked."

"Finally." Goran's shoulders sag in relief. "And we'll keep looking for Timun."

"We will," I agree. "But we'll need to get someone else down here in the meantime."

"I'll bring someone down at first light."

We step into the middle of the destroyed temple, over broken stone and dried leaves, and I grab Goran's wrist. The world shifts under our feet as we hurdle home.

TEN

CASSIA

My brain can't process any more numbers. Not yet. Maybe after some fresh air and a change of scenery. *Maybe.* Searching for something useful in these books seems more futile by the minute, and the book Theo gave only creates more questions. At least the myths are interesting. I hug it to my chest as I step out the front door on my way to give rock skipping another shot.

I come up short before the door closes behind me. Goran drags his feet through the courtyard, gravel dust circling his brown boots with each step. A black hat sits cockeyed on his head, tufts of blond hair sneaking out from the edges, and mud is splattered halfway up his jeans. I've never seen him ruffled before, let alone grumpy. I want to look away but I'm drawn to him the same way I would be to a car accident. As he gets closer, I notice dried blood flaking in one of his eyebrows.

"What happened to you?" I ask, stepping off the stoop.

His laugh is tired as he rubs his face. Theo's ring hugs his thumb. "Rough night," he says.

"Apparently." I smirk. It's possible I'm enjoying his discomfort a little. "Theo working you hard, is he?"

He levels his gaze at me. "Cassia, about the book—"

"So that *was* you." I never actually suspected anyone else, but with the amount of work done in my bedroom, a dozen people had to have come in and out, including Astra. "Mind telling me exactly what's so interesting before my brain melts?"

"I need to know." He steps close enough that I hear his breath rattle in his chest. "I'm sorry to ask, but it's important. Why are you reading through the archives?"

My face falls, my thoughts scrambling. *Crap.* I can't answer that; he'll take whatever I say straight back to Theo. I'm not sure what the reaction would be, but I imagine it won't be good. If there was another way out that Theo wanted me to know about, he would've offered it to me already. Call me crazy for not taking their word on it. They can't suspect I'm trying to find a way to weasel out of an untimely death until I know for sure there is one. "Nothing. I'm curious," I say.

"No one is curious about the archives." He pulls his brows together. "No one."

"I am."

He lowers his chin, his lips pressed in a tight line. "Did someone put you up to this?"

Warning bells chime in the back of my mind. I knew he was too observant for my own good. "Put me up to what?"

"Are you trying to sabotage Theodric?"

I snort. "Are you crazy?"

"If you are…" He licks his lips. "If you are, I unwittingly helped the moment I left that book under your pillow."

My stomach hardens. I can't believe he would think that when, for the most part, I've minded my own business. Is it because I brought up the war at the waterfall? My anger got away from me one time, and, even then, I wasn't asking Theo to do anything about it. He's the only reason I'm alive. Doing something to him might affect me if we're connected. For all my reading, I still don't know how this works. Besides, even if I wanted to sabotage him, I wouldn't have the first clue how to go about it.

I step away from Goran to regain my personal space and fix him with a stare. "Are you serious? What do you think I'm going to do, blackmail him into saving the world with inventories?"

He squints. "I don't know. Are you?"

"No," I almost shout. "Goran, what are you talking about? Did you hit your head this morning?"

He closes the gap between us again. "Whatever it is you're looking for, tell me or the next person to ask will be Theodric."

He can't mean that. Goran wouldn't sick Theo on me for reading those books. If looking at them was an issue, he should have said something when he caught me red-handed in the kitchen. Instead, he told me I was welcome to them.

When I stay quiet, he shakes his head. "Fine. I tried."

"Wait." The fabric of his sleeve is damp beneath my grasp. I don't want either of them to know, but if I have to choose one over the other, Theo loses. "I'm not doing anything wrong."

"No?"

"I'm trying to find another option for myself." My voice cracks. I let go of him to rub my forehead, and he makes a small, unconvinced sound. "I swear. I mean, it's nice here and all, but I'm not confident I'll survive the wrath of the War God. There has to be another way out of this. If Theo decides to send me packing, I'd rather my destination not be the Netherworld, so I need to be ready to negotiate."

Goran stares at me, then slowly his features relax and he steps back.

"Speaking of books," I say when he says nothing. I hold the cover out so the foil sun reflects in his face. "How much of this is true?"

He brings a hand up to shield against the glare. "Where did you get that?"

"Theo." When he doesn't say anything again, I wave it side to side. "So?"

He clears his throat. "I'm not sure. I haven't read it. Maybe half?"

Half? Which half? Half of it is the straight truth or it's all lies inspired by the truth? "What about Oskar?" I ask.

"Oskar?"

"He pushed the pearl."

"Oh. Him." He squeezes his eyes shut and rubs at the corners. "We never met. He only lasted a few years."

An invisible hand squeezes my chest. That has to be a drop in the bucket to them. Theo may appear to be seventeen, but he's thousands of years old in my world. Does that mean Oskar lasted a day? A week? Did Brisa kill him instead of kissing him at the end of the story? Or does Goran mean a few years *here*?

118

The questions swirl through my mind until my pulse leaves me breathless.

"What happened to him?" I ask.

"He was ready to move on." Goran shrugs. I can't read his expression. Pity, maybe. His mouth opens, but footsteps crunching on the gravel slam it shut again.

"Hello." Astra's voice travels across the courtyard. She makes her way under the arch, her hair swaying in a high ponytail, Cy close behind. *Finally.* It's been less than forty-eight hours since she redecorated for me, but it feels like a lifetime.

"Perfect," Goran groans.

Perfect, indeed.

Goran starts to turn away and fear burns through me like a hot poker. "You're not going to tell Theo, are you?" I whisper. "I promise I'm only looking for answers."

"I won't, but you're wasting your time." He turns to smile at Astra and Cy. "Theodric is busy today. Is this important?"

"I'm not here for my brother," Astra says in her sing-song voice. "I came to see Cassia."

Goran gives a terse nod, shoots me a final look, and continues on his original path into the mansion. I shake away the weight of his final words and give Astra a bright smile. I almost mean it, but seeing Cy in my peripheral vision draws my thoughts down a darker path. *Later,* I promise myself. I'll corner him later. First, I have to play nice so Astra doesn't suspect I'm up to anything like Goran did.

"What happened to him?" she asks, eying the front door as it closes behind Goran.

"I think he's having a bad hair day," I say.

I laugh. She laughs. Cy does not. I shoot him a sweet smile and he scowls, wariness written in his features. He should be nervous. I hope he's ready for an interrogation of epic proportions.

⬤

Astra loops her arm through mine as we circle back around the perimeter of Theo's realm. Uncomfortable heat seeps through the thin fabric of her sleeve, but I force myself not to pull away. Gods must run warm—Theo has been the same—so I may as well get used to it. But sweat still beads on my skin.

My nerves spark as we walk too close to the edge. Solid ground simply ends, giving way to infinite fluffy white clouds. They never float up past the lip of grass and stone, as if they're merely a new substance to walk on, but all I imagine is Astra losing her balance and pulling us both over.

When I catch a glimpse of Cy from the corner of my eye, he's walking a good five feet from the precipice. He's trailed us the whole time, far enough away not to intrude yet close enough to hear every word. His presence is a heavy weight on my back, but I welcome it. It keeps me from having to look over my shoulder to make sure he hasn't scurried off.

It's been nearly an hour, and I'm not sure how much longer I can take the idle chatter. At least I'm not expected to do much in the way of reply. A question here, a comment there, and she keeps going. She's told me about each item in the bedroom, the fit Theo had when she showed up with it all, and gave a play-by-play of the work. I tune her out somewhere between curtain rods and carpet padding, focusing instead on how I'm going to get Cy alone.

"Cassia." Astra stops walking and guides my shoulders to face her. "There's something I feel you should know. It's rather shocking, so you'll have to agree not to do anything rash."

Cy takes a step closer then hesitates. Astra doesn't look in his direction, but I do. His face is stony. His head tilts forward like an invisible force is keeping him from charging. If he doesn't want me to hear what the goddess has to say, it's bound to be good. A breakthrough, even. I lean toward Astra and give her my full attention.

"I won't," I promise.

"It's your brother," she says. "Oren Stavros is alive."

Pain tears through me, tiny shards shredding muscle and bone alike. I clutch at the fabric over my heart. She can't mean that. Surely she's confusing him with someone else because that's impossible. I visited Oren in prison. I heard the judge read his sentence in the courtroom. His ashes sat in an urn on our mantle. There's no way he escaped death. None.

"No. My brother was hung for treason," I whisper.

"He wasn't." Astra takes my face between her hands. Her fingers smooth over my cheekbones. The heat is there but I barely feel the touch. Her glossy lips move again, but it's hard to hear her over the nest of hornets buzzing through my head.

"What?" I squeeze my eyes shut until the droning fades. "I don't understand."

"Your brother was taken to a prison camp in Volkana after they raided the Kisken prison. Your government let the country think his sentence was carried out to avoid paranoia and riots," she says carefully.

121

My stomach lurches. That can't be true. It's too big a thing to cover up. Volkana has no problem rubbing their victories in our faces. They enjoy taking credit where it's due. Besides, why would they want Oren? It doesn't make sense.

"No, he's dead," I insist.

"Love, he's not." Her expression softens, glossing over with pity. "I would never hurt you with a lie like that."

It's all I can do to stay on my feet. *Oren's alive.* He's been alive this whole time, suffering and alone, as a Volk prisoner. A thought slams to the front of my mind, and I suck in air like I'm drowning. Astra can't be the only one to know who my family is. "Does Theo know?"

"Of course." She pauses. "I'm sure he planned to tell you."

Doubtful.

"Perhaps after the war," she adds.

Possible.

He knew. This whole time he knew Oren was alive. Volkana isn't like Asgya. They don't treat their enemies like human beings. When the war is over, only a handful make it out of the country, just enough to avoid war crime accusations. The odds my brother would be one of them are slim to none, especially since they wanted him badly enough to kidnap him from solitary confinement in a maximum security prison And then lie about it.

"How do I save him?" I breathe. "Theo will help if I ask, right?"

She releases my face, taking my hands instead. "You can ask him."

The doubt in her voice makes my head spin. "But you don't think he will."

She shakes her head slowly. Oren's wide smile floats to the surface of my mind. What does he look like now? Are his ribs showing from hunger? Is he

122

in one piece?

"Theodric doesn't want to give up his control, and I have a feeling your brother is important to Volkana," Astra says. "He knows classified information and could be used as leverage."

"Leverage over who? My country is as good as gone, and the people left think he's dead." My voice strains. "Theo said…he said it's my right as a sacrifice to…"

"He owes you nothing if he hasn't accepted you as a bride," she says.

Tears brim, casting me into a quivering landscape. I focus on the next thing that might save Oren to keep them from falling. "What does that mean? If he accepts me, he'll have to help? He won't have a choice? I thought he already accepted me when he didn't kill me in the temple."

Astra nods. "After things are consummated, he'll be obligated to help all of Kisk, including displaced Kiskens like your brother."

"Whoa." It feels as if someone rammed a two-by-four into my gut. I fight against the nausea and pull in shallow breaths. "That's n ot…I c an't…You mean *consummate* consummate?" My face blazes with embarrassment at the thought. "No. Absolutely not."

"Would it be so bad?" she asks. "The two of you have a connection."

Of course it would be bad. Theo and I have barely had a real conversation. There's no way I'm sleeping with him. Not that he's interested. Not that *I'm* interested. I love my brother, but what she's implying…That I prostitute myself…There has to be a way that leaves me with my self-respect. "I can't," I say again. "What are my other options?"

Her red lips crack and she falters. "If your brother survives the war, you'll need a plan to prove his innocence. Even if you do, he's still likely to be targeted."

"Prove his innocence?" My voice is a high squeak. "You're telling me he didn't betray Kisk in the first place? But he was convicted by the High Court."

"No." She looks out over the floor of clouds. "He was doing what his superiors told him to do. There was a secret deal between Kisk and Asgya. Volkana was becoming too powerful on Asgyan soil. The Asgyans needed help. When Volkana found out, they twisted the truth and presented it to the Kisken people in a way that made Volkana look like the victim. Your government could have refuted it, but all evidence was conveniently lost."

My hands tremble. I'm not completely sure who I'm angrier with. Asgya for dragging us into their problems? Volkana for stealing Oren away? Or Kisk for purposely ruining my entire family? All of it in equal measure. And Theo. He did this. This has to be one of the scenarios he talked about, but I can't do anything from here. I *need* Theo to fix this. To fix everything: Kisk, Kiskens, my family's reputation. I can't do it alone.

"Theo will help," I say. Deep down I know it's a lie. He won't. I know he won't.

Astra exhales before pulling me into an embrace. "He won't take it well, so I'll ask on your behalf. I won't let on you know, in case it puts you in danger."

Puts me in danger. She's right. This could make him think I have stock in the war when I didn't before. He will think it because it's the truth. I return the hug with numb arms. "Will you?"

"Of course." She steps back and plants a light kiss on my cheek. "We're practically sisters."

I flinch, but if she notices she doesn't say anything. "Thank you."

"I'll go now. Wait a few minutes and Cy will walk you back."

124

Then she walks away, her ponytail swinging with each step. I stagger without her presence to ground me, but Cy suddenly materializes. I forgot he was with us. He eases me down onto the grass, far away from the looming edge. My vision tunnels to his face, and I dig my fingernails into his flesh until he's kneeling beside me.

"I was going to tell you last time," he says.

Bull. He wasn't going to tell me anything except that cryptic *beware.* If Astra hadn't interrupted us when she did, he likely would have talked a few more circles. And a lot of good his warning did to prepare me for this bombshell. Even if he *had* told me while we were standing in Theo's entryway, I wouldn't have believed it without the specifics Astra gave.

"Be careful what you do with this information," he warns.

"What does that mean?" I snap.

He bristles. "It means keep your secrets close and don't do anything stupid."

"And what exactly would be the stupid thing to do here? Hmm?"

He takes a deep breath. "Not everyone here wants the same thing. It's hard to know when you're being manipulated, but sometimes it's obvious for other people. You don't want to end up as someone's tool, especially not a god's."

That I believe. The question is who he thinks is manipulating me—Theo or Astra. Maybe it's him. Truth scrambles with fantasy and I can't tell the difference. I can't think. I can barely hear around the receding hum in my head.

"If Theodric wanted your brother out of that camp, he would be out already," Cy says. "If you ask for help, he's going to think you're here to control the outcome of the war."

I know! I flinch away from him. "If I can't ask and I won't seduce him,

125

what should I do? How can I leave my brother there to be tortured to death? I wouldn't be able to live with myself."

"He isn't part of your world anymore," Cy says in a calm voice. "If you want my opinion, leave it alone and let the chips fall where they may."

"You have no idea what you're talking about." All I wanted were answers, and I got those from Astra. I surge to my feet. "I'll never leave Oren to that kind of fate. Never."

He breaks eye contact with a heavy sigh. "Suit yourself."

"Thanks for your permission," I spit.

As soon as I'm through the front door, I feel it. An eerie stillness, tight and ready to burst. It locks my knees in place when I know I should turn around and run. I should hurry back to Cy and pretend I never came. But the door to the war room flies open and it's too late.

Theo looms over Astra, his body shaking from head to toe. "Get out," he booms. "Now."

"It's—"

"Out!"

The windows rattle and I dart into the far corner, wedging myself between the wall and a silver suit of armor. Astra peels out of the room. Her shoes slamming against the marble floor. Fear writhes at my core and I cover my mouth. When she sees me, she gives a small shake of her head and barrels outside. Cy pauses on his way under the arch, but that's all I see through the

126

window before Theo slams the door behind her. It quakes on its hinges, and I press myself harder against the wall.

"What?" he shouts in my direction.

If I look back at this moment and remember that I cowered in a corner, I'll hate myself. I step away from the knight and swallow hard. "I didn't say anything." I'm impressed with how steady my voice sounds.

He stares me down before spinning away. Maybe he'll change his mind about Oren when his temper cools down, but I don't have that kind of time. Every day my brother is in that camp is another day he's at the mercy of ruthless Volks. Each second is a second closer to death. He's already been there too long, and for what? Following orders?

"Goran!" Theo shouts.

My body jerks. Cy was right about one thing: I can't ask Theo for help. I swallow the lump in my throat as I consider my only other choice. My brother's life in exchange for my pride. It's worth the price; it has to be. I might be the only one who knows he's alive, and I'm definitely the only one who cares. I'm the only hope he has left.

ELEVEN

THEO

Pebbles skitter down the mountainside ahead of me in a chorus of clicks. It's the only sound other than my rapid breaths. No birds chirp, no animals rustle through the brush. It's as if they sense the danger lurking beneath their feet as keenly as I do. The bomb Volkana created, filled with antimatter, ready to be loaded on a bomber within the hour.

The hair on my arms stands on end. This has been a long time in the making. The amount of antimatter my new spy reported doesn't crop up overnight—but no one knew. Or *I* didn't know. Volkana had to be working on this long before Timun was drafted, but my lack of power blinds me. My sibling's eyes are wide open, though. None of them said a word. They may want an end to the war, but not like this.

I lock my shield in place as I reach the base of the mountain. The hangar's bay door is open, beige painted cement a bright spot among the gray stone. It's not very subtle for a secret bunker, but the four brown and green uniformed soldiers standing at the entrance with assault rifles don't seem concerned. I squint across the runway, the only thing that manages to blend into the mountain pass. More soldiers linger inside, less poised, like no one would be stupid enough to try stopping them. And if they did, they wouldn't get past their comrades.

I draw the blueprints from my back pocket and unfold the thin paper as I walk amongst them. My finger traces the stairwell. It's an easy shot down four levels to the basement, then I need to turn right at the end of a long hallway and enter the code into the keypad. Simple. But I can't help the empty feeling in the pit of my stomach. This is more powerful than anything I've disabled before. I have no idea how they've harnessed the antimatter, which means I don't have the slightest idea how to take it apart.

Waltzing between soldiers, I make my way farther into the hangar. Hot air blasts down from a vent in the ceiling to mix with the early winter chill. I look up as I pass beneath the wing of the plane and skid to a halt. A bright yellow sun glares down from the smooth metal. The blueprint crinkles in my fists.

Thieving bastards.

They're going to drop this thing out of a Kisken bomber. It's doubtful there will be anyone left to identify the plane, but, if there is, the blame will fall on the island. I fold the blueprint into something resembling a square and shove it back in my pocket without looking away from the sun. I never meant for this war to go so far. I thought I could do this. Prove myself. Finally. *Finally.* But my hands are bound too tightly.

A woman in a khaki jumpsuit strides through the heavy door leading to the staircase. Her head is bent to the clipboard in her hands, her dark hair wound into a tight braided knot. "Is the flight plan programmed?" she asks in Volk.

"All set," says a voice from inside the cockpit. "We have to do the walk-around and check the oxygen masks, then we'll be ready to load it up."

I tear my attention away from the pilot and charge for the open stairwell. This thing has to be disabled before they're ready for takeoff. Once the explosives team moves the bomb into the elevator, my only option will be to go along for the ride. If I mess this up, I'd prefer to do it in a fortified underground bunker instead of near a large population. War is messy. Lives will always be lost, but I do have limits.

The metal stairs give slightly under the pounding of my feet. I barely have time to register the sharp smell of ammonia before I've made it to the final landing. Red signs cover the door, their white block letters giving various warnings: *Authorized Personnel Only, Danger, Explosives in Use.* I drag in a breath and let it out slowly, pushing my shield forward to encompass the door. The shield throbs around me, almost a living thing, and I pass into the hall unnoticed.

Bright fluorescent lights bounce off stark white walls, blinding me for a moment. There's one guard halfway down focused on his phone. The shield buffers my footsteps as they echo through the corridor, and I clench my jaw. The passage turns exactly where the blueprint said it would. The solid door looms at the end of the hall. A red light glows on the keypad over the handle. *Two, seven, five, one, three.* I repeat the code over and over until I'm standing in front of the door. My finger is stiff as I enter the sequence. The light switches to green and I slip inside. Motion lights flicker. Once. Twice. My breath catches and I stop mid-step.

A long gray cylinder hangs from the ceiling, suspended by a dozen heavy cables. On one end, four fins split diagonally. From the other end comes a long, needle-like point. But it's the eight tubes branching off at even intervals that render me immobile. Gold Penning traps are held taught with wires at the center of clear containers. Another cord, thicker, trails from the bottom of the hourglass traps into the body of the bomb.

My chest constricts around a frantic heartbeat, but I force myself closer. At least the antimatter is in plain sight. If I remove the cylinders, perhaps there's nothing else inside to cause an explosion. I run my hand over the smooth steel, feeling each screw, each weld mark. When I rap a knuckle against the belly, the sound is short and heavy. *Not hollow.*

The band of my ring twists around my finger as I rub my thumb against it. If I'm wrong, if this goes badly, the ring will take me back when the final flicker of life flees my body. Not that I want to be blown to bits and pieced back together, molecule by molecule through dimensions, but it's better than what will happen to the people of Volkana. Or this part of it, anyway. Women, children, the elderly. Not every Volk has the soul of a bloodthirsty conqueror, even if they are a seedy lot.

I scrub at my cheeks as I circle the bomb. To do this, I need to calm down. Going at this with shaking hands could get everyone killed. The caps to the clear containers appear to screw on. The antimatter should be safe as long as it stays within the golden hourglass. I need to get it somewhere remote before the charge runs out and blows everything to bits. I grip the cap but my sweaty palm slips.

Stepping back, I take a deep, steadying breath. I need more time. There's no way to guess what's inside the main bomb when nothing like this has ever been achieved before. *Concentrate.* I can do this, control this. It's just a bomb.

I circle it again and rub my hands against my jeans. This time when I touch a cap, I twist harder. The steel shifts but maintains its seal. Voices rise in the hallway and I tense, holding my breath. I have to get the Penning traps out before they come through the door.

The container cracks as I twist again. I leap back but nothing happens. Then, as I'm about to reach inside and retrieve the antimatter, hissing begins in the belly of the explosive. It's barely noticeable at first, but it doesn't take long for the sound to grow. The rest of the canisters vibrate and a high pitched whistle fills the cavernous room. The breath I was holding back breaks free and I tear across the room, whipping the door open. There's no time to think. No time to be smart. It's too late to stop the blast. The only thing left to do is run.

My shields drop as my concentration shifts to escape. I barrel into the hall, through a crowd of Volks in armored suits. Their shouts of surprise quickly turn into something primal as the whistle spills into the corridor after me, but I'm already at the staircase. Their feet hammer behind me in a frantic, irregular pattern. I lose the sound beneath the thundering in my head.

I pummel back into the hangar in time to see the wheels of the plane shift between their blocks. The cement floor tilts. I shove my way between soldiers—some running in, some out. Some stand still with their fingers over triggers. The screeching reaches an octave higher than I can hear for half a second before a deafening boom shatters the silence. I'm already across the tarmac when the blast slams into me. The bone shaking shove thrums through my body in waves. The mortals won't be able to withstand it; everyone in that bunker is dead.

They did this to themselves.

I have to believe that as I race across the sinking ground. If it wasn't a Volk mountain erupting, it would be an Asgyan city. They never should have tried something this dangerous; they had to know the risks. And yet, I'm sorry I failed them.

Trees groan and topple with heavy cracks. The path back to the temple crumbles in on itself, swallowing everything in its way. A metallic creak rings through the air, a whining cry, and the suspension bridge leading to the capital snaps. I take a sharp right. Boulders rain down, trying to sweep me along in their race to the gorge. Some nearly miss me. Others slam into my side. My ribs howl in protest. Broken. Blood runs hot over my skin, soaking through my clothes.

I'm not going to make it.

I have to make it.

The ground bucks again. My head is full of faraway screams and sirens, rumbles and booms. I wince against it all. The soil heaves under my feet, and I fall headfirst into a new crater. I shove to my feet. A fist-sized rock ricochets off my temple. I fall backward into the fresh dirt. I have to get up.

Get up.

One more step. Get up and take one more. Then another and another.

My vision blurs. Thick fluid flows into my eyes, blinding me. I stumble to my feet and search for something to pull myself from the corroding ground. My ears ring. The rich scent of clay fills my senses. Each attempt to inhale is blocked before it reaches my lungs. Darkness creeps over my mind, shrouding all rational thought.

Focus!

Home.

Goran.

Cassia.

TWELVE

CASSIA

The flashlight slips in my hand as I direct the beam of light around Theo's bedroom. It's plainer than I expected—bare stone walls with bulky, hand-carved furniture similar to what was piled in my room when I arrived. A rust colored comforter is pulled and tucked neatly over a massive sleigh bed. A rich mix of spices lingers in the air with a strong undercurrent of steel, of Theo.

Time is running short, so I swallow hard and move farther into the room. It took two hours to seep enough clovlan moss from the woods to lace Goran's wine and another hour for it to knock him out. Theo could be back any second.

My hand shakes as I pull open the thick wardrobe doors. A stack of T-shirts runs down the center with dress shirts, jackets, and the like hanging on either side. Batting the fabric out of the way, I shine the light over every inch. Then I move to drawers full of pants and underwear, sifting through each precise pile.

Nothing.

I run a hand along the hangers until everything looks as it did before and puff a piece of hair from my face with a shaky breath. Theo can never suspect I was in here. It doesn't matter what was in the back of the book on the Ostran War or how much it left my head spinning. There are awful things behind that leather cover—things Theo never should have let happen. The end numbers are higher than any historian ever recorded, and for no other reason than power. Theo's and the Ostran Empire's. If it weren't for the pages at the back, every fiber of my being would be too repulsed to do what I need to for my brother. I could never pretend to like Theo, let alone allow him to touch me.

But those pages.

The regret, the doubt, the self-deprecation. The pain in each ink stroke as Theo acknowledges his brother was right about ending the war, and that, in defending his territory, Theo took things too far. He admits he deserved to have his power stripped, but he wanted his siblings to trust his judgment. And he's sorry. Sorrier than he ever thought possible.

The wardrobe shuts with a thud and I freeze. My ears prick as I wait to hear heavy footsteps rushing down the hall. When they don't, I exhale and tip-toe to the nightstand. There has to be something here to help me, to tell me how to move forward with my plan. We have to have something in common to use as a springboard, or at least something I can fake an interest in. The pad of paper, pen, and handful of hard candy tell me nothing.

I kneel and sweep the flashlight under the bed. Nothing again. I lift the black and brown area rug, slip my hand between the mattress and box spring, and squint behind furniture.

Nothing. Nothing. Nothing.

It's like he doesn't live here at all. Like he's a guest in his own home.

The shaking in my hands spreads up my arm, quivering. I flex my hands to bring feeling back into my fingers. There's no more time. Theo may have another side hidden under all that bitterness, but there's no trace of it here. I certainly won't see any sign of it if he catches me snooping through his things after drugging his adviser.

Flicking off the flashlight, I ease back into the hall. I cringe at the soft click of the handle and back away from the door. My fingers skim over textured wallpaper as I feel my way through the dark to the stairwell.

Nothing. The word clangs through my head. My lungs seize. They constrict more with each step until my bare feet hit cool wrought iron. *I'm not sure I can save you, Oren.* I barrel down to the entryway instead of back to my room, gasping for air. It feels as if someone is compressing me into a tight ball. A cold sweat breaks out all over my body and my vision tunnels to the front door.

I sprint across the marble and into the moonlit courtyard. Gravel digs into my soles but I don't care. All I care about is air. Precious, precious air. My legs threaten to give out. Without the strength to convince them otherwise, I sink to the ground and bury my head in my knees.

I'm not sure how long I sit, rocking, in the shadows. When I finally lift my head, nothing is different. The mansion, the Wall, the moon and stars, all of it is the same. Everything except me. I'm light, yet heavy. Weary, yet wide awake. Pins and needles continue to assault my limbs. I've aged a thousand years but somehow feel younger than ever.

This is more than I know how to handle, but I have no choice. Just like I had no choice when Oren was arrested or when bombs turned me into an orphan. All I can do now is the same thing I've always done—pull myself up and deal with it.

A soft groan drifts through the courtyard. I leap to my feet and squint through the darkness in time to see a figure collapse against the arch. One arm wraps around his abdomen while the other hangs limp at his side. His knees knock together in an attempt to stay upright.

"Theo?" I call. The figure straightens slightly but doesn't answer. I shift nervously between my feet. "Theo? Is that you?" I ask, taking a step back. It's too dark where he is—I can't be sure.

"Were you expecting someone else?" he wheezes.

Relief flutters in my gut but it doesn't last. Theo's body slides across the stone as his knees buckle. He catches himself before hitting the ground, and I step forward. A ripple vibrates along his silhouette.

"Are you okay?" I ask.

Theo pushes off the Wall. His feet drag across the ground, his ankles twisting and bending under his weight, as he staggers from the shadows. The hair on the back of my neck stands on end, and I inch further back.

Is he drunk? Can gods get drunk?

The closer her gets, the more I'm torn between helping and hiding. Then he looks up. Moonlight reflects off his blood-soaked features, and I gasp. The sleeve of his jacket is ripped open from shoulder to wrist. A wide slash stretches from his side toward his chest, the fabric hanging limp. His jeans are in tatters. The few places untouched by blood are caked with dirt and leaf fragments. His breath rattles as he passes me on the way to the mansion. I watch him with my jaw hanging open until he pauses at the bottom of the stoop. He bends at the waist and spits red into the gravel.

I take a few tentative steps toward him. Drunk I can handle—*avoid*—but this…I don't even know what this is. "What happened to you?"

"Where's Goran?"

I hesitate. "Sleeping in the war room."

Theo exhales, glaring at the three wide steps before him. His nostrils flare as he hoists himself up and falters through the front door. I follow behind, raking him over for the source of so much gore. There should be cuts, holes, missing limbs, *something* based off the amount of blood I'm looking at, but I see nothing.

Maybe it's not his. The thought sends a chill oozing down my spine. Someone must have met a horrible end tonight. Maybe a lot of someones. It wouldn't be the first time he massacred mortals; he did it twice in the Ostran war. Entire clans.

Theo leans into his hands on the credenza in the entryway. Another feeling melts the slush creeping through my veins before it has a chance to solidify. I can't leave him like this anymore than I could watch that Kisken man starve after he lost at Fate. I sigh, resigned.

"You should sit down," I say. I take his hand and pull him gently toward the sitting room. When he comes without an argument, tension squeezes my stomach. He would never let me drag him around under normal circumstances. As soon as he half-falls onto the couch, I step back and wipe my hands on my pants. "I'll get Goran." He shouldn't be too hard to wake up. *I hope.* I only knew the type of moss to use because of an unfortunate incident last year when there was no food. I force what I hope is an encouraging smile. "Hang on."

He grabs the hem of my shirt, leaving a streak of crimson on the blue fabric. "Let him sleep. I'm fine."

"You're fine?" I raise my eyebrows. "Have you seen yourself?"

His hand drops away and he leans into the couch. His head thunks against the strip of wood above the padded back. "It's just a little blood."

"A little?" I wave my hand at his body, a frantic movement desperate to expel energy.

He gives a tired smirk and closes his eyes. "It's fine."

Clearly he's lost his mind. Even if it isn't his blood, there's no way he doesn't need help. He can't even hold himself up.

"Cassia?"

I jump. "What?"

"You're staring," he says.

I fold my arms across my chest. Of course I'm staring; he looks like something straight out of a horror movie. "What happened?"

"If I tell you, will you leave me in peace?" he asks, garbled.

Leave him here to suffer by himself? "Yes."

"Volkana planned to drop a new, incredibly destructive bomb on Asgya. I disabled it." His shoulders roll forward and he rubs at his chest. "*Tried* to disable it. I'm not exactly an expert on antimatter."

140

My eyebrows shoot up. "You blew yourself up to save Asgya?"

"I didn't blow up, the mountain did." The corner of his lip twitches. "I happened to be on it at the time."

"I didn't know antimatter was a thing." I rub my thumb against the smudge on my shirt. *He stopped a bomb.* It's his job, I suppose, but until this moment I didn't realize what that entailed. I didn't know he would have to put himself in such danger to do it.

"It wasn't." A small groan chokes the end of his sigh. "It is now."

I inhale, my lips cracking to speak, but I'm not sure what to say to that. He saved countless Asgyans from death. A mountain exploded and I assume a few Volks lost their lives, but if they planned to use the same bomb on their enemy, I can't bring myself to pity them too much.

As long as Oren is still alive...

A metallic taste coats my tongue, and I realize I'm biting the inside of my cheek. I know war means death and destruction, but there has to be a line somewhere. Apparently Theo understands that too.

"Don't move," I say.

Before he can argue, I take off for the kitchen where dust-covered mixing bowls are crammed on the top shelf. I hop onto the counter and straddle the oven burners to reach them. Somewhere in my head, I'm screaming at myself to stop helping him when I can't decide if I hate him. *Look how things turned out when I helped the Kiskens after they exiled me.* It's a lesson I should know well by now: don't stick your neck out for anyone that wants to chop it off. Unfortunately, I don't know how to take good advice.

I rinse the largest of the bowls in the sink and fill it with warm water. On the way back to the sitting room, I stop in the bathroom and stuff a stack of folded washcloths under my arm.

Besides, this is something.

Kiskens wash their friends and family all the time. Not that Theo and I are either of those things, but we should be. We need to be for Oren's sake. I take a deep breath outside the sitting room and hold it. This is all I can do. If I can remember *why*, maybe I can manage the *how*. Exhaling, I step around the doorframe.

Theo is in the same place I left him, his chest rising and falling in a long, labored rhythm. I pad across the room and let the cloths drop to the floor. The bowl clinks against the wooden table we used for our game of Fate, and his eyes fly open. His piercing blue irises hold me in place. Something shimmers there—suspicion, fear, pain—that tugs at a cord deep inside me.

"What are you doing?" he grumbles. "It's late. Go to bed."

The spell breaks at the sound of his voice and I huff, shaking the first cloth out. I dip it into the water. "If you don't clean your wounds, they could get infected." I glance at his ripped sleeve. "Some of this *is* yours, right?"

"All of it is mine," he says coolly.

"I'm surprised you have any left," I mumble to hide my surprise. I wring the water out and bring the cloth to his forehead. He jerks away. "It's just water."

"It's just blood," he counters.

I sit back on my heels. "Are you going to let me help you or not?"

His mouth opens and I can almost feel the word *not* hover between us. Then he shuts it and leans forward with a small, pained grunt. I put the cloth against his forehead and swipe around his temple. He winces but stays still, his gaze focused on his lap. I focus my own on the path I'm tracing across his face and nothing else. Not the flexing muscles beneath his ruined jacket or the vein pulsating rapidly in his neck.

At least, I try.

It's more work than I expect. Each line smudges dirt and blood against his tan skin. Lines of water race from the cloth, ending in red droplets at his jaw line. They drip down onto the torn knees of his pants. It takes three cloths before his face is finally clean.

The angles aren't as harsh as I thought before. Beneath the scowl he constantly wears, is a touch of tenderness. I can see it now despite his clenched jaw and furrowed brows. The soft sweep of lashes as he keeps his gaze down. The gentle curve of his lips. Palpitations flutter in my chest, my head fuzzy with nerves. *Stop it*. It doesn't matter if he's attractive. I've accepted my mission and have to follow through without getting lost along the way.

"Hand," I say as clinically as possible. He clutches them tightly between his knees. "Hand," I say again, firmly.

He purses his lips before prying his hands apart. They come to rest on his knee caps. The fingers shake against the shredded denim, but I can't tell if it's from pain or if he's as nervous as I am. *Probably the pain*. His breathing hitches as I begin at the wrist.

"I can stop," I offer.

"It doesn't hurt." His reply is immediate, but the sound is little more than a breath.

A flush rises in my cheeks, and I keep working until there's no exposed skin left to clean. My fingers slide up the ripped fabric of his sleeve, and I bite my lip as I glance inside. My head swims in relief that there's no trauma. Blood is one thing, but carnage is an entirely different animal. I threw up all over the frog they made us dissect in biology class, which really added an extra oomph to my last year of school. Throwing up all over Theo would be even worse.

"Umm." I drop my hand and his gaze drifts up to mine. "Can you…"

He blinks, hesitation etched into every facial angle, then shrugs out of the jacket. His teeth clack together and his breathing quickens, but I pretend not to notice. The T-shirt underneath clings to each muscle and the gash in the fabric shows a hint of his unmarred stomach.

This is a bad idea. All of it. Horrible. But it's too late now, so I school my expression into indifference and stick a clean cloth in the bowl. After a steadying breath, I turn back to his arm. There's no way I'm asking him to remove any more clothing. After this is done, I'm getting out of here.

I start at the cuff of his T-shirt and slide down to his elbow. This time I actually manage to stay focused on the work as my stomach flops, but the work itself is distracting. His muscles are even harder than they look. My arm slows. His gaze is heavy, watchful.

"So." I hesitate. "You have super healing abilities, huh?"

"I'm a god," he says. His words brush hot along my cheek.

"Right." I chance a look up at him. "I forgot."

His breath rushes out in a surprised laugh. "Did you?"

My cheeks blaze. This is dangerous. But what did I expect? I would have an easy time getting close to him? This game comes with a hefty price. If I'm not careful, if I don't concentrate on the wrongs he's done, I might lose even if I win. "Well, I hope you didn't like this couch much," I blurt as pink water dribbles onto the cushion.

"Peroxide," he says.

I scrub at his skin, my strokes rushed and uneven. "As long as you don't try stuffing it in my room like you did with all—"

He tugs on the end of the washcloth, pulling it from my hand. "Why are you doing this?"

"I don't know what you mean."

The cloth lands on the table with a wet slap, pink water draining off the corner and onto the patterned rug. He gently tugs my chin up. The grime on his fingers is slick against my skin. "Yes." Once our eyes meet, there's no looking away. "You do."

I swallow hard. *No, I really don't.* I know why I should be doing this, but with the book, the bomb, and the pain on his face...It doesn't make sense. None of this does. It feels as if my thoughts are caught in a tornado, flinging everything a snarled mess.

Theo shifts on the couch, inching closer to the edge. His breathing changes again, different from before in a way that makes my stomach clench. When his hand falls from my chin, I suck in a breath.

I shouldn't miss the contact, but I do. I want him to touch me again. I want to touch him again too, but my excuses are gone along with the mess. My reason to be here at all has disappeared. Still, I find myself not moving, pinned by an invisible hand.

The room grows hotter until, finally, I can't stand it anymore. I push off the floor and Theo follows me to his feet. His palms sear my cheeks as he takes hold and backs me into the wall. My stomach somersaults, my heart threatening to beat from my chest. Then his lips crush against mine, demanding. Mine move in response, slow at first, but it doesn't take long to match his intensity. He tastes cool, metallic. I grip the fabric near his hips and urge him closer. It's still not close enough.

I can't breathe. I don't want to breathe.

Theo lurches away, stopping halfway across the room where he sways on his feet. I drag in a breath and use the wall for balance. My head roars. I can't decide if I want him to kiss me again or if I want to slap him for kissing me at all.

Again, a small voice whispers in anarchy.

"I shouldn't have done that," Theo rasps.

No. He definitely shouldn't have done that, but, more importantly, I shouldn't have liked it. "It's okay," I say in an uneven voice.

"Cassia," he says, part regret, part warning.

"Theodric, you're back." Goran rubs his cheek in the doorway, fighting a yawn. "How did it go?"

Theo turns his rigid back to me. "I died," he snaps, and storms from the room.

Died?

Goran takes in the red towels on the table and the discarded jacket before raising a questioning eyebrow in my direction. I shrug. I don't know what else to do, and I don't trust myself to speak yet.

"Theodric?" Goran calls, rushing after him.

I press fingertips against my throbbing lips. *Don't you dare. Don't you dare like him like that.* He's lying to me. I can't trust him. And if I can't trust him, I can't have feelings for him.

But it's good he kissed me; it's part of the plan.

Stick to the plan.

THIRTEEN

THEO

"What's taking him so long?" I ask, more to myself than Goran. "Why isn't he here yet?"

I've been waiting for Ebris for hours now. He'll have a long list to scream at me about this time, but I have to give him this one—I failed. The blast likely took out an entire portion of the mountain range and the Volk capital. I can't be sure without the report from Ubrar, but the lack of one is telling; either the site of the ruined temple is buried or my new spy is dead. Likely both. At least Volkana won't be playing with antimatter again in the near future.

But, as if that weren't enough of a disaster for one night, I kissed Cassia. An idiotic, impulsive kiss. Somewhere between the shock of death wearing off and the adrenaline still surging through me, I lost control. The worst part is, I didn't hate it. Her touch felt good. It lulled me into a dream-like state, almost as if I were floating. The tightness in my chest tethered me at first. It held me back until it didn't anymore. When she stood to leave, my anxiety morphed to desperation. The thought of being away from her sent panic racing through my body. I wanted to feel her warm fingers trail over me, dragging the ache from my muscles, until exhaustion pulled me under. I wanted—needed—to be close. Closer.

The same feeling grips me now. Embracing my spirit, crushing it. I rest my head in my hands and groan.

"Chin up," Goran says from across the room. "At least you saved Asgya. That has to count for something."

"I wouldn't start celebrating yet." I drop my head further and rest my forehead on the desk. My muscles are sore, raw from knitting themselves back together, and I stifle the urge to crawl back into bed. When my brother comes storming in here, I need to be ready. It will be bad enough facing him without making him wait. "Blowing up one country over the next isn't exactly a victory. I'm supposed to be impartial."

"You are impartial, but you're also bound to rules. You know, those things you like to pretend don't exist." He shuffles through a few papers. "You couldn't very well let Volkana wipe Asgya off the map. It's a hard blow, but Volkana will regroup."

"You're unusually optimistic about all this," I grumble.

He snorts. "And you're unusually upset about it."

I'm not upset, I'm tired. This war. The game with my siblings. Cassia. Goran helps as much as he can, but I can only do so much without my full power. If it wouldn't make me look weak, like I had given in, caved under pressure, I would finish the war by the end of the month and take some time to figure out the next familial thing I need to out maneuver.

A soft knock on the door sends lancing pain through my skull. I wince and rub my sternum as I shove to my feet with a steadying breath. It's not Ebris. He doesn't knock, he barges. The men wait for Goran to go to them in the Wall if they need something, which leaves only one person it could be. My muscles tighten. I can't face Cassia. Not when each place she touched me prickles like a living thing.

Goran stands, his arms rigid at his side. "You can't ignore her forever."

"I can," I say through my teeth.

He gives me a long look before plastering on a bright smile and swings the door open. "Cassia." He ushers her inside. "To what do we owe this surprise?"

She's wearing a flared black dress that hits her knees with her hair smoothed into a ponytail. Small wisps flutter around her cheeks. The cheeks I held last night. My breath sticks. I remind myself to breathe and sink back into the chair. *Trouble.* She's bad for me in every way, but it's too late. Sending her to the Netherworld now is impossible. I clench my hands into fists and hide them beneath the desk.

"Um." Her eyes flick to mine for the briefest of seconds before she points behind her. "Your brother is here. He asked me to see if you're available."

Goran and I exchange hard looks.

"He also said to tell you *not that brother*," she adds.

I sit up straighter and stare past her into the hallway. "What's *he* doing here?" I half-whisper.

Goran tilts his head and forces his smile wider until it looks like his mouth will split in two. "Be nice," he says without moving his lips. "You need someone on your side."

"He's not on my side," I hiss.

Goran raises his eyebrows. "He's not on Ebris' side, either."

Leander strolls through the doorway with dark circles under his eyes and a genuine smile on his lips. Always the smile. I can count the times on one hand I've seen him without good humor, and even then he has an air of pleasantness about him. It's infuriating. No one is that happy all the time, especially when you're stuck in the Netherworld sorting souls.

"Hello, Theodric." He nods to Goran in acknowledgment. "You don't look pleased to see me. Is this a bad time?"

Any time is a bad time to deal with death.

I blow out a breath and try to relax my facial muscles into something less agitated. "It's been awhile."

"I've been busy." Leander scans the maps along the far wall behind Goran and clasps his hands behind his back.

"I can imagine." That's also my fault, but I can't say I'm sorry. Leander knows it's the cost of war as well as I do, so there has to be another reason he's here. "What brings you out of the Netherworld?"

Leander slips into one of the wooden chairs across from me and picks at a knick on the edge of the desk. "I always seem to forget how straight-to-the-point you are."

"I'm happy to remind you." I rub my temples, willing away the start of a headache. Another one this morning will put chinks in the wall I built to keep the high priest out.

"Maybe I wanted to see a friendly face," Leander says.

"So you came here?" I motion to the room full of weaponry and battle tactics. Nothing about my realm says *friendly*, least of all me. "You might have better luck visiting Astra. Or Drea—she adores you."

"No one could accuse you of being welcoming," he says in a flat voice. His smile falters, but the corners remain raised. "But I'm not here for a social call. I know Ebris already told you to stop stirring up the war."

"And?" I snap.

He stops picking at the desk and flattens his hand. His lips drop into a line. "What are you doing, brother?" he asks softly.

Resentment rages through my body, making me numb. "My job." His mouth opens, but I keep talking before he can get a word out. "I *did* stop stirring things up as Ebris asked. I ignored the war. I gave the mortals a chance to sort things out themselves, and look how well that turned out."

Leander throws his hands in the air. "You were supposed to guide them toward peace, not wash your hands of the entire thing. You dug them in too deep for them to crawl out alone."

The mortals dug their own hole; I simply provided the shovels. I'm too limited without my power to do more than that. The men and women in charge have to step up to the plate if they want a cease fire. I can help, but I can't simply will the war away anymore. I grit my teeth. "You overestimate my influence," I say.

"This is serious, Theodric." He glowers at me. "How did they figure out how to use antimatter?"

"Are you implying I had something to do with that?"

He blinks once. "Did you?"

"Get out," I growl.

"You don't intimidate me." He leans back in the chair and crosses his arms. "The mortals should be afraid, but not me. Unless you plan to work me to death, in which case your plan may be a glowing success."

I fix him with a cold stare. He must not realize how many lives were saved last night. If he did, he wouldn't go down this road.

"The entire city of Ubrar is gone. Do you know what the population was?" Leander asks.

He stares at me, impassive. I don't reply. Partially because, no, I don't know the exact population and partially because it's still less than the Asgyan target.

"I do," he says. "Three hundred fifty-six thousand one hundred and twenty nine. Care to ask how I know that number?"

"Not—"

"Because they all showed up at the same time last night. The entire city, Theodric. Including two of your spies. They send their regards, by the way. One of them was in fatigues. Are you sending your own to the front lines now? It's only fair, I suppose."

Timun. There hadn't been time to pick back up on his trail. I press a fist into my rolling stomach and take a shallow breath. "It wasn't my intent to set the bomb off."

Leander shakes his head. "I understand your need for war, but you have to think about what you're doing."

"I know what I'm doing. I can't predict everything the mortals will do." My voice is quiet. I'm not sure how things got this bad so quickly, but I have to do something before everything spirals out of control. I won't have a repeat of last night on my conscious. "Without being able to see them like you do, I'm left with educated guesses."

"Theodric." Leander leans forward. His fingertips pale as he presses them on the edge of the desk, his nail beds turning white beneath the pressure. "This isn't like the old days. You can't keep doing this. Ebris—"

"Ebris is holed up in a castle with his harem, ignoring what we do until the prayers of the high priests become too much for him to enjoy himself," I snarl.

"And what of your high priest? Can you not hear him?"

Thankfully, no.

Leander stands, thrusting a finger at Cassia. "*Look.* Do you see this? Do you see her?"

My back snaps straight. I forgot she was in the room. Her gaze cuts into me, her face haggard, and my bones turn to lead. "She's rather hard to miss," I say evenly.

"The mortals consider it barbaric to sacrifice livestock to us now, but Kisk sent you a bride. Don't you see how desperate they are?" he asks.

"Men are always desperate during war." I glance at Cassia again. At her dropped jaw. Her wide eyes. This doesn't concern her. I should have asked her to leave before talking to Leander; I knew what direction the conversation would take. "Goran, take Cassia outside."

Goran extends a hand to her, but she skirts around him into the hall. He follows, whispering a string of indistinct words. She says something in return, and her sandals clip rapidly against the tile. Goran's boots thud in unison and I sag into my seat.

When the chorus of footfalls fade, I turn back to Leander. A tremor begins deep in my abdomen, vibrating through me until I feel as if I'm humming. My nerves are too frayed, my body too bruised, to have this conversation.

I clear my throat. "I didn't create the evil in the world. Sometimes mortals—"

"Don't." Leander wilts. "Don't pretend you're doing this for them. You're doing this for you, and you always have. Drea may have given you the chance for this war by starting the famine in Asgya, but you should have stopped Volkana long before it got to this point." He holds up a hand, his wrist bending in defeat. "And before you start defending yourself, Asgya still had enough food to survive if they planned things right. You let Asgya walk unnecessarily into this war."

I shrug. "Of course I did."

He shakes his head. "You needed to scale back before it got out of hand. Even if all the troops leave Kisk tomorrow, the islanders are scattered, monuments lost, their culture destroyed."

Most of their culture was destroyed when Asgya colonized them. It's only recently, sixty years after the treaty for their freedom was signed, that Kiskens started regaining it. I rest my elbow on the arm of the chair and cover my eyes. *No headache, no headache, no headache.* "You're the God of Death, Leander. You understand everything fades with time."

"I accept death," he says quietly. "I don't revel in it."

I don't reply. There's nothing more to say. He's here instead of Ebris to put me on a guilt trip when I already feel terrible. No one will believe I didn't purposely set the bomb off, so there's no point trying to convince them I'm innocent.

"Can we take a second to talk about the girl?" he says, breaking the short, uncomfortable silence.

My already tight shoulders stiffen. "What about her?" I ask.

"She's alive, for starters."

My fingers dig into my temples. "Ah, yes. I told you she's hard to miss."

"Joke all you want but you know this is going to be a problem," Leander says.

I flick my hand at him. "I haven't accepted her as a bride. What does it matter if I keep her around?"

"You're breaking the rules," he warns.

"I'm *bending* the rules. It's called a loophole and it's fully recognized by Ebris himself." I made sure my brother was aware of it a long time ago. If he wants me to live by the laws, he has to as well. Which means allowing this.

Leander leans forward. "Why keep her if you have no intention of accepting? Isn't that cruel?" he asks begrudgingly.

It's absolutely cruel. I sit up and grab a pen, tapping it on the reports before tossing it back on the desk. It isn't fair to keep Cassia here. Alone and scared. But I'm selfish. As cruel as it is to make her stay, I can't fathom her leaving. It doesn't matter why I'm interested anymore. I'm not sure when it stopped being important, but it did. It's the most dangerous thing I've ever done, ever felt, but I only have to keep her at a distance until the war is over. Then any obligation will become null and void.

"Weren't you just lecturing me about sending you too many souls? Do you want another one?" I ask.

He tilts his head. "Ebris may force you to help Kisk regardless. You can't keep her and not show your appreciation."

"If I sleep with her, I'll help. If not, there's nothing our brother can do." He can try but I'm no stranger to standing my ground. It's what got me into this mess. I sigh. This is why I never kept a bride before. First Astra presses me to save Cassia's brother, now Leander to save Kisk. Ebris won't be far behind, and it's only a matter of time before my other sisters put in their two cents. I have too much on the line to risk Cassia ripping the rug from beneath my feet.

Leander hesitates and inches to the edge of his seat. "I'll take her," he says in a halting voice.

My body bolts upright, sparks dancing in my vision. "What?"

"If you don't want the inconvenience or the obligation, I'll take her." He looks away and shrugs. "She can stay with me."

My heart flies into an erratic pattern, assaulting me from the inside out. Cassia isn't a thing to be passed off—she's a person. She's my person. "Don't be ridiculous."

He scowls. "Why is it ridiculous? You tossed away hundreds of sacrifices. Why is she any different?"

"No," I say in a hard voice.

He blinks, his features slipping back to their usual carefree visage. "All right. I don't want to fight with you. Ebris is angry enough for the rest of us, but think about toning things down. Pacify him a bit." He moves toward the door. "But, Theodric?"

"What?" I snap.

He pauses in the doorway with his back to me. "Another mass killing and I *will* take sides," he cautions.

My muscles twitch in denial and I nod once. Goran is right—even if Leander isn't in my corner, he isn't in Ebris' either.

"I'll keep that in mind."

FOURTEEN

CASSIA

The entire city of Ubrar.

My whole body shakes. Last night Theodric told me the mountain exploded, not the Volk capital. I knew people lost their lives but had assumed it was the military or the scientists that created the bomb. And there I sat, feeling sorry for him when he blew up a bunch of innocent men, women, and children. I didn't just feel bad for him, either. I was actually grateful he risked his life to save Asgya. How could I forget who he is? He doesn't deserve sympathy. I should have let him soak in his own blood all night on that uncomfortable little sofa and wake with a crick in his neck. Most definitely, I shouldn't have enjoyed kissing him.

But I did.

And I want to do it again.

Bile rises in the back of my throat. *What is wrong with me?* I have to make him think we have something, which means the kissing is a good thing. The tight, bubbling anticipation in my stomach when I think about doing it again is definitely not.

The rough stone of the mansion scratches at my bare shoulders as I sit against the outer wall. I bite the knuckle of my index finger to keep from screaming. I need to talk to Cy again and ask if these feelings are a side effect of the sacrificial ritual, but I doubt I'll be seeing him for awhile. Not after Theo kicked Astra out the way he did.

"I know the way, Goran." Leander's voice drifts from the open door. It's cheerful again, the sound rising and falling in a lyrical tenor. "I'll see you next time."

Goran calls a goodbye from deeper in the house, then Leander is on the stoop. I press myself back against the stone and bring my legs up to my chest, tucking my skirt behind my knees. An oversized garnet pot hides me from plain sight. The bristly branches of the potted shrub allow slim slices of Leander's face to peek through, and I twist my head to study him.

When the door shuts, his shoulders slump, his head hangs, and he massages his forehead with both hands. There's definitely a family resemblance, but Leander looks more like a boy than a divine being. Strange, since he's older than both Theo and Astra. While his clothes cling to a fit body, maybe of a twenty-year-old, the edges of his face are softer. His nose ends with a rounded tip. When he cornered me outside the Wall on the way in, I noted the same ice blue eyes as the others, but there's no cunning spirit there. It's just him— someone without any walls to hide himself. He is what he is, and what he is seems almost…sad.

There are a dozen different names for him in Kisk. Some call him *The Great Thief*, others *The Murderous Cheat*. *The Demon* is the most popular these days. They say he crawls from the ground covered in black tar with wings ten feet wide and pointed teeth to devour souls. But watching him from my hiding place, his body swathed in sunlight with shadows haunting his eyes, all I can think is, *Death isn't so scary.*

Without warning, Leander's gaze snaps in my direction and his hands drop to his sides. I can't help noticing his lack of a weapon, but surely the God of Death doesn't need one. My pulse beats wildly in my chest. I take that back, he's a tiny bit scary.

His full lips pull back in a smile. "Cassia, right? Sorry, I forgot to ask earlier."

"I wasn't spying on you." I scramble to my feet and brush the gravel from the back of my skirt.

His laugh is light and musical. I feel myself blush. "I didn't assume as much," he says. "But if you were, I doubt you'd find anything of interest."

"I think that would depend on what I was looking for." I walk around the shrub and hug my abdomen. Maybe intimidating is a better way to describe him. Or maybe he's not intimidating enough, because, while I'm not sure what I meant to imply, I do mean it when I smile.

He ambles down the steps in a red plaid shirt and holds his palm out to me. I set mine over it in the Kisken greeting. I stare at our hands, my brows lowering. It's like touching an ice sculpture. Could he be cold because he's Death? But he's still a god. If they run hot, he should too.

"I apologize if we scared you in there. I'm not usually so rude, but I had a long night," he says, pulling away. "I had hoped to talk some sense into

Theodric before Ebris resorts to extremes, but he's..." Leander waves a hand toward the mansion.

"Impossible?" I smirk. "I brought the war up once and he abandoned me at the waterfall."

Leander shrugs. "Well, you're still here, which is more than I can say for the others. You must be doing something right."

I'm fairly certain I'm doing everything so, so wrong. Most people would bite the bullet and ask Theo for help instead of manipulating him. If I had anything other than my brother to lose, I'm not sure I would take the risk. Theo will probably hunt down everyone I care about if he finds out what I'm up to. If there's one thing I believe from the mythology book, it's that gods don't take betrayal well.

"Not caring if he helps Kisk seems to be my best quality," I squeeze out.

Leander's face flashes with something I can't quite decipher. "And do you care about the citizens of Ubrar?"

If I don't care about my own island, I shouldn't care about a Volk city, but I do. It's easy to write Kisk off after what they did to me—I almost feel like they deserve it—but Volkana did horrible things too. More than Kisk has. They stole my brother and killed so many people. I blow out a frustrated breath. "It's different," I say unevenly. "The people that died were innocent."

Kiskens were too. My eye twitches.

"You do care, but that's okay. That's *good.*" Leander sighs, his smile falling. "If it's any comfort, I do believe Theodric had good intentions, but antimatter is volatile. I don't know how the Volks contained it as long as they did."

I'd like to believe that. A small part of me does, but I'm not sure if it matters.

I have to keep my purpose in sight without getting involved with messy extras. Even if the messy extras include ground-shattering kisses. *Especially* if they do.

"Even if you claim you don't care about your country, you should know that the rumor is the Volks were planning to use a stolen Kisken plane to drop the bomb," Leander says.

I gasp. "What? Why?"

"To pass the blame, I assume. There were too many souls to process for me to thoroughly question them." His lips curl slowly and a curious gleam passes though his eyes. "I have a lot to catch up on today, but it was good to meet you, Cassia."

"You too." My mouth is dry as I speak, my concentration only partially on the words. Theo saved Asgya from death and Kisk from taking responsibility. I don't want it to matter.

Don't allow it to matter.

It matters.

"Maybe there's a bit of hope for my brother after all," Leander adds, walking backward toward the Wall.

A nervous chuckle escapes my chest. That's two people that think I'll bring Theo hope, but what does he bring me? Misery and death? I can't do anything for Theo; he's too cold-hearted and set in his ways. Maybe the hope Goran and Leander see is my potential to trick him into accepting his first bride and putting an end to all this insanity. If I succeed, that only helps with this war though. I'll hold no sway in the future. He'll never take my concerns into consideration, especially when he brushes off his siblings so easily. And that's assuming I live long enough to see another conflict ignite.

"Thanks for the rat, by the way." Leander calls as he passes under the archway. "For the record, I enjoyed receiving it almost as much as you enjoyed sending it."

My mouth cracks, ready to defend myself, but I stop when Leander winks. His warm laugh carries across the courtyard. The tension drains away, running down my limbs and into the rocky ground, then I'm laughing too. The sound fades as he walks away, his back a bright speck weaving toward the temple.

"What's so amusing?" Theo asks from behind me.

I jump, my smile dropping. All the strain that fell away a moment ago rushes back, settling into place like a well-worn glove. Goran's beside him, watching me wearily.

"Nothing," I say. He would never understand my hesitation to kill a beady-eyed rodent when he has no problem murdering people.

"It has to be something," Theo says. An emotion other than anger hovers between each consonant. "I've never heard you laugh like that before."

I narrow my eyes. He can't be serious. Is he...? He is. He's jealous. "Of course not. You haven't exactly made this a barrel of fun for me," I say before I can stop myself.

Theo works his jaw. "Give us a minute, Goran."

He doesn't need to be told twice before spinning on his heel and disappearing into the bowels of the mansion. Theo stares at me with a look that manages to be both cold and uneasy at the same time. I'm not sure whether to make up an excuse to run or hear what he has to say. Running seems like the more logical choice now that we're alone, but I hesitate a moment too long. He shifts his weight, balling his fists, and joins me on the gravel.

"I thought you blew up a mountain," I blurt. It's better than talking about the kiss, even though I should be trying to convince him it wasn't wrong.

His chin lowers and he looks away. "You shouldn't have been there for that conversation."

"Well, I was." I cross my arms, feeling brave. "You leveled the capital?"

"Not intentionally." He lifts his arms and exhales sharply. "That place was a cesspool anyway. The world is better off with it gone."

I dig my fingers into my arms to keep from doing anything rash. The end game is more important than enemy lives being taken. They're gone and there's no changing that, but Oren is alive. He's still in that camp and I need to stay on Theo's good side to save him. *Lucky for Theo.* There's a big piece of my mind I'm dying to give him. Mainly about his apparent lack of a conscience and total disregard for human life.

"If you don't want to end the war, why would you stop the bomb?" I ask. "Wouldn't it kick things up a notch?"

His head snaps toward me. "I never said I didn't want it to end and I certainly don't need to up the ante."

My next question lodges itself in my throat. If he wants it to end, what is he doing? Digging his heels in to prove a point *again*? Maybe he should reread his letter to himself after the Ostran War. He can't want control so badly he's willing to destroy the world. "I don't understand."

"Don't." His voice rumbles through me. "I'm doing what I was made to do. You don't need to understand."

I hold back, stuffing the anger into a tiny bottle while repeating *Oren, Oren, Oren* over and over in my head. The glass shatters. It rips through me, reopening old wounds and tearing new ones. Words fly off my tongue before the sentences have a chance to fully form in my mind. "Did you ever consider that explaining your reasons to people instead of brushing them off would allow them to understand? And maybe, just maybe, if they understood where you're coming from, they might be inclined to change their own thinking. Maybe they would compromise and work with you instead of against you."

His eyes flash but I refuse to listen to him tell me my opinions don't matter. They do matter, if not to him than to myself. I storm into the mansion. *Stupid, arrogant jerk.*

Wanting to understand his motives doesn't mean I'm questioning his authority. If I were, I would've come out and said it like his brother did a few minutes ago. If there's any hard evidence he's doing the right thing, I would love to see it so I can stop feeling like such a mental case. Because, even now, beneath the rage boiling in my veins, is a seed of doubt telling me he isn't so bad.

I am *a mental case.*

A hand snags my upper arm, yanking me backward into the sitting room. The door slams behind me. Before I can break away, before I even have time to realize it's Theo, he's kissing me again. The determination of last night is gone, replaced with something stronger, angrier. My lips freeze against his. Then his fingers curl into the base of my ponytail, his thumbs skimming the edge of my jaw.

Fire explodes in my chest. I grip the front of his shirt and tug until he's pressed against me, then pour my own anger, my own confusion, into the kiss. The cool taste of steel, the hot rush of body heat. I soak up every bit of it.

Then, too soon, Theo breaks away and nearly stumbles over the edge of the rug. "This can't happen," he says, his voice gruff. "I can't afford this."

"*You* kissed *me.*" My voice is barely there, breathy and stunned. "Twice."

His chest rises and falls in rapid succession. He steps closer, then back, and leaves without another word.

I snatch a throw pillow from the window seat and slam it over my face. The scream that tears from my throat vibrates my entire being. His words shouldn't be a dagger to my gut, but they are. I have to get out of here and clear my mind. Somewhere away from these walls, the smell of metal, and the sensation of Theo that lingers in every crevice. I drop the pillow to the floor and run.

Sharp pain lances up my back as I land hard for the eighth time. I lay, panting, in the velvety grass. Blue sky consumes the world around me. The rush of the waterfall roars in my ears, and, even at this distance, its mist clings to me.

Theo was right. I can't climb my way into Brisa's realm. The cliff is slick with mildew, making it impossible to maintain a grip. Each of my fingernails are split and bleeding, and I'm ninety percent sure I broke a toe. I should be glad I didn't break anything else after the last twenty-foot drop.

If only the ledges were a little wider. If the rocky barrier was a little further away from the fall's spray. I slam my fists into the dirt. *Nothing is impossible.* I take a deep breath and push up to try again.

FIFTEEN

THEO

My blade whirs through the air. A heavy whoosh. A clang as it collides with Goran's. He spins, ducking, and we circle each other again. I pull in fast, deep breaths, letting them out slowly as I smile. It's been too long since I've felt the weight of steel in my hand. Too long since the vibrations of each clash have coursed through my body.

The corded hilt is rubbed smooth from years of use, molding itself to my grip. An extension of myself. I swing downward. Goran blocks it with little effort and a smug smirk plays on his lips.

"Am I going too easy on you?" I ask.

He shoves my blade off his. "Have you ever?"

I advance. Left. Right. Center. He blocks them, the last only by a hair. I step back, adrenaline thrumming through me like a second pulse. A sense of freedom washes over me as I take the offense again. The blade cuts upward and nicks his arm. His foot shifts out of form. I grin and drive down on him with relentless force.

Goran's boots grind into the gravel. His smirk is gone, replaced with grim determination. Each blow he checks sends him back another step. He grunts and attempts to regain his stance but there's no time. I swing over my head, and he drops to his knee, raising his sword to protect his head.

"Yield," he huffs.

I lower my arm and step back, brushing the hair from my forehead. One match isn't nearly enough to pound out all of my stress, my anger, but I give Goran a minute to catch his breath. He's immortal but still human, and we haven't sparred since the war began. I roll my shoulders and wait while he bends over, resting his hands on his knees.

"You settled the new spy?" I ask.

He nods. "I inserted him as one of the missionaries helping with the cleanup."

I lean against the Wall and sigh. The reports will likely be sporadic until the roads are clear. When things settle down, I'll see about finding the exact point the temple ruins sat so the reports can be left there. Until then, he'll have to leave any news in the nearest known temple site nearly fifty miles away.

Goran stands and stretches his back. "Did you hear from Ebris while I was gone?"

"No."

I'm not sure which is worse—listening to Ebris or waiting to listen to Ebris. It's been an unnerving few days to say the least. I expected him the morning after the explosion, then the next day and the next. That he wouldn't come at all never crossed my mind.

Steel hisses in my ear and I duck. Goran's sword bounces off the stone behind me. I swing sideways as I rise, aiming for his hip, and he blocks it. Our blades grate as he twists his around mine. I hold tight, refusing to lose my weapon, and hobble backward to gain my footing.

I dig my boots into the gravel, balancing on the balls of my feet. A flash of silver arches toward my brow. I bend my knees, leaning back, but the tip grazes the bridge of my nose. The shallow cut stings. A drop of blood beads and I smile.

Now we fight.

I slam my sword down on his as it passes my shoulder and he spins away. He stays on the offense. Lunging and thrusting. I parry, flipping my sword over his. Then I'm behind him. He darts instinctively to the side before I can launch my own attack. My body hums. If I challenge Ebris to a fight like this, I might win. The fight against my brother would undoubtedly be harder, but the outcome isn't as important as the chance to draw blood.

I jerk sideways to goad Goran into striking, but he refuses the bait. We circle each other, matching step for step.

The frustration that's been eating at me flows down my arm. Into my hand. The hilt. Infusing the sword with a rabid passion. A shout rips from my throat and I lunge forward. Goran raises his blade with both hands to block. I beat down on it. Strike after strike. He growls his own aggravation, unable to move. Unable to fight back. Only defend. Then he pushes forward. His arms quake under the pressure.

My breathing changes, the careful rhythm lost. I grind my teeth together as he matches my last strike with one of his own. Our blades slide against each other in a shower of sparks. He dives forward, his sword aimed at my knee as he attempts to slip under my arm. I slam my hilt down between his shoulder blades and feel the impact right before he skids across the gravel on his stomach.

I lower my sword, huffing. "Intact?" I ask, using our code word to be sure the other is able to continue.

He shifts to his knees and wipes a trickle of blood from his eye. "Intact."

Nodding, I readjust my breathing. Fast and deep in; slow and steady out. My teeth almost clack in anticipation as Goran climbs to his feet. He holds his hand up to signal he isn't quite ready. Then, with a deep sigh, his hand drops and his sword rises. We lunge at the same time, our swords colliding.

I leer at him through the crossed blades. "You're out of practice."

"Whose fault is that?" he asks.

We push away from each other, circling, and dive again.

"Stop!" Cassia's voice pierces the courtyard.

Goran and I freeze mid-step. She races through the arch in the Wall and skids to a stop a few feet away. Water drips from her hair, her soaked clothes clinging to her body. Scrapes cover her arms and a gash in the knee of her jeans is outlined crimson.

My heart drops and I lower the point of the broadsword to the ground. I almost sheath it, but any fear it might inflict has already been done. Only she doesn't look frightened. She stands straight, her hands pressed against her chest. Her pupils swallow her irises whole as she stares us down. My grip pulsates on the hilt, squeezing and relaxing.

"What happened to you?" I ask.

"None of your business." She drags in an uneven breath. "Are you two trying to kill each other?"

Goran follows my lead, lowering the tip of his blade, and presses his lips together to hide a smile. It doesn't work for long before a short laugh breaks free. "Even if I wanted to kill him, do you think I could?" he asks.

"But…" She blinks, her cheeks flushing, and looks past me to Goran. "But you're bleeding."

He lifts a finger to the cut on his forehead. It comes away red and he shrugs. "A small cut. It'll be healed by dinner."

"Right." Cassia turns her narrow gaze to me. "Are you seriously hitting him with that thing?"

"Technically, that happened when he fell." I push my sleeves up past my elbows and take in each cut on her skin. Every bruise and welt. It twists something inside me. "Goran's been fighting with me for four hundred years and hasn't lost life or limb yet."

"Is that supposed to make this okay?" she asks in a high voice.

It should. Especially since Goran's not the only one who has shed blood on this gravel. He's bested me on more than one occasion, but we know when to stop. Where not to swing if the other doesn't look capable of stopping it. I need to be more mindful—Goran won't simply heal from a fatal wound like I will, but we're long past routine drills. We've been doing this dance long enough to have an honest fight.

"It…" I look at Goran for help, but he's too busy trying not to laugh. "No one's in any real danger," I say.

She glances at my sword and lets out a small hmph before turning her back to us. "Playing with swords. *Real* swords," she mumbles under her breath. "Morons. *Oh hey, friend, let me hack at you with this giant knife.* What kind of—"

She's too far away for me to hear the end of the question. When the front door slams behind her, reverberating through the courtyard, Goran buckles with laughter. I bite the inside of my cheek to keep from joining him. Her reaction might be amusing, but the way she looks isn't.

"It's good to know women haven't changed *that* much since I was alive." Goran flexes his fingers, gazing down at the marks on his hand. "She sounded like my fiancée every time I returned from training with a new mark."

I twist the tip of my sword into the ground, watching the gravel shift around the gleaming silver. Killing all my brides left me without reference, but others have commented on it enough to know he's right. I tend to forget Goran has a past. People he left behind when he came here to save his men.

"I know you're having a rough time dealing with the situation," he adds, "but I rather like her."

I slam my sword into the scabbard. "No one asked you."

"You like her too. You just don't want to admit it," he says, still smiling. His eyes shimmer with satisfaction. "If you think I don't know what I almost walked in on the night of the explosion, you're wrong."

My body jerks at the memory. "It was just a kiss. It won't happen again," I grumble. He doesn't need to know it already has. Avoiding Cassia has been working well the last few days, but she seems to be cropping up everywhere I go. I'm running out of excuses to get away from her. When I heard her tell Goran she was going to the brook this morning, I thought it was safe to fight here.

"It's not the end of the world, Theodric." Goran uses his thumb to wipe the trickling blood across his eyelid. "You're wasting a lot of energy trying to keep her at a distance. If you don't want to give up the war, limit yourself, but there's no reason not to enjoy each other's company."

Except every time I'm around her I want to do more than I should. Twice now I've lost control. Kissed her. It's not like me. I've met pretty girls before. Talked with them, ate with them, been with them. None of it has ever left me with such an empty void in my chest or an utter desperation to fill it. Each day the yawning crater aches more and more until it hurts to breathe.

"Do you think she's sincere?" I ask.

Goran's quiet for a moment. "Are you asking if I think she's lying about her intentions?"

I brush loose pieces of hair from my lashes. "Do you?"

"I think she's angry that her fellow Kiskens killed her, and washing her hands of them is her way of coping." He pauses. "She thinks her whole family is dead, so it's easy for her to do. When her anger fades, she might think differently. But at the moment, I think she means what she says."

How long does this method of coping last? Has the anger faded already? Is that why she kissed me back? Twice? When I came back hurt, she seemed genuinely concerned, and it was easy to fall under her charm. I couldn't help the kiss. But then she laughed with Leander. *Leander.* The only god people fear more than me. I know from that day in the temple that she's afraid of death, so even if he's a people-pleaser, she should have been wary.

"Goran?" I hesitate. I'm not sure what I want to ask or if I should ask anything at all.

"Control yourself until the war is over." He claps my shoulder. "You'll have no obligation to help Kisk during the next war."

No, but I'll want to. If I let her in, I won't want to let her go. The desire to make her happy is already spilling over. It's overlapping the war, muddying what's right and wrong.

"Relax," Goran adds.

Impossible. The West is running wild. Ebris is undoubtedly seething in his castle, plotting his next move against me, and Cassia is stealing what little sanity I have left. Or maybe it's my decision to stay away that's driving me insane. Maybe Goran's right and we should spend time together. Planned time without an opportunity for things to go haywire. *Chaperoned* time because I've never trusted myself so little.

"I need your help with something," I say.

SIXTEEN

CASSIA

My eyelashes catch in the knit fabric tied around my head, forcing them shut. The world narrows. I lick my lips and gingerly put one foot in front of the other to bide time. There has to be a way to escape. Somehow. I'm not even sure how we came to this. They don't know about all my attempts at scaling the cliff. If they do, they've known since the day of the sword fight because I haven't tried again since.

Apparently, I need a new set of life rules.

Rule Number One: When someone says be careful, listen. Don't ask questions.

Rule Number Two: Don't try to outsmart ancient gods. They've seen it all. They'll know.

Rule Number Three: When one of said gods produces a blindfold, run. Run fast.

It's a little late to worry about any of that now. I may not *have* a life much longer. Theo's hand rests gently on my upper back, guiding me forward, and I have to wonder if this is how cattle feel being led to slaughter. As much as I want to rip the blindfold off, deep down I can't help thinking it's a blessing. Not seeing death come is probably for the best, but I can't escape if I can't see. Even if I can see, it won't be easy going against Theo. Then there's the question of where to go.

If I could get his ring…But that's impossible. He's faster than I am. The second he sees me reach for his finger, I'm done for. Besides, I have to get *away* from him not close enough to grab his hand.

When the moment is right, I'll have to risk everything and bolt. I welcome the darkness as a friend, letting my other senses kick into overdrive.

There's a soft brushing sound, the front door opening. Someone takes my hands from the front. Thin, raised scars crisscross against their skin. Goran. I swallow hard and allow him to guide me down the steps with Theo's hand still hot on my back. A breeze carries the earthy scent of the woods on the other side of the Wall. A thud. The door shutting. Crunching gravel as we reach the courtyard.

Bile rises in my throat. They must be taking me back to the temple to finish me off. A shiver runs down my spine. *Okay. It's okay. Just wait. Don't panic.* The second the gravel gives way to dirt and we curve to the right, I'll make my move. It's the closest we'll get to the woods on the way, and the best chance I'll have of losing myself in the trees before they catch up.

Theo's hand moves to my shoulder, pulling me to a stop. *No.* They can't do it here. The odds of making it through the arch without them blocking the way are slim to none, let alone all the way to the forest. My mouth fills with saliva, my hands shaking. *Don't panic.*

Theo's fingers work the knot at the back of my head and the blindfold falls away. I squint as the sun stings my eyes, raising a hand to hide the glowing orb, and focus on Goran between my fingers. He doesn't look grim like he did the last time, but that doesn't mean much. When he smiles, my breakfast threatens to reappear.

"What's going on?" I ask. Goran waves a folded piece of paper between us. "Should I know what that means?"

"It's a scavenger hunt," Theo says from behind me.

I open my mouth but my brain sputters in a thousand directions. Whatever I was about to say sticks in my throat. It feels as if every molecule of air is electrified. Like it's waiting to sense a sword swinging in from behind or an arrow whirling from the rooftop. *A trap*, my mind screams, but when I look at Theo, he's concentrating on his shoes instead of me. If he were going to kill me, he would at least *look* at me, wouldn't he? For all Theo is, he isn't a coward.

"What?" My voice is barely a whisper.

"You said you enjoyed them." He stuffs his hands in his pockets and shrugs. Veins trail along the muscles in his arm as he flexes. "I'm not sure if it's exactly the same as the ones you're used to..."

The blood drains from my head. I stumble back and plunk down on the bottom of the stoop. He isn't going to send me to the Netherworld. He doesn't know my plan to seduce him or my backup plan to run. This is a surprise. He did this for me. I wave a hand in front of my face to fight the increasing vertigo.

"Are you all right?" Goran asks.

I shake my head. "I thought you had changed your mind about letting me stay," I mumble. I'm in no condition to conjure up a lie about why I'm seconds from passing out. It's enough to leave out the why.

"You didn't tell her?" Goran asks in a rushed whisper. "You can't be that clueless."

"It wouldn't be a surprise if I told her," Theo whispers back.

I pull in deep breaths. *Get yourself together.* Theo put this together for me, and I can't throw it in his face. The kissing gave me hope, but after not seeing him for days, I was beginning to think seducing him was a fruitless venture. Maybe it won't be so pointless after all. My plan can't fail because I'm afraid of Theo's reaction, or worse, that I'll fall for him after one more kiss like the last. I shake the numbness from my hands and ease my way back to my feet.

"I'm fine." I rub at the glossy scar on my neck. "Really, I am," I add when neither of them speak.

"I had a whole speech ready," Goran says with a shrug. "But, here."

I rub my fingers over my sweaty palms and take the paper from his outstretched hand. "So this is a...scavenger hunt?" I try to hide the skepticism in my voice and glance at Theo. "You remembered."

"Of course," Theo says.

Of course. Ha!

Goran steps back. Theo's hand twitches as if he wants to grab him and force him to stay close, but he balls it into a fist instead. I flick the edge of the paper with my thumbnail. *Interesting.*

"Am I doing this alone?" I glance at Theo from under my lashes in what I hope is a flirtatious look. I feel ridiculous for it. Like I'm wading through rough water without knowing how to swim and there's no one to offer me a lifejacket. "Or do you plan on helping?"

"Goran planted the clues," Theo says as if it answers the question.

My inner voice screams *no*. I don't want his help. He'll ruin the memory of this for me, and I have precious few good ones left from before. But my body is a traitor. My heart races, my stomach flutters, and I fumble while opening the last fold.

"All right." I swallow and look at the clue: IPSOKSNR PCIGK. Theo steps up beside me, his heat reaching out to merge with mine, and I force myself to stare at the letters. "It's an anagram."

"Something about rings?" he suggests.

My gaze slides toward the black ring around his finger, but I force it back to the paper. There's no getting it from him, and I shouldn't consider trying until my job is finished. Maybe if I get away with saving Oren, I can pry it off Theo in his sleep. I'll have the necessary access if this goes right. I smother the idea and mentally cross out letters, rearranging them into anything that makes sense.

This would be a lot easier with a pen.

"Corks? Do you have a wine cellar?" I ask.

"I don't." He tilts his head and is silent for a moment. "That would leave *skipping* as the only choice for the first word."

"Hm." I gasp. "Rocks! Skipping rocks."

"The brook," he says.

His breath skims my cheek and my breath hitches. I crumple the paper, stepping around him. "Come on."

The path to the cliff is familiar now. It's the same trail leading to the bucket of flat stones I use as a cover for spending hours away from the house. I duck under branches and hop over fallen trees without much thought, sparing a moment to be glad I chose jeans and sneakers this morning. Theo's right behind me, but I'm sure he's pacing himself. There's no way, with his long legs, that I'm faster. I appreciate the thought though. As much as I don't need him to let me win, I did solve the puzzle. Claiming the next clue feels like my right.

And there it is, nailed to a wide oak tree with twisted, sweeping branches and bright green leaves clinging to its bark. I beam at Theo, the biggest I've smiled in a long time, and pluck it from the trunk.

"Did you ever do it?" Theo asks quietly.

The steady rise and fall of his chest draws my attention. *Stop it.* But my focus lingers anyway. It's better than looking him in the eye while thinking he's attractive and risk him reading me too well. "Do what?" I ask as I unfold the new clue.

"Skip a rock."

My head snaps up, sure he's making fun of me, but he's waiting with genuine interest. *Okay. Commit to the plan. Act better; be believable.* "Not even close." My laugh flows naturally, almost as if I don't have to try. "One day."

"One day," he echoes.

His hand inches closer to mine and the energy dances between us. *Do it.* But then it falls back to his side. Pain scratches at my chest and I focus on the paper. This is no time to get emotional.

"It's a riddle," I say. Riddles aren't my forte, but it's easier if I listen. "Can you read it out loud?"

Theo slips the paper from my hand and I still myself to better concentrate. A faint ringing fills the silence before Theo speaks. The first syllable to pass his lips rolls over me and I shiver.

"Soldiers fight and soldiers fall, lords of war plan it all. From this height we know the sea, but soon enough you'll need a key. Mountains and roads are in your sight, but from here it's only trite."

"I have no idea," I admit.

His lips never stop moving as he repeats it again and again. The longer I wait, the more in his own thoughts he becomes. A tight, writhing knot grows in my lower stomach as I watch him. My hand flexes, eager to reach out and wipe away the small crease between his brows.

"Any thoughts you want to share?" I ask instead.

"Lords of war has to refer to me," he says in a rush.

I nod. "Do you use a key for anything?"

"Have you run into a locked door?"

"No." I narrow my eyes. *Don't make me smack you again.* "That doesn't mean you don't have some mythical key to the universe."

His laugh is distant, his mind still on the riddle. "Wouldn't that be nice?"

I lean against the tree and rip a large pronged leaf from a low branch. It curls against the breeze as I roll the stem between my fingers. Theo doesn't move but his lips never stop, although his murmurs are too quiet to hear now, and I flush. The memory of what those lips feel like on mine is palpable. A twisted ring of want bands my ribcage.

It's easy enough to remember the lies Theo's told when we're apart, but when he's nearby it all fades away. I should ask him to help my brother; it's the right thing to do. I can't forget about the things Theo did in the past, but I can choose to move forward. He's capable of doing better, I know he is. In the moments when he's not caught up in winning the war or the power struggle with Ebris, I catch a glimpse of a different person.

Ugh. Why does this have to be so complicated?

Theo jolts and I spring away from the tree. His smile builds, brightening his face. "The key on a map," he says, grinning. "It's the maps in the war room."

I've only been in the war room once, the day Leander came, but it isn't any less oppressive the second time. Tall windows line most of the back wall, letting in massive amounts of natural light, but it feels too harsh. Yellow, curling maps cover the right wall and an unbroken table near it is plastered with crisp ones, colored with blues, greens, and browns. Endless binders line bookshelves. A massive circular table with a variety of colored glass pieces takes up the entire center of the room. I trail the scrolled edge with a finger as Theo plucks the next clue from the edge of a map.

"What is this?" I ask.

Theo hesitates. "The War Table."

"Oh." I lift a blue sphere from the black stone base and hold it up toward the ceiling. Slivers of light penetrate the edges, shimmering, dancing, across the smooth curves.

"You're holding ten thousand Asgyans in your hand," he says in a carefully controlled voice.

My grip twitches and I rush to put it back in the exact position while forcing my hands to remain steady. "Sorry."

"It's useless now." He approaches the table, eying it like it might move of its own accord. "When I...when my powers were taken, it became nothing more than another piece of furniture. I only use it now out of habit."

Red and blue pieces are grouped together on opposite sides with a few spaced between, mingling with each other. This is the war that destroyed Kisk, laid out in the most anonymous way imaginable. I exhale from a small crack in my lips. The lack of a third color doesn't escape my notice. "What does the clue say?" I ask.

He rounds the table, stopping in front of me to read it, and I ball my hands to keep them where they belong: at my sides. The struggle strains my muscles, aches my bones, until it's too much. My body doesn't give my brain a chance to object before moving.

I shoot to my toes, my hip bumping the table. The glass trembles along the surface. Theo's eyes dilate a split second before I make contact, then mine slam shut. A warm haze descends on the room. My senses slowly fight through the horror of what I did, and panic swells in my chest when he doesn't respond.

Then Theo lifts me from the floor, setting me on the war table. Pieces tumble across the table in series of sharp clicks, and I'm lost to the kiss.

He bends to reach my face, cupping the back of my head, and I ball my hands into his shirt. The sensation is familiar now, as if we had been doing this for years. Low, deep kisses that end feather-light. His stomach hardens beneath my knuckles and I release his shirt, splaying my hands over the fabric instead. The same struggle to breath surfaces and I embrace it. Pulling it close, and Theo closer. It suffocates me from the inside out.

A cough breaks through the fog and Theo leans back, his lips swollen. His jaw muscles jump and he sets the paper on my thigh. "Goran," he says, blocking me from his adviser's view. "There you are."

"Forgive me," he says, sounding completely unapologetic. "I thought maybe you were having a hard time working things out."

Theo takes a handful of deep breaths, each rippling over my cheek. "We're fine," he says.

"I'll leave this here then." Goran shuffles in the doorway and disappears.

Theo's shoulders slump and he rests his hands on either side of my legs. "Cassia."

"I know," I breathe. *What an idiot.* Did I really kiss him? Have I lost all common sense? "You didn't want to kiss me again."

"That's all I want to do," he whispers in my ear. "But I can't. Not yet."

I smother the urge to lean into him, burying my face in the slope of his neck. Instead, I place my fingertips on his collarbone and gently push him away. The paper flutters to the floor as I slide off the table. The hunt is over before it's finished, but I bend to pick it up anyway.

A soft mew travels from the other side of Theo's boots. I pause as a fluffy, gray cat, no bigger than my hand, bounces over to weave through my ankles. "A kitten?"

Theo glares down at it, still struggling to collect himself. "She's the prize."

I lift the squirming kitten. She stares at me with large green eyes as I stand. "You got her for me?"

"I thought…" He sighs, running a hand through his hair. "I thought you must be lonely here."

I hug the kitten, her tiny claws catching in the fabric of my shirt. "Thank you."

"You're welcome." His voice is composed again, polite, even if his expression isn't. He dashes into the hallway, and I follow as far as the door.

"Did you have fun?" Goran asks in a bright voice.

"Shut up," Theo growls as he passes.

I'm torn between following and staying put, but the kitten snags my skin in an attempt to crawl to my shoulder. "No, no," I say quietly, pulling her from my body before she can dig her claws in. It doesn't matter where Theo found her, or if she's secretly some alien creature the mythology books forgot to mention, my heart is exploding.

Tomorrow.

Tomorrow I'm going to ask Theo to save Oren. I can't do this to him. It isn't fair to either of us. If he won't help, I'll find another way. *There's always another way.*

I kiss the kitten's fur. "I think I'll call you Moki."

SEVENTEEN

THEO

Red ink scars the map as Goran leans over the table, drawing circles with a compass. I read the coordinates slowly, watching them take shape one after another. A sense of dread lurks in the shadows, waiting, hoping, for my suspicions to be confirmed.

"What are we looking for?" Goran asks after creating the eleventh mark.

"Brisa sunk an Asgyan fleet. No survivors." We didn't have a chance to discuss the reports before I shoved a pen in his hand, but Goran isn't the one I need to talk to about this. My sister is. I read the last set of numbers and let the list float to the floor. Two are in the middle of the ocean, but the majority linger near the Asgyan shoreline. "These are confirmed tidal waves in the last twenty-four hours."

Goran sets the compass down and drums his fingers on the table in a steady *thump, thump, thump.* "But Brisa doesn't like to get involved with this sort of thing. Are you sure it wasn't coincidence? The ships could have been in the wrong place at the wrong time."

"Does it look like a coincidence to you?" I ask. There's never this many waves hitting at once, let alone in a concentrated area, not without earthquakes or volcanic activity to stir things up. Technology would have warned them to get out of the area before it was too late. This isn't bad luck. "I'm going to go talk to her."

Brisa will tell me the truth; she always has. Ebris can punish us for breaking the rules, but not for breaking confidence. Not outright, anyway, and Brisa can hold her own.

When I turn to leave, Cassia is in the doorway with the kitten at her feet. "Hey." She wrings her hands and a smile twitches uncertainly on her lips. "Are you busy? I need to talk to you about something."

I open and shut my mouth. If it's about yesterday, I don't have time to hear it. Ever. I'm just glad Goran did as promised and looked in on us. I don't want to think about what might have happened if he didn't interrupt. "I'm actually on my way out," I say.

"Oh." Her expression falls. She looks behind me to Goran, then the table. "Later then?"

I hesitate. I've never heard her voice anything but strong. Wary, maybe, or nervous, but never quiet. "I'm not sure how long it will take. I'll find you if it's early enough."

"Any time is fine," she says.

I step around her, careful not to brush against her, and bite back a humorless laugh. There's nothing she has to say that can't wait until the issue with the ships is finished. I'm absolutely not going anywhere near the third floor to wake her in the middle of the night. "Maybe."

I step from my alcove in the water temple and into the main room. Blue and gold mosaic tiles splash the walls. They curl into waves, shining as if wet. The air holds a salty edge to it. Enough that I taste it on my tongue. A long banner drapes over the altar with pearls and shells carefully woven between aqua beads. Brisa perches in the middle of it, swinging her legs to a choir of delicate clicks. Dark, curly hair frizzes around her. She's wearing a denim shirt with a pair of shorts and looking much too relaxed for having killed two thousand Asgyans.

Her thin lips quirk when she sees me approach. "It took you long enough. I was beginning to wonder if you would come at all."

"Of course I came." A choked breath flies from my chest, and I grip the railing separating the altar from the pit. "I needed those ships, Brisa."

Her bare feet slap against a cobalt floor as she slides from the altar. "I took the smallest fleet."

"The smallest," I echo. Something desperate cracks beneath my ribs, but I can't let it surface. Not in front of anyone. Not even Brisa. "It was the Asgyans' last set of destroyers. You didn't have to take any ships at all."

Her blue eyes flash and she circles the pit to put distance between us. "I did," she says flatly. "I'm sorry."

It's all I can do not to grab her thin shoulders and shake the truth from her.

Instead, I match her trek around the pit until we're face to face. She'll tell me. *She will.* If this is what I think it is, the game has moved to a whole new board. New rules, new hurdles. New traps.

"Ebris put you up to this, didn't he?" I ask.

Her hand lands on my forearm, squeezing, but she won't look at me. "It would be easier for all of us if you listen to him."

"That isn't a no."

He did it. I know he did. He hasn't been by to scream at me because he knows it's pointless. I don't listen, but everyone else does. Having my powers stripped set an example for the others, so of course they do as they're told. It won't take much to turn them all against me. To rig the war and make me look worse. Untrustworthy. To make it impossible for me to ever crawl my way back to full strength.

"I sent you as many signals as I could without being suspicious," she says.

She didn't do a very good job of hiding it. If Ebris is paying as much attention as I am—and he is—he saw the same pattern I mapped out with Goran minutes ago. If Ebris gave her a choice to sink the ships, she might have been straightforward about it, but, from her passive-aggressive help, it's obvious she wasn't. Our shared hatred of authority, of being held in check, makes her my favorite. That doesn't change the fact that those ships are at the bottom of the ocean.

Or that my brother is sabotaging me.

"He'll destroy everything to get his way," I blurt. It's foolish to talk like this in the temple. Ebris could be listening, but I find it hard to care. "I'll have to ally Asgya now. A country from the East. Maybe Butaelo could be persuaded in exchange for access to—"

"Theodric, no." Brisa lowers her voice. "Are you kidding? You can't bring another country into this mess. There are other ways to fix this without making matters worse."

"An ally is the only way to save them now." I pace across the shimmering floor. If I don't do something, Volkana will seize the opportunity to strike. They can't be allowed to own the entire West. If they become a superpower, more than Asgya will be lost.

"*You* are supposed to help them. Not Butaelo," she says.

My anger blasts into fury. Everyone seems to be convinced that the only way to end the war is to undermine me at every turn. I *am* trying to help, but everything I do is trampled, ground to dust, by actual power. "You seem to have forgotten that I can't do what I should. Ebris saw to that himself."

She gathers her mass of hair in her hands and lifts her gaze to mine. A calculating smile parts her lips. "As a favor to me, don't get another country involved. Ebris is already losing his patience with this *cursed* war. I don't think you'll enjoy whatever he has planned if you don't listen."

The way she said *cursed* strikes a chord in the back of my mind. I narrow my eyes and she narrows hers back. The hint of an idea clouds within me, urging me to give it shape.

"What's a single ship going to accomplish anyway?" she adds. I stare at her with a blank expression. She sank a single fleet, not a single ship. "Come on," she mouths.

Heavy locks slam into place. No military ships will fight alone, but another kind will. One in particular. One with a captain who everyone believes is cursed.

"All right. For you," I say, monotone. I kiss her cheek. "I'll figure something else out."

Cassia's laugh floats into the entryway followed by a small foil ball. A gray blur dashes from the sitting room after it. The kitten skids back and forth on the marble floor in pursuit until it flies under the credenza. She throws herself on her side and stretches a front leg after it with tiny grunts. A determined little thing.

If only the things I'm chasing could be so easily caught. I scratch at the stubble on my cheeks. Goran isn't going to like the new plan. It's irrational. Unreliable. *Brilliant.* There's a fifty percent chance it won't come to fruition anyway. My skills of persuasion aren't exactly effective without a sword. But, luckily, with these people, it may come to that.

"I still can't believe Theodric got you a cat." Astra's voice bangs through my head.

"I can," Cassia says. My shoulders relax slightly at the vote of confidence. There's a short pause and Cassia steps out the door. "Is it stuck under there, Moki?"

"Moki?" I ask.

Cassia twists to look at me with a hand at the base of her throat. "You scared me." She laughs, slightly breathless, and color rises in her cheeks.

Astra murmurs something from inside the sitting room. I strain to listen, giving only a nod to acknowledge what Cassia said.

"When did you get back?" she asks.

"Just now." The undercurrent of a man's voice replies to my sister.

Cassia steps closer, following my gaze toward the open door, and lowers her voice. "Is everything okay?"

"It will be," I answer. Moki scampers back without the ball and attacks the laces on my boot. Her claws pick into the leather, leaving a pattern of tiny holes. "Is Goran in there?"

She nods. "With Astra and one of Ebris' men."

"What?" My voice bounces off the walls. I push by her to find Goran standing rigid between Astra and an unknown man with sandy hair. Their conversation screeches to a halt, and the man bobs his head in my direction. "What's going on here?"

"I had some things to bring to Cassia," Astra says in a sweet voice.

I clench my fists. "If Cassia needs anything, I'll get it for her myself. You need to leave."

She smoothes a hand over her pencil skirt. "I'll stay awhile longer."

"No." I don't trust her when I'm here to monitor the visit, and I'm not about to leave her alone in my house. I can't have her rushing back to Ebris to tell him I'm up to something, either. "Leave."

Astra presses her lips into a thin line, but she doesn't argue again. On her way out, she stops to whisper in Cassia's ear. Cassia nods. Then Astra is gone. I fight the raging urge to demand answers from Cassia. There are more important questions to ask.

"And you?" I snap at the man. He bobs his head a second time and holds out a sealed envelope. A cool rush of nerves prickle over me as I rip it from his hand. "Go."

He makes it out the front door in record time. When I see his figure pass through the Wall, I inch farther into the room toward Goran, who might have to hold me back from storming my brother's castle with my sword in hand. The black wax crown holding the flap down snaps beneath my fingers. I read it out loud:

Theodric—End this. I don't care what the outcome is as long as the fighting stops. If things aren't moving toward a conclusion by the end of the week, Brisa will swallow Kisk whole, Drea will extend her famine, and I'll personally see to Volkana. You won't like what will happen to you and yours if I have to get my hands dirty.

The note crumbles in my fist. I definitely won't like what will happen, but I can't let him steal this war from me. He's taken too much already. I will win this even if it means he kills each of my sacrifices.

Not all of them.

I glance at Cassia, chewing her lip in fear, at a stony-faced Goran. Ebris won't go that far. He can't—not like he did with drafting Timun. Whatever happens to me, it isn't his place to manage my household.

"Worried about your homeland?" I snap at Cassia. I regret the question as soon as I ask it. This isn't her fault.

"What?" Her chest heaves. "No, I'm worried about *me*. What exactly does *you and yours* mean?"

My heart rams against my chest. Each beat bruises and breaks. There are countless cruel things my siblings and I have done, but to threaten each others' sacrifices? Especially now when we receive so few. When I need them more than anything else to function as the God of War.

"It means," Goran answers slowly, "Theodric isn't the only one throwing the rules out the window."

"Ebris isn't going to lay a finger on anyone. He's trying to intimidate me." My voice wavers. "Come on, Goran. We're leaving."

Cassia steps forward. "Wait."

There's no waiting. No talking. No time. I need this plan in action by midnight.

"We'll be back," I say. "Don't let anyone else in."

Without waiting for her to agree, without making sure Goran is following, I march back toward the temple. This has to work. As ridiculous as it seems, it has to work. It's time to put an end to the war before every mortal dies to prove a point.

We're halfway there when Goran clears his throat behind me. "What was that about?" he asks.

"Ebris is sabotaging us." As I say the words, I feel the weight of their truth. I've known it longer than I'd like to admit.

His stride falters. "Brisa told you that?"

"She didn't have to."

Goran gazes sideways at me. "But she didn't *tell* you that?"

"It doesn't matter." I wave a hand through the air. The letter proves it, and I'm finished talking. Now is a time for action, not debate. "I found a way to replace the destroyers."

Goran looks me up and down. "This should be good."

"Do you remember Hex?"

193

He steps in front of me, walking backward toward the temple with his hands raised in the air. "Not the pirate?"

I grin. "The pirate."

Technically, she's Asgyan but claims no country as her own, so it won't bring anyone new into the war. But with her cannons, she'll be able to take a few players out of it.

◆

Shadow Cove puts Ubrar to shame. Not in size but in questionable principals. As the Asgyan pirate capital, it's expected. Especially since the authorities gave up on this place long ago. It's easier to ignore it. Sail around. Keep away from this section of coastline. The pirates are happy enough to stay within their borders to keep the place from drawing ire, but it's another thing if you go waltzing into their territory.

I keep my shield up as we brave the rocky coast toward sloping asphalt roofs and chimney stacks that cough pillars of gray smoke. Folded black sails dot the sea. Smaller motorized ships are tethered to the piers. It reeks of dead fish, making each breath uncomfortable. We reach the edge of the cove, landing in stagnant mud, and I lift the neck of my shirt to cover my nose.

It was never like this in the past when I came between wars for a bit of fun. For all they got up to, the pirates kept their houses from leaning and roofs from caving. The ground was always maintained. Not anymore. The steel watchtower Hex lives in one of the only buildings that doesn't look like it would blow over in a strong wind.

"I'd like to say one more time what a horrible idea this is," Goran grumbles. "The soldiers will never trust them."

"The soldiers will never know." The creaky wooden staircase leading to Hex's door sways under foot. I tell myself it's my imagination, but my knuckles are white on the railing. "Think of them as a new kind of militia."

He grunts. "More like money-hungry mercenaries. Hex will want something for her trouble."

"She's a pirate, Goran. Of course she will." And if she agrees, she'll have it. I drop the shield and pound on the door with the heel of my fist.

"Who is it?" screeches a woman on the other side.

"An old acquaintance."

Goran scoffs. "She's going to shoot us on sight."

The door flies open and a woman in her early forties stands before us in a bathrobe covered with ducks. Her blond hair is braided tight to her head, freckles sprinkled over her nose, and she clutches a cup of steaming coffee in one hand. "*You.*"

"Hello, Hex," I say. "How's the knee?"

Scalding coffee splashes my face. My teeth grind against the sharp, blistering pain. I wipe it off, flicking the liquid from my fingers. *I should have seen that coming.*

"Like I said five years ago, I didn't touch your gold," I say. There's no reason for me to steal from her or anyone else. I only wanted a few rounds of cards that night. Her first mate took the chest while Hex was surveying the ship for damage. But, naturally, the blame fell to the stranger in the crowd. Pirate loyalty and whatnot.

"Like I said five years ago, go screw yourself," she growls.

She moves to slam the door, but I slap my palm on the aged wood. "What would you say if I told you there's a way for you to make it back tenfold?"

Her hazel eyes bore into me, her chin lifting. "I'm listening."

EIGHTEEN

CASSIA

The whisk scrapes against a glass bowl, dragging yellow goop up the sides. This is the fifth attempt at making Theo's ridiculous tabowi crepes, and I'm ready to throw the whole thing across the room. It shouldn't be this hard. It's a thin pancake, for crying out loud. I stab at the egg and milk mixture. I have no idea what I'm doing wrong, but the batter keeps rising.

Luckily Astra went overboard with ingredients.

Not only did Theo listen to my answers when we played Fate, but he paid enough attention to know I needed a friend. Beneath all his anger is someone with feelings. Far, far beneath, but it's there. Somewhere. I want to do something nice for him in return, and if it butters him up a little before we talk, all the better.

I didn't get a chance to ask about my brother earlier, and my pulse flutters like a caged bird, tense and unsettled. The conversation will only take five minutes, but his response will last a lifetime. However long that may be after I get the question out. My guess is about two minutes. I've accepted the odds, but the uncertainty of it all keeps me firmly in its grip. Doubt has imbedded its claws too deep to allow sleep to take me.

Even if Theo agrees to save Oren, he's not going to stop the war. Ebris will step in and do whatever it is he plans to do. Maybe kill me or cart me off somewhere to do who knows what. I beat the egg mixture faster until bubbles foam around the edges of the bowl and slam the runny whisk down on the counter. It'll be okay. Maybe Ebris will take pity on me and end it quickly. Leander seems nice enough. If he rules the Netherworld, how bad can it be? I'm supposed to be dead anyway. My time here was a bonus. I got to sleep in a comfortable bed, eat decent meals, and take daily showers. I should be glad I got the chance.

Yet, I'm not. Because I'm not ready to give up living. When the time comes, I'll fight Ebris with whatever I have at my disposal.

If I could just get this recipe to cooperate...

I toss the bowl of dry ingredients on top of the liquid with more force than necessary. A puff of flour rises into the air, and I bat it away from my face. The edges are swallowed to the bottom first, and I watch as the surviving granules shift across the surface. I swipe the whisk off the counter to stir. The batter thickens and sticks between the wires hoops. I bang it off and try again. It sticks a second time. I stab at the concoction as a muffled scream lodges in my throat.

"What are you doing?" Theo asks.

The whisk flings from the batter, a chunk splattering my face. *Ugh.* Of course he would come down here in the middle of the night and catch me failing miserably. I pull the sleeve of my sweater over my hand and wipe the goo from my cheek without turning to face him. "Me? What are *you* doing down here?"

Mature. I wrinkle my nose and fidget with the bowl. Too much flour, I think. Or maybe not enough milk. Why am I so bad at this?

"I can't sleep," he says.

He moves closer, the familiar chink of his boot buckles missing. His confusion radiates at my back as he takes in the spilled sugar, broken egg shells, and cutting board covered in deep purple tabowi juice. When he leans over my shoulder, his chest bumps against my arm and I glance up for the first time. He's not wearing a shirt.

I resume poking at the solid ball of dough to hide my blazing cheeks. If how he looked with a shirt on is any indication of what he'll look like without one, it's better to focus on anything else. The feelings I have for Theo came out of nowhere, slipping into the cracks of my determination with each hint of a smile. Every rare laugh. Every kiss. I didn't understand any of it until I understood all of it.

Theo isn't horrible, he's broken. The only difference between us is that I pretended things would get better while he fought to regain his normal. A little too hard, maybe, but everything he knew was ripped away. If anyone can understand that, I can. I won't be another shackle on his wrist. So, with my plan of seduction out the window, it's better to avoid temptation altogether. At least until after I ask about Oren.

"Is that tabowi?" He runs his finger through the pool of juice. "Where did you get it?"

I nudge the wooden crate full of bumpy, hard-skinned fruit on the floor with my ankle. "I asked Astra if she could get some."

He shifts away and grabs one off the top. "Why?"

"Well…" Heat blisters its way up my neck and into my cheeks. I didn't plan to tell him why. I thought I'd do a few trial runs, present the food in the morning, and let it say thanks for me. "You said you liked them in crepes, so I was trying to figure it out," I mumble. It sounded like a much better idea in my head. In my head I actually knew how to cook.

Theo's quiet beside me while I pick tacky strands of dough off the whisk and drop them into the garbage beneath the counter. His body stills. I'm too afraid to look up and see what he's thinking. The tension rakes down my back, a million pins pricking at once. When he shifts to lean against the cabinet, I jump. I try to hide the jerky movement by throwing out the ruined ingredients, but it makes it more obvious.

"Why?" he asks.

"Why what?"

"Why are you making the crepes I like?" His voice is quiet, his eyes daggers in the side of my face.

I rub my wrist across my forehead. Clearly I'm making them because he likes them. Well, he won't like *these*, but it's the thought that counts…I hope. "I wanted to say thank you. You know, for Moki."

"Cassia…"

I sigh. "I know—they're not right. I've never actually eaten a crepe before, let alone made them, so I'm stuck guessing. So far I've only made a mess, but

I'll keep trying. If I live in the kitchen until it's time to leave, they may be edible. Astra brought a lifetime supply of ingredients so—"

"Leave?" He pushes off the cabinet with more grace than I could ever hope to have. The dim under-cabinet lights cast deep shadows across his face. The way his brows lower he almost looks worried, but it must be my imagination. "Where are you planning to go?"

"The note. Unlike you, I believe Ebris." I wave the dirty whisk through the air. Like Goran said, I belong to the War God. As much as I hate the thought, Ebris is going to think the same way. "I'm yours, aren't I? Which means when you don't end the war, and you won't—" I pause to glare at him—a challenge to him to deny it. "I'm in the line of fire."

"Are you?" he asks, shifting closer still. "Mine?"

I twist the knob of the griddle to off with a deep breath. *This again.* Can't we agree to be friends and leave the possessive pronouns out of it? "So I've been told," I mumble.

"Listen." He's at my side, pulling the utensil from my hand. He pushes the warm griddle to the other end of the counter. "Ebris talks a big talk, but he won't hurt you. It's just a way to get to me. To make me bow to his demands. He isn't so callous as to take my shortcomings out on someone who hasn't done anything wrong."

It feels like I have. At some point in my life, I must've done something so terrible that I ended up in this situation. Dead parents, a framed brother in enemy custody, murdered as a sacrifice. Karma is having a field day with me. *No.* I cross my arms over my chest. I didn't do anything, and it's time I stop feeling like I did.

"Do you believe me?" he asks.

That's the question of the century. I want to, but it's hard when he's keeping something so important from me. "Goran said Ebris is changing the rules, so there's no way you can know that for sure," I say.

"Stop." He takes my hands, removing them from my arms, and turns me to look at him. "I know how to deal with my brother."

I snort. If that were true, he wouldn't be where he is today. My eye twitches; that wasn't a fair thought. "Are you going to do what he says?"

He turns sideways. "I spent the day helping Asgya. It could be seen as a step in the right direction."

That doesn't mean he's working toward an end, just that he's buying time. I shouldn't complain either way. Even if I wanted to, I couldn't with the way he's cradling my hands. His fingers curve gently around my wrist, his thumbs caressing my knuckles. I focus on the building heat there instead, sneaking a peek at his chest. Being alone with him, close to him, it doesn't make this any easier. I have to ask him about Oren now while I still have the mind to speak.

"I need to talk to you about something." I force myself to pull my hands away.

"Cassia." His voice is low, almost a whisper. "Do you *want* to leave?"

"No." I'm surprised by how much I mean that. It wasn't that long ago I was trying to scale a cliff.

His shoulders slump as he exhales. My attention catches on the movement and travels down to his bare abdomen. A shiver races over me. No one looks like this in real life. Hard abs and corded muscle like that require massive amounts of airbrushing. Then again, this isn't real life. He's the God of War. It's exactly what I should have expected. Should have but, somehow, didn't. It robs my lungs of oxygen. Before I can look away, he moves closer. His breath tickles my forehead and my body hums with energy.

"Theo, we really have to talk about—"

He leans down, cutting me off, but hesitates before making contact with my lips. His eyes are startlingly blue this close with the tiniest flecks of silver. When I don't move away, his mouth presses against mine. The gentleness catches me off guard. The kiss is a question seeking an answer. My answer. I lean toward him, responding with confidence. Sparks shoot to my core in a way they hadn't before, lighting the embers there. It's a slow burning fire, a careful scorch, that's no less consuming.

All I know is the taste of him as he pulls me flush with his body. One hand presses against my lower back. His other hand snakes into my hair, and I push up on my toes to better meet him. My fingers are cool against his arms, and his scent mixes with the sweetness of tabowi fruit. His fingers blaze against the strip of skin at the hem of my sweater, and I draw a sharp breath.

"Should I stop?" he asks, husky, his lips still half pressed to mine.

Probably. But I don't want him to. It feels too right. I wrap my hands around his neck and pull him back to me, deepening the kiss.

His hand glides further up my back, searing a trail up my spine. My hands slip down his chest, feeling every rippled muscle, and his grip tightens in my hair. He moves back until my waist presses against the counter and lifts me up. I circle his hips with my legs. His mouth travels across my cheek and down the side of my neck. His breath is blistering. My body will explode if I don't get closer, but there's barely any space left between us.

Rules, lies, and obligations be damned. I want him. I want him in every way and to never let go. When he guides my shirt over my head, leaving me in a tank top, I shake with nerves. My whole body is lit from the inside out.

"Are you cold?" he whispers.

"No talking." I dart forward to kiss him again. The distance is too much. He doesn't argue. His hands find my waist and I curse the fabric between us. I brush my fingers down his back and a small, hungry sound escapes him. His body presses closer, unconsciously pushing me back until I'm forced to place a hand on the counter to keep from falling.

My ribs throb under the pressure to contain my frantic heart. If Theo lets go now, I'll burst. I loop my free arm around his back, holding him close with my thighs, and savor each second, so afraid this kiss will end like the others.

Theo pulls back enough to look me in the eye, his pupils blown wide, and brushes the hair from my face. "Cassia, can I…Can we…?"

Yes, yes, yes. But if we do this, he'll be obligated to help Kisk, and I know how much he'll hate it. And, by proxy, me. I want something different for us.

"But you said—"

"I don't care," he breathes. His fingers glide over my collarbone.

The little resistance I'm clinging to wanes. Why does this have to be so complicated? I know what I *want* to do but…"But what about the war?"

"I don't care." His breath shakes, his arms trembling against me. "You're the only war I can't win. The only war I don't want to."

A chill runs up the length of my body. My insides quake. I can't decide if I want to laugh or cry, but I don't do either. Instead, I lean forward and kiss the soft spot behind his ear.

"Take me upstairs."

NINETEEN

THEO

A line of sunlight cuts through a crack in the heavy curtains. Black and brown fibers weave through the rug beneath my feet—some places still vivid while others are worn dull from years of traffic. I rest my elbows on my knees as my gaze follows the interlocking border.

Cassia's presence burns at my back. She's curled under the sheet, her hair spread over my pillow, and the scent of jasmine clings to my skin. Each of her breaths, soft and steady, pulsate through me. A battering ram to my chest. A sharp twist in my stomach.

She didn't steal my control; I gave it to her. I know it's time to end the war, so there isn't much to hand over, but I did it nonetheless. This may make Ebris think he's won, that I'm about to remove the main battleground from play only because I have to, but it doesn't matter. It can't matter. It's done and there's no taking it back. There was a choice last night and I chose her. I would make the same decision again. I shouldn't regret it—I don't—but it doesn't make the consequences any easier to swallow.

I blow out a long breath and push to my feet. Opening the wardrobe, I take a white T-shirt from the top of the stack and pull it over my head. I grab a gray button up to go over it and a pair of black jeans. I cringe as the row of buttons on the fly jingles. I'm not afraid of facing Cassia. Not really. But, what if *she* regrets it?

When I turn around, my breath catches. The pillow is at an angle as Cassia half hugs it with her chin tucked toward her chest. A bare shoulder peeks out from under the sheet. Her lips form a soft *O* and an ache begins in my chest. It seems impossible someone could be this beautiful. That, in all my time visiting her world, I've never seen someone come close. It's as if there's a light shining inside her. Bright. Flawless.

From the moment I saw her in Kisk, she's been a fighter. Strong in her own way. A soldier in her personal battle. Caring. Impulsive. Difficult. And she chose me. After everything, she still chose me. It's almost too hard to believe.

We could have lived as separately as possible. I think that's what she wanted at first, and definitely what I wanted if she was going to stay at all. I tried to stay away and went so far as to talk Goran into interrupting us during the scavenger hunt. But each kiss begged for another. The distance chipped at my foundation, ravaged my being. Perhaps she only came to me out of loneliness before, but it doesn't feel like that now. We moved together perfectly. Instinctively and without hesitation.

I've never been so wholly consumed by anything before. The thought sends goosebumps racing over my skin. I never knew it was possible to be so happy and terrified at the same time. I ease back onto the mattress and graze her cheek with the backs of my fingers. I wish we could freeze this moment before reality takes the reins. Before I have to go to the war room. Before she has the chance to tell me last night was a mistake. I only want this moment, replayed forever, in the quiet hush of the morning.

Cassia's face twitches beneath my hand, and her eyes flutter open. She sits up with a gasp, holding the navy sheet tight to her chest. Her hair sweeps over her shoulders. "Theo."

"Morning." My smile flares into place, and I trail a finger down the length of her arm. She shifts, her face skewing into a wince. "Are you okay?"

"Fine." She brushes my hand away. "I'm…fine."

My stomach lurches. Here it comes. I won't be able to stand hearing it yet. *Ever.* Numbness spreads up my arms the longer she's quiet. Each second is torture. Every breath more painful than the last until she finally looks at me.

"Theo," she says again, this time with an edge. My pulse echoes in my ears. *Don't say we shouldn't have done that. Please don't.* "I know what last night means for you and how much you didn't want this to happen."

The relief of what she didn't say feeds my panic. Last night meant everything to me. She has to understand that before she says another word. I lean across the bed and take her face in both hands. "Look at me." A few long seconds pass before she listens. "It's true. I never wanted to lose my control, and I've never given it up for anyone before."

"Because you killed them," she blurts. "We played one stupid game of Fate, so for some reason you couldn't do the same to me. Now look at what happened." A hollow laugh rattles from her throat.

I press my lips to hers so hard it hurts. When I pull back, it's only enough to meet her gaze. "I'm glad we played that stupid game. I'm glad you're here. *Right* here. I'm not sorry."

She takes a sharp breath, ducking her head. "But now you have to help Kisk."

"I already decided to end the war. That's where I was yesterday—finding a way for Asgya to fight back. It's gone too far, and I can't risk my family doing anything more to make matters worse. I know you don't care about the Kiskens, but they'll be saved too. As many as possible." I take a deep breath. There's no point saving the island now outside of accepting Cassia's sacrifice, but it's part of the deal. "If you came here to save them, to steal my choices, I wouldn't have touched you. This battle ended for me when you told me to do nothing for the island. I didn't want to admit to it back then, but I don't want to fight this anymore."

I kiss her again, softer, and her lips push back in response. My body goes numb to everything else. She has to believe me. *She has to.* I will the truth into her as I draw closer. This is right, no matter the price. I'll gladly pay it a thousand times over.

After a second, her fingers touch my shoulder, gently pressing me back. Her eyes travel over my face. Searching. Penetrating. Urgent as if the answer she's looking for is the only thing that matters in the world. Finally, she exhales, the corners of her mouth quirking, and softly shakes her head. "If someone told me this would happen the day I got here, I would've thought they were insane." She places a gentle hand on mine. "I don't want you to think I didn't want this, Theo, but I'm worried you'll resent me for it later."

I sag against her, pressing my forehead to hers, but my chest is still uneasy. There's no way I could hate her. Not when I willingly gave her this control over me.

"Never," I breathe.

"Theo?" She hesitates. "There's still something I need to talk to you about."

Sadness tinges her words. Low and uncertain. I can't listen to her doubts without being destroyed. Not right now. Not yet. I would be lost. Shattered. Any hope I hold of something better for the future—better than endless games with my siblings and desperate grabs for power—obliterated. It would break me beyond repair. *No. Not yet.* I'll hold onto this happiness as long as I can. *Longer.*

"I better get to work," I say before she has the chance to blurt out my death sentence. I break away and shrug the dress shirt on over the T-shirt. "Goran and I will likely be gone a lot over the next few days."

"Why?" She balls the sheet tight in her fist. Her body angles to follow my trek around the bed, color splashing her cheeks.

I occupy myself with the shirt buttons. "Whether we meant for this outcome or not, I still have to honor my obligation to you." It won't be easy considering how aggressive Volkana is. Even after the debacle with the antimatter, they're rallying men on the northeastern tip of the country, ready to attack. I'll manage though, with Goran's help. Somehow. My sword rests beside the headboard, and as I lean down to grab it, I kiss her cheek.

"Promise me something," she whispers.

I hesitate. "What?"

"Don't get blown up again."

Warmth explodes in my chest and I smile. "I'll do my best. You're welcome to stay here and get some rest. It'll be well after dark when I get back." *If I return tonight.* This may take longer than I expect, considering I have my siblings to deal with on top of everything.

She rests a hand over my wrist as I buckle the sword to my hip. "We can talk later though, right?"

Fear snakes through my veins. Each palpitation pushes it further into my soul until the dread nearly sends me to my knees. Instead, I lean over her and plant a final kiss on her left temple. "As soon as I have time."

Goran bends over the round war table, stretching to reach the center. Glass pieces are arranged across the board, a new color sprinkled amongst the red and blue. *Green.* But Kisk has no fighters left to put on the board.

"Good, you're up," he says. He straightens his back until it cracks and surveys his handiwork. After a moment, he reaches down and moves another piece.

I carefully pick my way over to him, more nervous than I should be. It seems like an easy enough thing to tell him the war is changing. It's not. I've held so strongly to my resolve that I'm not sure how to let it go. I want to, I need to, but once I say the words out loud, everything will be different.

"I expected you earlier." Goran fights a yawn.

I stand across the table from him and lean my palms on the scrolled edge. "It's barely past dawn." My eyebrows shoot up as I scan the board. There are more Kisken pieces than Kisken people on the island, let alone soldiers. "We have a lot to do today," I hedge.

"Oh, I know." He continues shifting pieces as he grins like a madman. "My room is right down the hall from yours."

Of course it is. I work my jaw side to side and keep my gaze safely on the table. At least I don't have to explain myself. He doesn't have to look so smug about it though.

"I think I have a plan," he says, holding back a laugh.

"You have a plan already? How long have you been down here?"

"I'm neither blind nor stupid, Theodric. As much as you bristled at the idea, I knew this day was coming. I thought after the war, but I started working on this just in case. Also, since you asked, I've been hiding down here all night." He slides a blue glass airplane on a thin pillar along the far edge of the board and smirks. "*All* night."

I laugh. I should have known Goran would support whatever happened, but it's a relief to be met with humor instead of resignation. "When this is sorted out, we should talk about rearranging rooms," I say. *Assuming Cassia isn't planning on crushing me into a fine powder.* She's tried to talk to me about something so many times that I can feel the weight of it resting on my shoulders.

"Indeed," he says in a light tone. "I'm happy for you."

The reds and blues and greens on the table blur against the black base. This changes everything. My entire life. But it also changes his. "Should you be?"

"Of course." He lowers his brows. "You should be happy for yourself as well."

I grunt, noncommittal, but I am happy. For the first time in a long time. "Where are you getting all the Kiskens?" I ask.

"The Volk and Asgyan prisoner camps." Pride lights his expression. "They'll need time to heal and regain their strength, but most of them should be able to shoot a gun."

I hold my breath, staring at the red cube in Volkana. Their largest prisoner camp, nestled at the base of a mountain before the terrain gives way to desert, houses Cassia's brother. It isn't part of the deal to save him, but that doesn't mean I can't. I don't have to be obligated in order to do something like this. I never did. I'm allowed to do something for the sole purpose of making someone else happy. Making *her* happy.

"Cassia still doesn't know her brother is alive," I say slowly.

Goran stares at me across the board without a word, and I shudder. The truth of it gnaws at me. I should have told her a long time ago, but I didn't want it to influence her decision to abandon Kisk. And maybe her opinion of me, as well. My body grows tight, high-strung and ready to run. Cassia might not be able to forgive me for hiding the truth or for letting him stay in that wretched place. I flex my hands in and out of fists to fight the numbness there. She isn't the only one with something to say later. There can't be any more lies.

"You don't have to tell her you knew the whole time," Goran suggests. "Tell her we stumbled upon him while freeing the others."

It's reasonable. Without my abilities, I don't know everyone that survived. "I can't lie to her," I admit. Reality threatens to suffocate me. I could lose her for this. "If she finds out from someone else, it will only make it worse."

Goran shrugs. "Well, the Asgyans treat their prisoners humanely, so they'll more likely take the brunt of the work. The ones from Volkana will need the most care. I believe Colonel Stavros would be a good man to lead if we can get the others to trust him, but I don't know his physical or mental state. It's possible he's dead by now." He scans the board. Distant. Unseeing. "Either way,

I think this plan will work. The men and women will be desperate not only to save their island, but destroy their enemies. They'll find the energy somehow."

Some will. Some will not. But it's the best chance we have.

"We'll start here, then." I touch the camp where Oren is. "If the Colonel is going to lead this campaign, he'll need the extra time to rest."

Goran sighs. "You know what this means, don't you?"

"What?"

"We have to talk Hex into smuggling thousands of men and women back into Kisk."

I fight a smile and tap his shoulder with the back of my hand. "I'll let you break the news to her."

TWENTY

CASSIA

True to his word, it's been days since I've seen Theo. The only reason I know he's been back, is because he sneaks into my room each morning to kiss my forehead. He stands there for a few long moments, staring at me, and I itch to open my eyes for a small glimpse of him. The scent of cool steel, sulfur, and the ocean linger in my room long after he's gone. The image of him after the explosion haunts me. I want to make sure he's in one piece, but it feels more important not to. Like the moment, in all its frailty, is somehow holding Theo together when he needs it most. To wake up might break whatever spell is keeping this thing he and I have from imploding.

But I can't avoid him or the conversation we need to have forever.

Soon, whatever feelings Theo has toward me will be lost, cracked beyond repair because lying by omission is still lying. His entire choice to be with me was based on it. He said himself he wouldn't have touched me if I wanted to save Kisk. I'm sure saving my brother falls into the same category, and I can't deny the truth that I *had* meant to steal his control. If my own feelings, my conscience, hadn't gotten in the way, I would have.

I'm not sure how to tell him I know Oren is alive. There's no good way to go about it, so I suppose I'll just say it. I'll say it, then I'll ask Theo to save him, because, either way, whatever we have will be finished. My body strains against the thought of this being ripped away.

I shift under the covers and press the heels of my hands to my eyes. I won't cry. I did this to myself and deserve whatever heartache I get. Plotting behind someone's back always backfires. I never realized how high these stakes would be.

I roll over to where Moki is curled, sleeping on one of my pillows, and snuggle my nose into her sort fur. *I'm strong,* I remind myself. *Stronger than this.* I repeat it over and over until, eventually, I fall back into a fitful sleep. A sleep full of nightmares teeming with fierce blue eyes, reptilian masks of crimson and gold, and glinting silver swords.

♦

When I wake, I'm soaked in a cold sweat. I shiver as I toss the covers back. The misplaced guilt I felt for over a year in Kisk never came close to this. Raw and chafing, it courses through me like liquid fire. I can't do it anymore.

Today, I tell Theo the truth.

I fling open the wardrobe to find my own kind of armor to go up against the War God. I need something that makes me feel confident, unshakable.

This might even go well enough for me to get my own volume in his archives. I imagine the jerky handwriting on the inside cover. *Cassia: Kisken Liar Extraordinaire.* With a sharp breath, I settle on a pink lace top with a pair of dark jeans. With a quick scratch to Moki's head, I hurry to shower and dress.

Then to the entryway to wait.

And wait.

And wait some more.

Hours tick by, but I don't move from the foot of the stairs. My stomach growls, still accustomed to unnecessary daily meals, and I press a hand over it. The fingers of my other hand strike in quick succession on a step while I tap my shoes against the marble floor. I take a series of deep breaths. I'll be here when Theo gets back if it kills me. Then maybe he *will* kill me, but knowing I'll lose someone I love feels the same as being dead.

My heart skips a beat. It's the first time I've let myself think that word. *Love.* Over the last few days it's popped into my mind over and over, but I've kept it locked it away. Loving someone means giving them the power to hurt you. It's handing them your soul and asking them not to tear it to pieces. Admitting to myself that I love Theo now is dangerous; I'm about to be run through the shredder. But I can't help it. I do. I love him.

A shadow shifts across the floor, and I leap to my feet in time for Theo to shuffle through the door, running his fingers through his hair. My whole body tingles at the sight of him. Each heartbeat echoes in my ears. I can't tell him. I can never tell him.

I have to tell him.

My stomach knots violently and I grab the banister to stay standing. Theo's shirt collar is stretched, one sleeve unrolled, the cuff hanging loose around his wrist. He kicks the door shut with the heel of his boot and releases a heavy sigh. My hands tremble as I watch him. He stands with his head bent, hair stiff with saltwater, and his eyes closed for so long I think he's fallen asleep on his feet. I bite my bottom lip and remind myself why I've been sitting here all day: to seal my fate, for better or worse.

A small, tired grunt travels across the entryway and I move forward as if pulled by invisible strings. "You're back," I say, wiping my hands on my pants.

Theo's body jolts, a smile already breaking through the lines of fatigue etched on his face. "Cassia." It's a whisper, carved with longing, that tugs me closer. Then his arms are around me and I'm enveloped in his warmth. "I feel like I haven't seen you in years," he says against my neck.

His fingertips glide over my collarbone. I laugh to hide the shiver cascading over me. "Only days." *So many days.*

"Only?" He pulls back and kisses me, soft and slow. "Have you been all right on your own?"

I've managed to keep myself busy and finally got a rock to hop once before sinking, but I don't say that. My face twitches, threatening to fall. I make myself smile instead. "Nevermind me. How are you?" I scratch at the stubble on his cheek. He smells of fire and stagnant water. "You look like you need a break."

"That's exactly what I need." The weight of his hands settling on my hips grounds me. "But first I'm going to take a shower." He shifts down and kisses me again. "Then I'm going to do more of this." He leans closer, pressing a hand at the small of my back. My fingertips light over the erratic pulse in his neck. After a moment, he smiles against my mouth. "I'll be right back. Don't go anywhere."

As he circles me to reach the stairs, he keeps a hand on my waist, turning me with him, drinking me in. His smile melts away my anxiety. There's warmth in his expression, tender and excited, that I've never seen before. I don't understand it but I recognize it all the same. He cares for me. I'm not sure how much or if it's the same as I care for him, but it's true. Absolutely true.

Theo finally dashes up the stairs and I nearly collapse as the water kicks on in the bathroom. *Okay.* I sigh. This is going to be harder than I expected. My thoughts scattered when he touched me. He looked at me as if I've become his entire world. To never see that look again…

From the corner of my eye, I see motion through the front door. A bright red figure moves in the courtyard, another following in black. Considering the new circumstances, I'm not sure I trust surprise guests. I dart into the sitting room and peek around the floor-length curtains. My jaw drops. *Astra.* With Cy trailing behind her, his arms crossed.

Not now.

She's the only one with the ability to hurt me before I hurt myself. When she told me about my brother, she was trying to help, so I'm not sure why panic buds in my chest. She won't tell Theo. This has to be a friendly visit, nothing more, but a raw, nagging worry makes me slip behind the curtain as they burst through the front door.

The curtain pools around my feet, wrapping me in heavy folds, and I hold my breath. Astra's shoes clap across the floor. She calls out for Theo, then me, before wandering into the sitting room. She stops and my breath stops along with her. I dig my fingernails into my palms to keep myself from shaking. If the curtain moves, I'm done for.

"Wait here," Astra says. "I'll find them."

Her heels recede into the entryway, calling for Theo again, but I stay against the windowpane. The glass cools my skin through my clothes. Cy could easily rat me out for ignoring Astra if I come out of hiding now. I swallow hard. He warned me to be careful with the information about my brother, and I did the exact opposite. He had to believe me when I said I wouldn't sleep with Theo or I'm sure he would've warned me about that too, because it was an absolutely horrible idea. I can't tell him how right he was on top of everything else.

"She's gone," Cy says. "You can come out, Cassia."

I gasp, then groan. "How did you know I was here?" I ask, pushing the fabric aside.

"I saw you looking out the window as we came up the steps. It was easy enough to assume you didn't get far." He studies me like he's seeing me for the first time. "The Bride of the War God, slinking about her own home."

"Shut up," I hiss. My face burns at the insinuation. And the title—I can't bear the title. "What are you doing here?"

He motions to me with both hands. "We received word of the good news," he says in an even voice.

"What?" I knew the other gods would know eventually, but I didn't expect anyone to swing by to applaud us. I mean, who does that? *Oh hey, congrats on the sex.* No. Just no. I haven't even processed it. It happened, I know it happened, and I'm happy to have been with Theo, but it opened a bigger can of worms than my virginity. A can chock full of death and despair. I can only handle one massive, overflowing emotion at a time.

"Is there a newsletter?" I grumble.

Cy arches an eyebrow. "I didn't think you had it in you."

"What is that supposed to mean?" *I know what that means.*

"You play the game well for having so little experience." He looks over his shoulder at the doorway before stepping closer and lowering his voice. "You should have let your brother go."

"I told you, I can't, but that's not why—"

"It doesn't matter why." The first sign of anger creeps into his tone. "What matters is that you handed your god over on a silver platter. One slip up, one move out of place, and Ebris will find him in breach of contract. He's been dying to banish Theodric to the Between since the Ostran War."

"Why do you care so much what happens to Theo?" I snap.

"I don't." He blinks, startled by his own words. "Not any more than I care about the other gods, but I'm tired of seeing innocent people get caught up in this feud. Ebris is more cunning, more destructive, than the others put together, and no one has the power to put him in his place. It would have been nice to see someone else win for a change."

I want to ask what Ebris did to him or maybe did to Astra, but it doesn't matter. None of this other stuff matters. If Theo will be banished for not keeping his obligation, if the Between is as bad as the mythology book made it sound, he can't find out the truth until the war is over. When it ends and his duty to Kisk is complete, I'll tell him that I knew since the beginning. It will kill me inside to keep it a secret, but I can't turn back time. It will make me look so much worse in the end, but it will have saved him from himself. It's the least I can do.

"This isn't a game, Cy. Real lives are going to be affected by this," I say.

Theo's life. My life. "You have to help me keep this a secret."

"What? No." He shifts backward. "I told you to be careful. This is your problem now."

"Please," I beg.

"I'm not going to volunteer the information, but I won't lie for you," he says in a tight voice. "I have myself to think about."

"Yourself?" I scoff. Irrational anger digs at my already sore insides. "Are you sure you're not worried about Astra?"

He glares at me, almost at the door now. "Astra is a goddess. She knows how to take care of herself."

"Cy—"

The sound of Astra's heels cut into the conversation, clicking in quick succession until she's standing in the doorway. "There you are." She beams.

"Here I am," I say flatly.

"Oh, my beautiful little darling." The soft ends of her hair tickle my arms as she sweeps me into a hug. "You're perfect. I always knew you were."

Suspicion slithers through my mind, oozing into my limbs. I pat her shoulders and find she's lacking her usual heat. I break away, unsure what she's saying. The words themselves are innocent enough, but not the heavy, meaningful aura behind them. She smoothes her hands down my face and holds me in place.

"Now we can put all this behind us. Cy's country will be saved. Your brother will be rescued and—"

"What?" Theo asks, his voice murderously low.

Astra's hands fall and the room grows so still my whole body surges in

221

time with my heart. He can't find out like this. *Not like this.* Sweat beads along my forehead. It must look like a conspiracy from where he's standing. Like I schemed against him with his own sister. My blood drains to my feet. My voice is lost.

"You know your brother is alive?" Theo asks carefully.

I want to scream that my brother has nothing to do with anything. I want to tell him the other night happened because I love him, not because I wanted to trap him. I want to fall on my knees and beg for forgiveness, to explain that I had made desperate plans for this when I first found out but changed my mind. But I can't because he'll never believe a word of it.

"I know it as well as you do," I say defensively. He lied too, after all. I'm not in this deception alone.

"How?" His face falls somewhere between shock and rage. "For how long?"

"The second time Astra came to visit," I choke out. "But—"

Theo grabs Astra's wrist. "How did you find out?"

"I have ways of—"

"Get out," he booms, shoving his sister toward the door.

"Theo," she says in a high voice.

"Get. Out."

He walks toward her until she backs out the front door and slams it in her face. Cy is already gone. My knees wobble and I know…I know how this will end. Was there ever a doubt? I may love Theo but that doesn't mean he loves me back. Even if he did, he won't forgive me. It isn't in his nature. Especially when it comes to the one thing he fought so hard to hold onto. The second he gave me control, I rammed a knife into his back, twisting and tearing at his flesh.

222

When Theo returns, the shock is gone but the rage is still there. It ripples through each movement as he strides toward me. His nostrils are flared, his veins popping under his freshly scrubbed skin.

"Theo?" I step back, hitting the shield of a white statue. I hold my hands out to keep him at arm's length. "Theo, listen."

"What have you done?" His voice quakes with each syllable.

"I can explain," I say. "It's what I wanted to tell you. I *tried*, Theo. More than once, but you were busy. And…and you didn't tell me, either."

He's so close I can hear each labored breath, feel the stir of it in the air. "Tell me I'm dreaming. Tell me it isn't true," he begs. "Tell me and I'll believe it."

How I wish I could. "It wasn't like that," I say in a rush. I jump as his hands slam down on either side of my head, gripping the corners of the shield. "At first I hated you for keeping it from me and, yes, I wanted to use you to save him, but I changed my mind. I couldn't betray you like that when I had real feelings for you."

"Real feelings?" He barks a laugh. "You're going to keep up the charade? It's done. You've been caught."

"It's not a charade." A handful of hot tears roll down my cheek before I can stop them. "In the kitchen, before we went upstairs, I brought up the war. You had a chance to stop, but you didn't want to any more than I did. I know you felt that I wanted you that night. *You*. Nothing else." I reach to touch him but stop before making contact. "Our being together has nothing to do with Kisk or my brother."

"Maybe not for me." His arms tremble around me. "But for you, it had *everything* to do with it."

"It didn't," I whisper. A sob lodges in my chest, but I shove it down. "Did I want my brother out of a country that's known for torturing people? Of course. I tried to ask you for help, but you were too busy to talk. Or maybe you were avoiding me, I don't know. I *tried* Theo. I did."

Wet pieces of hair quiver against his forehead, his gaze distant. Disbelieving. Hurt. "I would have done it for you," he says quietly.

My breath quakes, a shiver to each exhale. "Theo, please listen."

"I would have, but I won't now." He leans away from me, a new type of fire dancing in his eyes. "Let Ebris do what he will. I'm going to let Volkana slaughter every Kisken they can get their hands on. When they're done, when you know your brother and every other islander is dead, I'll show enough mercy to let you meet them in the Netherworld."

Bile rises in the back of my throat. This isn't the Theo I know—this is a new person. *No.* This is a god.

"You don't mean that," I whisper.

"Oh." The statue's shield shatters beneath his hands, puffs of powdered plaster coating my shoulders, and he shoves away. "I do."

My knees buckle and I slump to the floor in a heap. Theo leaves me there without so much as a second glance.

I knew he would likely hate me, but to kill an entire race of people? Even if he loathes the fact that he accepted me, the deal is done. Ebris won't let him break the agreement. Cy admitted that much. I stumble to my feet.

Unshed tears blur the room, then the hall, the courtyard, and finally the temple. I'm not sure how I made the short walk but, when I reach Ebris' altar, I collapse. I can't travel through the portals myself without Theo's ring, but the note to Astra went through. Maybe my prayers will too.

Using the stone wall, I push myself back onto my feet and fumble with the small gold hoops in my ears. There's no box on the altar to place them in, so I cup them in my palm and press the jewelry onto the wooden surface.

"Ebris, King of Gods, please accept this tribute." I swallow hard, unsure if this is right. I've never prayed a day in my life. There's an equal chance I'm insulting him as there is I'm honoring him. "If you're there, if you can hear me, I hope you'll listen."

TWENTY ONE

THEO

Heavy rain pelts Gull Island, a long outlying strip of land belonging to Kisk, but I barely feel it as I make my way down the hill. I'm too numb. Too angry. Too blindsided to care that freezing water soaks my clothes. My mouth is full of the acrid taste of betrayal. Metallic. Bitter.

Cassia knew.

She knew almost from the beginning. Before the first night I kissed her. Is that why she kissed me back? Why she took care of me after the explosion? It has to be. She avoided me before that. I've been around long enough to know the difference between true compassion and false sympathy. At least, I thought I did. The concern on her face as she washed me seemed so real. Maybe I'm too far out of my comfort zone to know anything anymore.

But there are still two things I'm sure of: war and vengeance. My siblings have played me long enough. I'm certainly not going to let a mortal do the same. Ebris be damned. I won't let Cassia steal everything I've worked for. If he wants to banish me to the Between, he can fight me for the chance. I held onto some of my supernatural strength and am better with a sword. I certainly won't make it easy for him.

"Theodric, I didn't expect you back for hours," Goran calls. His voice is barely audible over the splatter of rain. He rushes toward me from the edge of the camp where the escaped prisoners are holed up and wipes the water from his face. "The men have all been seen by medical now. Eighty percent are able to hold a weapon." He stops short and scowls. "What happened?"

I stop at the edge of the barren crop field, now nothing but mud. Brown tents stand erect in neat rows, ten wide and twenty deep. Ten thousand Kiskens are beneath those canopies with the last five thousand due to arrive tomorrow. Some hobbled about on crutches when they got here. Others are missing limbs. Still more are unable to get off their cots. A piss poor army if I've ever seen one. Easy to destroy. I'm not sure how I saw promise in them earlier. Wishful thinking, perhaps.

"What happened?" I repeat in a hard tone to keep my voice from snapping. I want to lean on Goran, if only for a minute. To share the agonizing pain of having my insides ripped apart. But I can't; I won't. Cassia doesn't deserve to bring me that low. Instead, I'll kill her brother before moving on to the rest of her kinsman. "Where is Colonel Stavros?"

"In the center tent," he says. I brush past him and he darts after me. "What's going on? Have we been discovered?"

I grip the hilt of my sword. The cool metal is reassuring at my hip. Unwavering. A trusted friend. The only one I have other than Goran. I fix my interest on the one tent that breaks formation, rising up in the center of the rows. "I'm going to do to him what I should have done to his sister that day in the temple," I rumble.

Goran's shock sparks at my side. "*What?*"

She lied, I almost blurt. The truth sticks in my throat. I can't forgive her. I won't. Manipulation is something I've come to expect, but I truly thought she was different. If Cassia wants to trap me into one course of action, I'll show her the power of a god. Even one as reduced as I am.

"Cassia knew about her brother. That's why…"

"What?" Goran shouts. "How? When? *How?*"

"Astra told her." I breathe heavily, the rain pouring down my face. "She's known long enough to deceive me."

"Wait."

Goran steps in front of me and I almost run him into the mud for it. "What?"

"Are you saying she did this on purpose?" he asks.

I glare at him. His disbelief is salt in my open wounds. Cassia is good at this game, too good if she fooled us both. I crack my elbows, pulling my attention away from the throbbing in my chest. "Of course she did."

"Theodric." He must catch the pity in his own voice and rubs at his mouth. "I'm sorry. She didn't seem like…I never expected it from her."

I raise my eyebrows. *Seem like what?* I want to ask but I'm too afraid of the answer. "Neither did I." I step around Goran and continue toward the center tent where the commanding officers will plan the salvation of their island.

"You can't kill the Colonel," Goran wheezes. "We still need him if we're going to save Kisk. He's the highest ranking officer we have."

"We aren't going to save Kisk."

"We aren't going to save Kisk," he repeats, halting between words. "We *have* to."

"I won't lose, Goran." My grip tightens on the hilt. "I can't. I've come too far for some mortal to swoop in and snatch it away."

"Listen to yourself. This isn't a win-or-lose situation. Ebris will never let you see the light of day again if you don't hold up your end of the sacrifice," Goran warns. "Don't let yourself fall into this trap."

I've already fallen.

I storm into the tent, my shield up, and gag as the stench of rotting meat slams into me. A man in a tattered gray jumpsuit cradles his right arm to his chest. His head, covered in bald patches and jagged scabs, rests on the pole behind the bench.

Goran flies in behind me. "Colonel Oren Stavros," he huffs, motioning to the broken man, "is one of the twenty percent unable to fight. He has a mind for strategy though and can still lead from behind the scenes. Please, Theodric. In four hundred years, I've never asked you for anything, but I'm begging you not to do this."

The Colonel can't be more than twenty-five, promoted for the sole purpose of leading the aide missions to Asgya, but his paper-thin skin ages him. Protruding bones make him almost skeletal. Yet, somehow his features are so like Cassia's that it's hard to look at him. "No," I say.

A man in a matching jumpsuit ducks into the tent with a tray of medical supplies. Bandages, scissors, an assortment of medication. "Sir," he says. "Doc sent me over to check your arm."

"It's fine, Gregor," the Colonel says. A weak smile cracks his parched lips. "I doubt that woman's credentialed anyway."

Gregor carries the tray with shaking hands. Greasy hair falls across his cheekbones. "She may be a pirate, but she's better than those hacks in the Shell."

"It's hard to be worse than a butcher." He shifts with a groan. "Like I said before, they can have my arm in the morning."

Gregor sets the tray down on a warped tabletop and tugs the Colonel's wounded arm away from his chest. He turns green. "No offense, sir, but this can't wait."

The Colonel tugs the bits of worn sleeve down but there isn't enough material to hide the gash on his forearm. Pus oozes from blackened skin. Nothing on that tray will do any good. It needs to be amputated before the gangrene spreads.

"Plenty of men have issues more pressing than this thing," the Colonel says. "They can chop it off at dawn if it makes them happy, but the others need to be taken care of first."

"But, sir—"

"Find Major Buros." He coughs and nods to the medical supplies. "Take that and tend to someone else." When the man hesitates, he adds, "That's an order."

"Yes, sir," Gregor whispers. He lifts the tray with a bowed head and turns.

"Wait," he calls in a hushed voice. "Do the men from the other camps still think I'm a traitor?"

"We're working on it, sir," Gregor says apologetically. "They'll understand soon enough and will follow you when the time comes."

The Colonel waves him off before collapsing against the post, but he watches the silver tray until it disappears from the tent. An image of Cassia giving the emaciated man half a loaf of bread flashes through my mind. I squeeze my eyes against it, willing away the rawness in my chest, and pull my sword from the scabbard.

"Theodric," Goran pleads. "Don't do this."

I grind my teeth. "I won't let Cassia get away with betraying me, and Astra needs to see what her meddling leads to."

Goran steps between me and the Colonel, shaking his head. "I don't know what happened, but this isn't something to do out of anger. If you kill him, there's no going back," he says. "Not with Ebris and not with Cassia. They won't forgive you."

My mind flashes again. This time to Cassia climbing out of the pit. The petrified look on her face as I nearly took her life wedges between my ribs, splintering the bone. I should have known she would do something like this. I tried to murder her. There's no way she could care for me.

"I don't want to go back," I rasp. "Even if I did, it's already too late."

"If you insist on killing him, at least wait a few days," Goran urges. "When your temper has cooled, speak with Cassia again. Get the whole story first. You can't bring her brother back to life if you find out there's a misunderstanding."

That he thinks there could be a misunderstanding is laughable. I know what I heard. I saw the challenge smoldering beneath her fear. I lied to her as much as she lied to me. I know it, she knows it, and the crushing weight on my shoulders knows it. Even if there is something I don't know yet, something that will make her appear innocent, I'm not sure I can believe it. My heart is stone again, shielded by an iron fortress. Impervious to charms or excuses. A barrier keeping me on track.

"*One* day," Goran says.

My pulse convulses against its newly formed walls. Pounding to be free. I glance at the Colonel as he takes labored breaths on the bench. "Damn you," I growl. "One day. If his arm doesn't kill him by morning, I will."

Goran exhales, pushing back his dripping mop of hair. He thinks this will buy time to salvage the war. He's wrong. I'll spare one man for a single night, but the plan to sabotage the island hasn't changed. I glare at Cassia's brother, then throw a final look at my adviser.

"Don't expect the remaining prisoners to arrive in the morning," I call over my shoulder. "This war is still mine."

The Cursed Jewel is docked between the Kisken mainland and Gull Island, its massive black sails tethered to their masts. The rain isn't falling here, but a heavy fog coils across the ship's deck. I squirm in my soaked clothing. The crew is too busy unloading supplies to notice me sprint up the wooden gangway unshielded, but Hex doesn't miss a beat. She greets me at the rail with knotted, windblown hair and a deep frown on her sun-kissed face.

"You better be bringing my payment," she snaps. "There's no other reason for you to step foot on this vessel."

"Half before, half after, like we agreed," I say. "You'll see the rest when the job is done."

She crosses her arms. "Which job is that exactly? The attacking or the smuggling?"

"Turn your men around." Disgust swirls around me like a cloak. "Keep the supplies, sell them. I don't care. As long as you sail away from here. You'll receive payment when you've reached an eastern shore."

"Which eastern shore?" she asks without moving her jaw.

"*Any* eastern shore. Don't come back until word of Kisk's fall is heard in the farthest corner of the world."

"You've got to be kidding me." She glares at me. "First I'm supposed to attack Volk ships, then you have me smuggling Kiskens, and now you want me to disappear? What do you think this is? Rent-a-Pirate? I have an empire to run."

"I'm making you richer than you ever imagined." I step closer, my hands in fists. "Do it. Now."

Her laugh is a bitter, piercing sound. "I'm not going anywhere. Keep the rest of your money. We're done. We'll drop the rest of the cargo and return to the cove."

I sneer. "Do that and I'll make sure Volkana comes for you as soon as they've mowed down every Kisken in their path."

"Try me." She shoves my chest with her fingertips. "Who do you think you are?"

A god!

"*Theodric!*" My head snaps toward the source of my name, the hair rising on my arms. Brisa stands at the bottom of the gangway, shielded from the pirates. "Get down here," she snarls through her teeth.

I turn back to Hex and point my finger in her face. "Today."

The pirate's shouts follow me all the way back to shore. She's still going when I trail my sister around the corner of a boat house.

Once we're out of sight, I throw my shield in place and Brisa rounds on me with unwarranted fury. "Are you completely insane?" she snaps. "What are you doing? Do you *want* to live in the Between for the rest of eternity?"

"I won't let Ebris banish me," I snap.

"Oh, lose the cocky attitude." She steps closer, leaving an inch between us. "You might have been a challenge to Ebris before, but now you're as good as mortal. He'll toss you in there like a rag doll."

Her words scorch through me. While it's true I'm not as strong as I should be, as I was, I'm nowhere near as weak as a man. I have the will to beat Ebris. The determination. It's about time someone did it. He can't run around unchecked because the others are too afraid to stand against him. I've never been scared; that's why he hates me.

"Stop this suicide mission and get your act together. Listen to Goran. Make the right choices. Like it or not, you have to save Kisk," she hisses.

"I have to do nothing," I shout, spittle flying. "You stood there in the middle of the Ostran War and let Ebris do this to me. He *asked* me to wage that war, and, in return, he took everything from me. I played nice for centuries to earn back what's mine, and all I've gotten in return is suspicion and games. More *games*." I press a hand against my sternum. Scar after agonizing scar rest there. The latest wound—Cassia's cut—is still wide open, and Brisa has the audacity to give me orders.

"If no one else plays by the rules, there's no reason I should," I say.

"This is exactly the type of drama I try to avoid." She squints up at me.

"I don't want to see you banished, okay? But don't blame your poor choice of a partner on Astra." She holds her palm up when I open my mouth to speak. "Yes, I know all about it. Astra came crying to me after you kicked her out of your house. She thinks you're going to kill your new bride and that it's her fault. You chose Cassia, Theodric. This isn't some fairy tale where you get to ride off into the sunset. The girl hurt you, I get it, but *boo-hoo*. Snap out of it and do your job."

My ears buzz. I can't breathe. The weight is too crushing. Doing my job is all I've ever tried to do. All I've ever *wanted* to do. They're upset because I refuse to let them hold my leash anymore, but they haven't seen anything yet.

"Stay out of my business," I say. Then I turn and walk toward the main island. Toward the Asgyan and Volk troops. The Kisken revolution will end before it ever gets off the ground.

"Don't say I didn't try to help you," Brisa screams at my back.

TWENTY TWO

CASSIA

All my tears have long been emptied into my pillow, leaving me dry and aching. Raw. I haven't cried like that since Oren's supposed execution. Not even after the bombings. I've lost track of time, drifting in and out of sleep, but the sun is bright as it filters through the sheer curtains. I'm tempted to pull the covers over my head and ignore the world a little longer. I have nothing to get up for; my brother's likely dead by now, and it won't be long before I am too. But I can't waste what little time I have left wallowing. I'm not a wallower; I'm a doer. Not that I know what to do. I've lost any shred of influence I had with Theo, and I'm stuck in his realm until he decides to send me away.

"Goran?" I call in a hoarse voice. He's been sitting quietly outside my room for an hour now. He gave up trying to talk to me awhile ago, but I sense his steady presence through the door. Apparently he brought breakfast again. It smells similar to the one he brought me my first morning here. Bacon and eggs. A hint of coffee. My nose is too stuffed to be sure, but I really hope the last one is right. "Are you still out there?"

He looks like hell—dirty, matted, and bone-tired—when he ducks his head into the room. "Yes."

I sit up and rub my nose with the back of my hand. "What are you doing out there? Shouldn't you be helping Theo destroy Kisk?"

Goran pushes the door in and leans against the frame with his arms folded, fists tight against his side. His blond hair is weighed down against his head with random tufts rising above the rest. "I've come to see Theodric as more than a god in the last four hundred years. We're friends." He studies the carpet. "But I'm not interested in helping him dig his own grave."

My chest caves. Theo is going through with his threat then. I'm still not sure how I feel about Kisk, but I hate that Kiskens will be destroyed *because* of me rather than in spite of me. I'm the traitor here, not Oren, but he'll pay the price for my foolishness. Maybe he already has.

"I'm also worried about you," Goran adds.

"Me?" I choke back a sob. "You should be glad to see me go after this."

His gaze cuts to my face, his expression hard. "I don't believe you did what Theodric thinks you did."

A sudden, desperate weightlessness sends me stumbling from the bed. I right myself and hold my breath, my lips parted, waiting for the punch line. If Theo doesn't believe me, there's no way Goran does. *But maybe.* At least he seems willing to give me an opportunity to explain.

"Did you?" he asks.

"Maybe. I don't know." My throat is like sandpaper as I swallow. "What exactly does he think I did?"

"That you conspired with Astra. That she told you to manipulate him into accepting your sacrifice for your brother's sake." His eyes bore into me, searching for the truth but hoping for one version of it. "Maybe for Kisk too."

"I didn't do anything for Kisk," I mutter. My shoulders slump under the burden of his stare. "I didn't do anything for my brother, either, but I wanted to. I was *going* to."

Goran steps closer. "But?"

"But." My cheeks burn and I heave a sigh. "But my feelings got in the way, and I couldn't do it."

"You did, though," he says cautiously.

"I know," I mumble. The reminder pricks at my center. "But my intentions weren't...this."

There were no intentions. Other than the fleeting moment I brought up the war in the kitchen, I didn't think about anything other than Theo until I woke up the next morning. Even if I hadn't changed my mind before we slept together, I wouldn't have had the willpower to stop. If that makes me a horrible person, so be it.

"Is Oren dead?" I ask after a long silence.

Goran shoves his hands in his jean pockets. "He wasn't when I left."

My stomach churns. "But he will be?" I don't need to ask to know the answer, but I can't help wanting to hear it confirmed.

"I sincerely hope not."

"Did Theo honor your sacrifice?" I blurt in a raw voice.

"What?" Goran's eyebrows shoot up.

I perch on the edge of the bed, too weary to continue standing. "When you came here, did he honor it?"

Goran's silence rings in my ears until he finally nods. "I led my troops to a fort without knowing the enemy took it days before. After retreating to an old tower, we came under siege, but we were too outnumbered and weren't properly supplied. Theodric got them all out."

Jealousy swells inside me. Why couldn't things have been that simple for me? The least Theo could've done was save Oren if he didn't want the war to end. "Can you help me?" I ask. I'm fairly certain I know the answer to this question too.

"I've done all I can," he says quietly. "He won't listen. Maybe when he calms down you can explain yourself."

My eyes drift to the blue walls, the corners blurring. I've done all the explaining I'm willing to do. Theo won't calm down. Not for a long, long time. A thousand years have passed since the Ostran War, and he's still holding a grudge for what happened. Humans will probably be extinct before he even thinks about hearing me out.

"Thanks, Goran." I blink. "I appreciate your vote of confidence."

He leans into the hall and produces the breakfast tray. "Don't start giving up now."

"I won't."

I offer him a small smile as the tray lands on my lap. He's wrong; I have given up. It took years from the first blow to tear me down, but it finally happened. I've lived through more sorrow than joy in my sixteen years. I'm tired and alone and I can't handle anything else. I can't.

After Goran leaves, I set the tray on the nightstand. As hungry as I am, I have no appetite.

"Where is he?" A man's voice booms up the staircase to the third floor. It reverberates off the walls of my room, sending my heart flying into my throat. *Ebris.* It seems like forever ago that I heard him argue with Theo in another language, but I would recognize his tenor anywhere. I stumble over the rug and grab the footboard to keep from face planting. My pulse echoes in my ears as I thunder down the steps.

"I want to see him *now*," he shouts.

My palms are slick against the railing. *Did he hear me*? If Ebris was listening to my prayer, it obviously wasn't received well. Maybe I should be running in the opposite direction.

"He left." Goran's back is to the bottom of the stairs when I round the final spiral. His hands are held away from his sides, and I pause a few steps from the landing. "I can't get him back. He took the ring."

"I can go," Leander says.

My breath catches. I'm not an expert, but I doubt the King of the Gods needs Death as backup. Not unless he wants me to have a VIP pass to the Netherworld. I shouldn't have asked for leniency for Theo by putting the blame on myself. What did I think Ebris would do? Send me to my room without dinner? I bite my bottom lip and back up the staircase slowly, barely moving in fear the motion will be noticed.

"A lot of good you did the last time," Ebris snaps. "You said you were hopeful the war would end. That it looked like he would accept the girl."

"Well, I *was* hopeful and he *did* accept her," Leander says calmly.

"For all it was worth. You—" Ebris roars. "Show me his plan to destroy the island, or I swear I'll flay you with my bare hands."

Goran steps aside and motions to the back of the mansion. "He smashed the war table, but you're welcome to see for yourself."

"See what?" Theo strides through the front door and the world slows. He brushes a bit of dust from his sleeves and the crisp scent of Kisken winter drifts up the staircase. I watch as the familiar powder lifts, dancing with each subtle movement in the air.

Oh, Theo. What did you do?

I want to run to him, wrap my arms around his waist and tell him how sorry I am. I want to tell him I love him and I never meant any of it. I want it so badly my whole body shakes, but it's impossible. We both made sure of that.

"Enough is enough, Theodric." The King of the Gods darts into view, his chest nearly bumping Theo's, and I stifle a gasp. Brutality shadows Ebris' features. His teeth are bared; his square jaw locked. "How many times do I have to say it?"

Theo's face contorts with a fury so deep, he's hardly recognizable. "This is *my* choice. My role to play. You've taken enough from me."

The veins in Ebris' neck throb. He isn't as big as Theo, but I don't doubt for a moment he holds more strength in his fists than Theo holds in his entire body. I've seen what he can do without trying. "This is a new era," Ebris says.

"We can't entertain wars for your amusement anymore. Did you see what that bomb did to the mountain in Volkana?"

Theo laughs, a harsh sound. "Did I see what it did? I was blown to bits stopping it from reaching its destination."

"If you were minutes later, it would have hit its target."

"You're worried about my part, but no one seems to know how the Volks learned to harness antimatter," Theo spits.

"Don't you dare try to pin this on me."

My heel slips as I back up another step, and both gods whip their heads in my direction. Heat floods me, roasting me from the inside out. My legs have trouble remembering how to stand and my arms hang limp at my sides. If it weren't for my skin, I would be a puddle at their feet.

"You're owed your country and you shall have it," Ebris says to me. His head tilts stiffly back and forth as if restraining himself is taking all his willpower.

"She won't." Theodric glares at me with cold, hard eyes. It's so different than the way he looked at me twenty-four hours ago that my brain strains to accept the new truth all over again. "After dusk, there won't be a Kisk left to save. Whoever wins the battle will win the island."

"Kisk *will* keep its freedom," Ebris says in a flat voice.

"There's no chance of that happening. Volkana and Asgya will come at them from both sides, outnumbering the Kiskens seventy to one."

A tremor rolls over Ebris, power humming through the air around him. "Goran, ready counter measures. I'll take care of this myself."

Goran bolts toward the war room without a moment's hesitation, and I struggle to breathe.

"Throwing you in the Between won't change anything, will it? I want to more than I've wanted anything in a long time. It's what I had planned, but I know you, Theodric. You'd come out two, three thousand years from now hungry for retribution and more determined than ever to get it." Ebris steps back, his body tight as a bow string. "You'll trade places with Leander until you learn the true price of war."

"What?" Theo and Leander shout in unison.

Ebris holds up a hand. "Leander, you'll work with Goran to put things right after I save Kisk. He seems quite capable. And you," he points to Theo. "You'll be chained in the Netherworld. Let's see how well you greet the souls of the people you've condemned to death. When you appreciate human life instead of treating them like pawns, we'll see about letting you out."

Theo's face is tight, but I can't tell if it's anger or dread. War is his life. He'll go crazy sorting people into neat little rows day after day, but Ebris has a point. He treats war as if the people aren't real. They're nothing more than pieces on his war table to be shuffled around at will, but I was more than that. Goran still is. Ebris can't see the caring part of his brother, buried deep beneath the pain and need for control, because he isn't looking.

Perhaps if I hadn't lied, or I had been able to properly explain, we wouldn't be in this situation and Ebris would have to come around. Maybe not with this war but with the next. I can't accept responsibility for what Theo's doing out of spite, but I know my part in it. I started down the path to this end weeks ago when I convinced myself that using him was justified.

Aren't we the same? Using people without a care for who gets hurt in the process. Theo is simply working on a grander scale.

Theo's hand shifts to the hilt of his sword. My mouth runs dry, my muscles seizing. He can't seriously mean to raise it against Ebris. But he will. I see it in each taught line of his body.

"Wait." I fly down the steps and find myself between Theo and Ebris. The air is thicker here, overpowering, and my limbs go numb. "The only one who can fix this in time is Theo. He knows all the players and where they are. Goran and Leander would only be able to make educated guesses. No offense," I add to Leander. "And Theo will only make things worse in the Netherworld. Souls would probably get lost or sent somewhere they shouldn't."

I'm babbling now. I have no idea how the Netherworld works, but I'm sure if anyone can mess it up, it's Theo. And he'd likely do it on purpose to prove another point.

"They'll manage," Ebris says slowly.

"I'll go," I whisper. The image of Oskar pushing the pearl across the seabed rises to the front of my mind. I say it without looking at them, without thinking, because, if I do either, I will lose my nerve and collapse in a useless heap. "I'll help Leander sort the dead in Theo's place. I'm his partner now, right? As his bride, I carry the same weight. Let me go instead. With Leander's help, everything will run smoothly and Theo can bring peace to the West."

"He'll learn nothing from that." Ebris says it dismissively, as if I have no idea what I'm talking about. He's right. I don't. But I do know Theo, and Theo knows war.

"I agree to it," Leander says. I search his face for a hidden meaning, but his expression betrays nothing. He steps forward rubbing one hand nervously against the other. "She's right. He accepted her. By law, she can carry his punishment."

"It isn't your place to decide," Ebris says.

"This is about Theodric not adhering to the rules," Leander says. "If there's ever a time to uphold them, it's now."

Heavy silence snuffs the oxygen from the entryway. I clutch at the hem of my shirt to keep from reaching out to Theo for comfort. He's so close I would barely have to raise my arms to touch him. His body heat shimmers against me, but I have to stay strong. This is what I deserve for my role in this disaster, for lying and being too cowardly to tell him the truth about Oren when I first heard it. Ending the war, bowing to Ebris' demands, is his punishment for lying to me.

I draw in a shallow breath. If Theo were anyone else, I would hope this would make him realize I wasn't trying to be dishonest. That I do care for him. But he's Theo. I can't have such lofty wishes.

"Fine," Ebris grinds out. "You have three months to end the entire war with Kisk a free country. If you fail, she stays in the Netherworld permanently and you'll go to the Between."

"No," Theo growls.

"No to which part? It's a fair deal."

"She stays here."

I glance up before I can stop myself. Theo flushes. He's purposely not looking in my direction, but he can't hide the edge of panic in his eyes or his too rapid breath.

Ebris shrugs. "Enjoy your time chained in the Netherworld, then."

Theo's forearm stiffens beneath my hand when I grab hold. "What are you

245

doing? You hate me now, so what does it matter? Let me do this." *For you, for me, for everyone.* For the living, who will be saved under an experienced god and the dead who will be able to pass on without trouble. And maybe, just maybe, this will stop guilt from eating me alive.

"No," he says again without meeting my gaze.

"Theo." I dig my fingers into his forearm. "Take this as my apology and go help Goran."

He works his jaw, his breath coming even faster now, but he doesn't reject the idea again. I want to heave a sigh of relief but can't manage it. This is the last time I'll see him for a long time, if I ever see him again. I want to leave on a better note. One where he tells me he isn't mad and he doesn't want to murder me after inflicting horrible pain. I want to tell him I understand where he's coming from. That I forgive him even though it's unforgivable. He's a god and that's a much bigger difference than I realized.

"Come on." Leander gently taps my shoulder. "I'll come back for your things later."

I nod. My fingers are stiff as I release Theo. My chest aches as I follow Leander out the front door, praying I don't faint.

Please, Theo, don't think to raise your sword against Ebris again.

I fight the urge to look over my shoulder as we cross the courtyard. If Leander were different, I'm not sure I would have the courage to go through with this. I take a shaky breath and focus on his narrow back. Whatever horrors wait in the land of the dead, I have to believe Theo's going along with his end of the agreement. Otherwise, this is all for nothing.

TWENTY THREE

THEO

Cassia doesn't turn around as Leander leads her from the mansion. I'm not sure I expected her to, but it doesn't hurt any less when it doesn't happen. I should stop this while I still can. Run after her and force her to stay. The Netherworld for a mortal is the same as the Between. I can handle the darkness—to spare her, I can. What I can't handle is her staying with Leander. I'm not a fool. I know how charming he is. There isn't a cruel bone in his body.

I lock my knees, curling my hands into fists. It shouldn't matter what she does anymore, what torture she endures, but my traitorous heart is shattering. They aren't even at the temple yet, and the ability to hate her has already left me. A taut string of anxiety takes its place.

Maybe this is for the best. Leander will treat her better than I ever have, and I won't have to live with the reminder of her betrayal every day. Because I couldn't have killed her. As angry as I was, as I still am, I couldn't have done it. Her brother, yes. Her country, without a doubt. Her? Never.

"You're lucky to have such loyal friends," Ebris snarls behind me.

We're alone now, so I don't turn from the window. It's easier to face the empty courtyard than risk breaking his nose with my fist. My hand twitches toward my hip. I can't draw my sword, either. Not if I want to see Cassia again.

"Loyal?" I scoff. Goran is, even if he refused to stand behind me in this. I don't know about Cassia, but Leander didn't do this for me. He did it because he's lonely.

"Don't mess this up, Theodric." Ebris moves to block the window with his wide frame. "I've been more lenient than you deserve. If you throw this in my face, you won't like the repercussions."

My nostrils flare as I match his stare. If he doesn't leave soon, I won't be able to hold myself in check. "I heard you the first time."

"Did you?" He steps closer. "Did you hear me the first time I told you to end this war? Or the second? What about the third?"

I slam my jaw shut. He's trying to goad me into ruining this, but I won't give him the satisfaction. I've spent so long trying to prove I'm in control that to lose it now would be a mistake. "I heard you," I say again.

Feminine voices cut through the courtyard, loud and screeching. I can't see over Ebris' shoulder, but I don't need to in order to recognize them both. "What now?" I mutter, sidestepping my brother. I fling the door open as Brisa drags a hysterical, sobbing Astra up the stoop. "This isn't a good time."

Brisa scowls at me from under her lashes and blows a curl away from her mouth. "You're welcome," she huffs. When the door slams shut, she tosses Astra away from her and leans on her knees. "She's a scrappy one."

The neck of Astra's shirt is torn. The cardigan over it falls off one shoulder and her long hair is snarled around her shoulders. Stray pieces lift with static. She wipes moisture from her cheeks, smudging the black trail of makeup, and backs away.

The air fills with unspoken things, writhing and alive. The anticipation cools my blood. I inhale to center myself and pack the anger into a tight ball.

"What are you doing here?" I demand.

"I'm saving your butt. Again." Brisa tosses a hand in Astra's direction. "Tell Ebris what you told me."

"I can't," Astra squeaks.

"For the love of—" Brisa straightens. "Do it or I will."

Astra shakes her head, her wet cheeks grasping strands of hair. My already rigid body stiffens into a statue. I've never seen Astra like this before. She's always been passionate, emotional, but I can't remember a time she was this upset. This terrified. She barely stumbled when I discovered what she encouraged Cassia to do. What could be worse?

"I..." Her narrow chin trembles as she looks at Ebris' feet. She clutches a thin chain hanging around her neck. "I *can't.*"

"Someone better," Ebris says.

"Did you ever wonder why you found Cassia so intriguing?" Brisa asks me.

I shift my weight between my feet. Of course I have. From the moment I saw her in Kisk I wondered. I kept her here to sort out the reason, but it got pushed aside the more I...the more time we spent together. So much so that I forgot to be curious. We settled into a routine, and then I was too worried about not kissing her to care *why* I wanted to. Another mistake.

My brain struggles to piece the puzzle together. The picture lurks beyond my grasp, fading in and out. Maybe I'm subconsciously protecting myself. Maybe I already see it clearly but don't want to believe it.

"What are you trying to say?" I ask.

"I did it, all right?" Astra's lyrical voice scratches my eardrums as she shouts. She holds her hands out from her sides, her fingers shaking. "The day I came to meet Cassia, I made you love each other."

I lurch back a step. She can't mean that. It's forbidden to use our powers on each other. She wouldn't dare. Besides, I know how I feel. *Felt.* Before Cassia destroyed everything. It wasn't manufactured. Except…Except I fought it. I didn't want to want her. I still don't, yet somehow still do. Maybe it wasn't my determination to keep control over the war but rather because deep down I knew it wasn't real.

"I did it for you," she adds in a rush. "You spend so much time shutting everyone out, Theodric. There's more to life than death and revenge. I thought if you could *see* that…" She hiccups.

"Astra." Ebris steps forward, his face slack. "If that's true, you've committed a crime worse than any Theodric has. We have to honor each other above anything else."

"Of course it's true. Why would I lie?" Her voice is pure venom. "I noticed Theo's interest in her that night in Kisk and told the zealots they would be forgiven for sacrificing her unwillingly. Theo's curiosity kept him from killing her long enough for me to give them both a small shove. Each time they saw each other, the seed I watered grew. Each time they touched, their feelings bloomed a little more. There wasn't time to wait for things to progress on their own."

My blood turns to ice, cracking my veins. Astra did this. It makes sense, but part of me rejects it as truth. It seems like so long ago I met the dirty girl with snarled hair and watchful eyes. This deception isn't Cassia's; it's my sister's. Astra played us both, and I let Cassia walk to the Netherworld because of it.

"Why?" I wheeze. "Why would you care if Cassia and I had a chance? Why wasn't there time?"

"For you." More mascara races down her cheeks in inky trails. Her lips curl in distaste as she glares at me. "And for Cy. I couldn't let you destroy his homeland."

"Cy?" Ebris hisses. "You did this to your brother for *him*?"

She jumps at his sharp tone. "He told me not to, but how could I stand by and let it happen? He can say he doesn't consider Kisk his home as many times as he likes, but I know he has to care."

"How could you stand by?" Ebris cracks a hand across her cheek. "The same way the rest of us have. We can't turn on each other. *Never* each other."

I pinch my lips tight. Correcting Ebris, telling him he's done nothing but turn on me, will only derail the situation. I need more. More details, more answers, more closure.

Blood beads in the corner of her lips and a low, inhuman, laugh climbs from her throat. "Don't act like you're any better, Ebris. I know what you did."

"You know nothing." A storm swirls in Ebris' eyes, the gray of his irises shutting out the blue. "Shut your mouth."

"You don't want Theodric to know you told the Volks how to harness

251

antimatter, but you've always been sloppy at covering your tracks," she spews.

It's as if the entire world has spun off its axis, spiraling into oblivion. I double over. My stomach threatens to heave its contents across the entryway. This isn't happening. It's too much. Too far. This is sabotage at its finest and so much worse than what Astra did. Thousands of lives were at stake that night, and thousands of others were lost.

"Are there any of you that haven't plotted against me?" I drag in a breath but can't seem to get enough air to fill my lungs. "You've been playing with me for ages, but now you're not even content with that. Are we to pit ourselves against each other?"

"Theodric." Brisa touches the back of my hand. "Breathe."

I dig at my abdomen. "What about you? What have you done?"

She squints at me. "I'll pretend you didn't ask me that."

"The deal is off," I growl at Ebris. "You stacked the cards and you *dare* lecture me about learning the cost of war?"

"The deal is already done." His mouth twists into a grimace, both smug and irate.

Just because Cassia is gone doesn't mean it's too late to change things. I can bring her back. The urge to draw my sword overwhelms me, but if I attack Ebris like every muscle is screaming at me to do, I won't win. Brisa, even Astra, will stop me if I try.

"I'll end the war because it's the right thing to do." A forced shiver shatters the chill within me. "But Cassia comes back."

"No."

I lunge forward and grab Ebris' windpipe between my thumb and index finger. "You *will* bring her back."

He swats me away like a fly. "I won't. You still need to understand what you're doing."

He speaks as if this is all my doing. As if he hasn't had a hand in creating this disaster. In drafting Timun or sinking ships. What else has he manipulated? What else don't I know?

A fevered laugh wracks my body. "You think because I have no true power that I don't have a way to ruin you." I don't, not yet, but if it's the last thing I do, I will remove him from his throne. "You aren't as invincible as you think you are."

"You're welcome to try," he says.

"Ebris," Brisa warns. "This isn't right."

"What *he's* doing isn't right," Ebris rumbles. "How many Kiskens are dead? How many men have crossed your ocean to certain death?"

"He's the God of *War*. He's doing what he's supposed to do." She crosses her arms with a huff. "You said yourself that we have to stick together. If you value anything about this family, you'll fix this."

Ebris glances at Astra. "She'll go to the Between. That's enough compensation."

"For her crime, yes," Brisa says over Astra's ear-piercing wail. "What about yours?"

He waves a dismissive hand. "There's no law to stop me from giving mortals new technology."

Brisa glowers across the hallway. "That isn't why you did it. Don't set the rest of us against you. You can beat Theodric as he is, but you can't take on the rest of us all at once."

Ebris stills, the smile slipping into nothing. He studies Brisa, watching her as he runs through a series of facial tics. *Deciding.* Trying to make up his mind whether or not she speaks the truth. If she would really stand against him—if they all would.

"Fine," Ebris barks. "End the war, then go get your whore."

I step forward, my fist raised to fly in defense of Cassia's name, but Brisa grabs my elbow. "And restore Theodric's power," she adds. "It's been long enough, and it's only making him rebel more."

"Absolutely not." The answer is firm, unyielding.

"Drea has already sided with me on this," she says. "With Astra in the Between and Leander being Leander, we're all you have left."

The line between Ebris' brows deepens into a crevice. His eyes dart around the entryway, ignoring Astra as she curls in on herself in the corner, rocking. "You wouldn't dare." It's almost a question.

"Wouldn't we?" she snips.

His jaw muscles twitch, but it's the only part of him to move. "I'll return them after you clean up your mess," he tells me in a hoarse whisper.

Then he grabs Astra's wrist, renewing her screams, and bolts out the door. It slams against the wall, cracking the glass. I grab the banister. *He'll return my power.* With the smallest hint of blackmail, of an uprising, Ebris is willing to give me my life back. It doesn't feel like much of a victory. It's more like a consolation prize. The price Ebris is paying to keep himself on top.

Be happy.

I should be; I'm getting everything back.

Almost everything.

"Are you okay?" Brisa asks.

My feet slip out from under me and I drop to the stairs. "No." The word is nothing more than a puff of air.

Brisa flutters around me, her hands reaching out and pulling back as if she can't decide whether she wants to hug me or slap some sense into me. Finally, she steps back with a sigh. "Goran! Get out here."

I'm not sure how long it takes him to listen. Maybe two seconds, maybe two minutes. My vision blurs as they stand in the middle of the entry. Their whispered conversation buzzes in my ears, but I tune them out. This isn't how I wanted to win. By default. I wanted to be trusted. To be welcomed.

But I'll regain everything once I finish the war. Everything except Cassia. Because, while I may be allowed to bring her back, that doesn't mean she'll want to come. And why should she? None of this is real. It's all part of some elaborate plot, and I treated her horribly.

Goran hovers in front of me and snaps his fingers next to my ear. "Can you hear me?"

I can. I don't want to, but I can. "The war was rigged, Goran."

"We'll survive it like we always have. This will pass," he assures me.

"Cassia." Her name rips from my mouth before I can pull it back into the dark hole where my courage once was.

He nods and speaks in a soft tone. "What Astra did doesn't mean your feelings aren't genuine. You know as well as I do that Astra can't force two people together if there isn't something there to begin with. So she gave you a nudge." He shrugs. "It doesn't change things. You still love each other."

"Do we?" My head falls back with a groan. "It doesn't change the fact that she used me."

"Get your head out of your arse. She went to the Netherworld to protect you."

"That wasn't for me," I whisper. "That was to get *away* from me."

"He's finally snapped," Brisa grumbles over his shoulder.

Goran frowns up at her. "I've loved and lost before. I know what you're feeling, Theodric, but you still have a chance to fix things. Pull yourself up, act like the god you are, and do what has to be done. You're so close." He clasps my shoulder. "After this, you'll be restored. It's the only thing you've wanted the entire time I've been here. Don't blow it in the home stretch."

"What if it's not the only thing I want anymore?"

"Goran?" Brisa grabs the back of her hair. "I think we broke him."

"Then we'll have to *fix* him," Goran says, keeping his focus on me. "Now, come on. Stop wasting time. Get in the war room and strategize."

TWENTY FOUR

CASSIA

The Netherworld conjures up all sorts of images. Ghostly spirits, eerie fog, and, of course, the infamous arch souls pass through to continue to their final destination. Wherever that is. I rub my arms as we cross through Leander's temple and glance over my shoulder for a final glimpse of the alcove leading back to Theo. A silent sigh pours from my chest. I can't think about him. He certainly won't be thinking about me. I take in the gray, unadorned temple without focusing on anything particular and follow Leander into the land of the dead.

Instead of a gloomy wasteland, I'm greeted with something so jaw-droppingly beautiful I pinch my elbow to make sure I'm awake. Enormous opaque peaks jut from the land, glittering beneath a muted sun. Blue and yellow shadows quiver across the white, rocky ground. Above, the sky is a dome of long, delicate clouds. A sweet smell lingers in the air, floral and fruity at the same time.

"Whoa."

"Not what you were expecting?" Leander asks with a grin.

I jump, not realizing I stopped on the threshold of the temple and my smile spreads like wildfire. Who would ever expect *this* to be here, of all places? My wildest imagination could never come up with something more amazing. "Not in the slightest."

"I'd offer to show you around, but I'm sure you'd like some time to adjust." He watches me carefully as he shuffles closer, stopping a few feet away.

I'm not sure if he's waiting for me to agree, but, honestly, I don't know what I'd rather do. I don't feel much like exploring, but sitting around twiddling my thumbs will give me too much time to think. And I have far too much to think about.

Finally, Leander bobs his head in the direction of an opal castle, complete with elegantly wrought balconies and pointed towers, carved into the side of a towering mountain. "After you," he says.

My joints creak with each movement, begging me not to go another step in that direction. Gorgeous or not, every cell in my body knows what this place is. I don't think there will be enough time in the world to adjust. At least at Theo's it looks like home. There's grass and trees and *life*. It's so still here, so quiet, goosebumps rise up against it.

I spin, taking in the endless kaleidoscope of color. "Um, Leander?"

"Hmm?" He falls into step beside me, his shoulders curled forward.

My stomach flutters. I don't want to ask this, not really, but I won't be able to relax until I do. If anything deceased pops out at me, I swear I'll drop dead and save everyone a bit of trouble. "Where are they?"

"The souls?" He places a hand in the middle of my back and gently steers me around a waist-high shard of crystal I hadn't noticed. I nod. "They can't cross the Black River."

I squint into the distance, twisting to look in every direction a second time. There's no river. There isn't even the sound of one, or another body of water for that matter. I clench my hands into fists. "But *where*?"

"The other side of the mountain. Don't worry, you won't have to see them. Occasionally you may hear something." He hesitates and gives me a twitchy smile. "When too many come through at once, it can be crowded, and they tend to be confused and angry. It's understandable after a disaster, but with the acoustics here, it can sound a bit…"

"Terrifying?" I offer. Because that's how I imagine a bunch of pissed off dead people sound. Any other answer will undoubtedly be a lie.

"Well, yes." He takes a deep breath, motioning with his hands as he speaks. "The river prevents the riots from spilling over, so you're perfectly safe on this side of things."

Perfectly safe. I can't remember the last time I was able to say that with any truth. It isn't that I don't trust Leander. His nervousness is actually reassuring, almost like he's more afraid of scaring me off than anything, but I don't trust the gods in general. Judging by what little I've seen, they shouldn't trust each other either. At all. And if you can't trust your siblings, who can you trust?

Not that I've been the best sister; I used to believe Oren committed treason. I should have known he would never do such a thing, but he never once told me he was innocent. Maybe he thought he didn't need to.

I peer up at the top of the mountain and bite my lip. *Is he over there right now?*

"Here we are," Leander says.

A wide, sweeping staircase reaches up to massive front doors that almost blend into the rest of the stone. Specks of green and blue glimmer inside the milky white walls like tiny magic lights. Glass columns run down each corner, showing hints of furniture on the other side. It's straight out of a fairytale, but I can't imagine living here forever. Not without the slightest hint of the real world. It's going to be impossible to forget where I am for a second.

Leander fidgets beside me. "Do you like it? We can make changes if you'd be more comfortable with something else."

"I've never seen anything like this before." The curved rock of the newel post is smooth beneath my hand. "I wouldn't dream of changing it."

There's a spring in his step as he climbs the two dozen steps. A boyish excitement comes over him, lighting his face. "I would show you the main rooms, but I have to get back across the river soon."

Of course he does. The end of a war can be equally as bloody as the beginning. Maybe more so. I bite down hard on the inside of my lip until a metallic tang touches my tongue and follow Leander through the doors, feeling hollow.

♦

Stalking might not be the right word for how I spend the next hour. *Lurking,* maybe. I prefer to think of it as inspecting the castle entrance. I lasted about fifteen minutes in the game room after Leander left. Neither the pinball machine nor a round of solitaire could distract me from the ear-ringing silence.

Then the thoughts came, one after another. Is Theo okay? Is Oren alive? Is Goran having a hard time keeping things on track? Do they miss me? Of course they don't. But maybe? The questions stacked on top of each other until the tower wavered and crashed around me. I couldn't sit there anymore with carnage scattered at my feet.

I run my finger along the delicate carvings in the opal wall. A patchwork of squares and circles chase the door up from the floor. There's no furniture in the hall. No paintings or statues. The walls speak for themselves. Beautiful. Cool. Suffocating.

It gives me a completely new respect for Leander. To come home to such a solemn place after working what I imagine is a stressful job has to be terrible. It's no wonder he agreed to my offer to come with him so quickly. He probably goes bat shit crazy.

"Cassia?" Leander's voice echoes behind me. "Is everything okay?"

My hands fly to my chest, resting over the permanent ache there, and I spin away from the door. If I knew he was back, I would have tracked him down whether he was busy or not. "I thought you left," I say.

"I did." He rubs his hands together before wiping them on his shirt. "There's a back way to the river to avoid going around the mountain."

"Oh." I shift uncomfortably between my feet. "Are you done for the day?"

Leander shakes his head, a dash of pink touching his cheeks. "I wanted to make sure you were all right." His laugh is quick and uneven. "Things got backed up while I was with Ebris, so I have to return."

"Take me with you," I blurt.

My stomach squeezes in revolt. For someone that wanted to avoid the dead, that came out much too hopeful. Clearly, I'm insane. I don't want to see whatever waits on the other side of the river. It's safe here; I should be glad Leander isn't making me go with him. That *is* the agreement Ebris made after all—to help sort the souls. But what if I do see Oren? The colors of the hall fade as fast as the blood from my face, but I won't take the question back. Knowing is better than wondering.

"Please?" I step closer to Leander and force a tight smile.

Leander stiffens and taps his fingers against his outer thigh. "I'm not sure that's a good idea."

"I need to make sure my brother is still alive," I tell him honestly. *Because if Theo lets him die, I'm going to march back over there and strangle him with my bare hands.* "I'll stay out of the way."

"He's alive," Leander says slowly. His blue eyes waver, almost as if each new thought fuels his uncertainty.

"But how long did it take you to get back here?" I press. "Five minutes is more than enough time to murder someone." My hand drifts to my neck where the ghost of the cut lingers. Theo almost killed me in ten seconds; he can absolutely finish Oren off in the same amount of time.

"You're not going to take my word for it, are you?" he asks after a strained silence.

I shake my head.

"All right, then." He snaps the hood of his black sweater over his hair, and his jaw works back and forth. "Let's go," he says without meeting my gaze.

My heart pounds against my ribs as I follow him through identical, plain hallways to a glass platform deep within the castle. When he throws a lever, the ground shifts, lifting us into a round shaft. I grip his elbow to steady myself, but soon the muted sun shines above us again.

The floor clunks to a halt at the top of the mountain. Everything is visible from here, layered with cascading patterns of pastel light. Below us a wide, ebony river cuts through the shimmering landscape.

"Stay close," Leander says. "And don't go anywhere near the arch. If you cross, there's no coming back."

This is a stupid, reckless idea. Leander can be trusted to tell me if my brother shows up. But I know myself too well; it won't be enough to take his word. Oren's been dead before. This time I have to see it with my own two eyes or I'll never believe it. I take a deep breath. "Got it."

He holds a steady hand out to me and leads the way down a steep, narrow shelf in the mountainside. Dread ripples over me the second I look down. *High*. So, so high. The three feet between the white stone and impending doom feels more like three inches. I exhale slowly through my mouth. Freaking out will only make this worse, and I'm not turning around. *I'm not*.

"There are some ground rules for your safety." When he glances over his shoulder, he's chewing on his lip. It isn't the walk making him nervous—his steps are sure and purposeful—but the strain is written all over his features. That alone should send me spinning on my heel.

"I'm all ears." Anything to keep me from thinking about the drop. Or Oren, Theo, and the dead people I'm walking toward.

"Don't let go of me on the river. *Ever*. There are things…Just don't let go of me." He stops and raises his eyebrows. When I nod, he moves again. "The souls can touch you, so stay away from them too. Actually…" He squints down the ledge. "Stay beside me the whole time. If anything happens with the war, it could get hostile fast. This way I'll be able to get you back across before anyone can hurt you."

"Done," I say as we reach the bottom.

The sweet smell is stronger here, pungent. A wail carries across the water so softly it's almost not a cry at all but a trick of the wind. I would let myself believe it if there was even the slightest hint of a breeze.

"Are you sure you want to do this?" Leander asks.

I look him in the eyes, a piece of my old resolve snapping back into place. *I've got this.* How different can the souls be? We're both dead. Maybe it won't be as bad as I think. Maybe...maybe I won't freak out.

"Positive," I say.

He reaches out, pauses, then carefully links our fingers. His knuckles lock our hands together when he tightens his grip. It feels like I'm touching a mannequin, smooth and cool, but there's strength in his raised tendons. For a moment I feel completely safe knowing he'll get me back to this side of the river.

But then we step off the bank, and my stomach lurches into my throat.

The Black River churns beneath our feet. Thousands of tiny whirlpools feed into each other, sucking and spraying, soaking the hem of my pants. I cling to Leander's arm with every bit of strength I possess and try to see through the haze of light-headedness. Whatever invisible thing is holding us up, I'm not at all confident in its ability to stop me from plunging to my death.

"It's okay," Leander reassures me. "I won't let you fall."

I narrow my gaze across the river. It didn't look this wide before. "So..." I want to talk about something—anything—but my mind is nothing but static.

Leander doesn't offer anything to talk about either, so I hold my breath until my feet hit solid ground again.

Leander eases his hand from mine and flexes his fingers. "We're here."

I keep a grip on his arm with numb fingers. The ground is the same as the other side, but I already knew that from the view at the top of the mountain. With a quick breath, I let my gaze wander up and tense at the sight of the arch. Twenty feet of black onyx looms between the bases of two mountains, hidden from the other side of the river. Simple, glossy, curved columns reach up to meet each other midair. I step toward it but Leander grabs my elbow.

"Stay away from the arch," he says softly. "Don't even look at it."

"Why?" A soul shimmers in front of me, and I gasp so hard I choke.

"Get back." Leander's voice deepens, carrying across the shore as more and more bodies close in. Their shapes flicker in the sunlight like liquid glass as they stop and stare. Some have solidified spots—cracks, chips, gouges. This is nothing like I imagined. Somehow it's simultaneously better and worse.

"I said, get back." The words rumble from Leander's throat and the souls disperse. "Okay." He exhales. "Remember to stay beside me."

I nod. Faces keep flashing in and out beside me, as if they're following our every move. Their eyes are colorless. Their lips turned down, their brows creasing. Resentment rolls off them in waves.

"They're confused," Leander says. "Don't let them scare you."

Scared is the understatement of the year. This easily qualifies for one of my top three terrifying moments, right after being sacrificed in the temple and before Theo overhearing my secret. Whatever restless emotion possessed me to come here drains away.

I open my mouth to tell Leander I want to go back when the arch catches my notice again. It pulls at my chest, calling to me, asking me to come home. *Home.* A woman stands on the other side in a black and white striped apron. A giant pink lily is tucked behind her right ear. A man stands beside her, his heavy black beard is in desperate need of a trim. *Mom? Dad?*

It's them—my parents. They're right there in vivid life-like color, exactly the way I remember them. My pulse quickens until the beats become one giant vibration. I release Leander's arm and my body falls into autopilot. My feet turn toward the arch. My legs carry me closer. One step. Two. My parents seem further away than they were a moment ago. Three steps. They wave me forward. I try to tell them I'm coming, but my mouth is too dry. Four steps.

A razor sharp sting burns my cheek and I stagger back. Leander stands in front of me, his shoulders rising and falling with labored breaths. His eyes are wild. Frenzied. "Son of a…" He shakes out his hand. "Are you with me, Cassia? Can you hear me?"

My arm feels detached as I lift a hand to my cheek. "Did you slap me?" I whisper.

"I'm sorry, I panicked." He drags a hand down his face. "You were fighting me when I tried to pull you back, and you didn't seem able to hear me. If you got to the arch, it would've been too late."

Tears distort my vision, but I refuse to let them fall. It wasn't real. It couldn't be real. An illusion, that's all. "I saw my parents," I say in a voice more bitter than I mean.

Leander blinks. "You saw them?"

"Through there." I motion to the arch but force my eyes to the ground, unable to bear the thought of seeing them a second time. "I think they wanted me to go with them."

Leander glances over his shoulder. His feet shift from my line of sight and he stands beside me. "You're the first mortal to come here without any intention of crossing," he says. "Forgive me. I didn't know it would affect you like that."

"Like what?" I rasp. "What *was* that?"

He takes my shoulders and gently steers me away from the pillars. The touch drags me back to reality. Tremors rattle my bones. My parents weren't really there, but they *were* here last year. They walked this shore, crossed that arch, as one of the shimmering souls. Did they frown too?

"It's different for everyone," he says. "Some souls see their house or a pet. Others see loved ones waiting for them."

My head twitches involuntarily back for one last glimpse, but Leander gives my shoulders a light squeeze. He's right. Looking is dangerous. "What's on the other side?"

He watches me with a sorry smile. "I can't tell you that."

I'm not sure if that means he doesn't know or if he isn't allowed to tell me, but it doesn't matter. Knowing might tempt me to turn around and run into my parents' arms before I'm ready to cross. It's better to imagine it's a dark, forbidding void and the souls are someone else's loved ones if I'm going to come back again tomorrow.

And I will. I've come this far without letting fear make my decisions for me. Because sitting in that castle alone every day will absolutely leave me certifiable by the time this is over, and because, while my parents are unquestionably dead, my brother is not.

"You're absolutely sure my brother isn't here?" I ask.

"I'm sure."

The relief that settles alongside my confusion is short lived. Grief I thought I buried in Kisk nibbles at my spirit. I need to be away from here, at least for today. Leander was right. I should take a moment to adjust to losing Theo before piling on other sorrows. I have an endless supply of tomorrows and right now, my entire being aches with weariness.

TWENTY FIVE

THEO

My fingers rap against the desk as one of my western spies, Jonah, pecks away at the keyboard. He gnaws on a toothpick as he types, glaring at the screen over a pair of black rimmed glasses. I try to quiet the storm brewing within myself. To sit still and wait, but it seems an impossible task.

This is a risky plan. If it works, it will fast track a peace agreement, but it feels like I should be doing more. Taking a more active path. Not finding incriminating evidence on Volkana to hand over to the International Committee of Warfare.

"No offense but that's not helping," Jonah says in a heavy accent.

I lean back in the leather armchair. He's been at it for hours, and each second I'm here is another the war still rages. Another that Cassia is in the

Netherworld. It took nearly two days to wade through the fog of Ebris and Astra's betrayal. Once I did, new hues colored the world. Things that were once so vibrant are now dull. Insignificant. I've been fighting for the wrong things too long, and I'm desperate to start fighting for the right ones.

"How much longer?" I ask.

"My Volk is a little rusty," Jonah says. "And this is the National Defense Headquarters, not your grandma's bank account. It isn't easy to hack into."

I scowl. "*Why* do you know how to do this exactly?"

He smiles without looking away from the monitor. "You want to know everything at a moments' notice, right?"

"Does it matter?" Goran fights a yawn.

I grunt and push out of the chair to pace the room. Anything to keep me from losing my sanity. I scan the plaques and framed awards covering the wall. Photos of the minister with other dignitaries. A plastic tree swallows an entire corner. Beside it, a half-full coffee pot sits on a short gray filing cabinet. I tug mindlessly on the silver handle of the top drawer, but it doesn't budge.

"Hand me a letter opener," I say.

Jonah continues typing. "Me?"

My eye twitches. Apparently once my sacrifices make a cozy life for themselves, they forget who they owe it to. "No, the other person sitting behind the desk," I snap, harsher than I intend.

Goran rounds the desk to rummage through its drawers, shaking his head. "Ignore him. He's having a bit of a rough time," he says, casting a steady glare in my direction. "Keep working."

A rough time.

I pop my knuckles. My own brother is a saboteur, my sister used her abilities against me, and the girl I have feelings for stabbed me in the back before leaving with Leander. If that doesn't entitle me to be a little testy, nothing will. Red hot betrayal was the only thing keeping me going those first few days. Tendrils of it still snake through my body, refusing to melt away, but I'm trying. Trying to make things right.

I grip the handle again and tear the drawer open with a loud, screeching bang. Goran curses under his breath but I tune him out. Arguing when I'm this anxious will undo my carefully wrought restraint.

I'm not sure what I expected to find inside. Office supplies, maybe, but not hanging folder after hanging folder stamped with red ink. *Top Secret.* My hand hovers over them, my brows lowered. No one would keep such sensitive documents in their office, especially someone as high as the minister of defense. The janitor could have picked this lock after hours if he had the mind for it.

"Interesting," I mutter.

Pulling a folder from the far left, I skim the pages. It's a first-hand account of the Kisken prison break at the start of the war. The further I read, the higher my eyebrows climb. Everything in this file is false, except the signatures and seals. "This says the Kiskens were torturing Volks in their prison, and the raid was to rescue their own men." I snap it shut. "No mention of taking Colonel Stavros or the others."

"The Kisken government covered that up." Goran stands grim in the blue glow of the computer. "No one would suspect..."

No one would suspect the Colonel is alive, no. Let alone that he was in

Volk custody. There's no reason to question his execution. If they did, the truth is likely buried as deep in the Kisken server as it is in the Volk's. I should have expected something like this from such a deceitful country, but I hadn't. I assumed the Volks avoided prosecution because of their more obvious lies, like the plane they were going to use to drop the antimatter. Not false documents they could hand over in a flat second.

I lay the folder down beside the coffee and grab one further down the line. A skirmish between Volkana and Asgya, allegedly started when Asgyans shot at them. Another, the taking of an Asgyan base, which was true enough, but the fire that burned it to the ground after wasn't electrical.

"Keep looking," I say to Jonah. The clack of fingers against keys drums against my ears. When I told Cassia war involves layers and layers of deceit, I meant it. Exhaustion bumps against the cracks in my determination. The sooner this war is over, the sooner I can get away from all the lies and live closer to truth.

"Almost got it," Jonah says.

Goran steps across the room and gingerly pulls another folder from the cabinet. "We should destroy these. They'll give the Committee a reason to doubt the truth."

A plan clicks into place as I run my finger over the tabs. "No."

"But—"

"Roll up your sleeves, Goran." A grin curves my lips. Volkana will tell the truth whether they want to or not. "We've got a lot of signatures to forge."

"Jackpot." Jonah leans back in the chair and stretches his arms behind his head. Icons flood the screen, red square upon red square. He leans forward and plugs a small black box into the tower. "Give me a minute and you'll have what you need."

"Print everything," I say.

"Everything?" Jonah echoes. "That will take more time than we possibly have."

I toss a folder at him and it flops onto the desk. "Find these, then."

"What are we doing exactly?" Goran asks.

"We're going to replace the false reports with the real ones." I grab a stack from the cabinet and hand them off to my adviser. "After I give the Committee the external drive, they won't be able to ignore this anymore. When they come to do an investigation, the minister won't be handing over falsified documents."

Goran studies me, a slow smile widening across his face. "I'll find the seal."

Splinters from a freshly shaved log slice my palms as I slam one end into rich Kisken soil. The outer wall of the fort stands fifteen feet high with the tops carved to needle-like points. It's almost complete, however rudimentary. There isn't the time or supplies to build a high-tech base right now, but the escaped Kiskens need something more secure than a field full of tents.

Brisa has kept the troops I sent toward Gull Island at bay, but it won't be long until someone is lucky enough to fly a path between the storms. And once the International Committee of Warfare arrives in Volkana to press charges, there's a chance they'll attempt a fast and furious backlash.

It's been a week since the information was handed over, so it could come at any time, especially if the Volks catch wind of the investigation. It wouldn't be smart, but Volkana isn't known for playing safe. Only playing dirty.

"Going back to basics, I see."

I freeze and let the next log thud to the ground. "Hello, Drea," I say without turning.

"These were perfectly healthy trees." Her voice is thin. Strained.

I clench my stomach against a groan and turn back to my work. Lift. Aim. Drive. The sun beats down on us, suctioning my shirt to my sweaty torso despite the crisp winter air. The last time I saw Drea, we argued about the Asgyan famine. She said I was making her point invalid. That the Asgyans would attribute all their sorrow to the war instead of learning to respect the crops she provides. I said facing possible death would make them appreciate each other instead, and, as her creations, isn't that important too? It hadn't gone over well. Not that I blame her. Being undermined is a horrible feeling. It hadn't felt that way at the time but, looking back, that's what I did.

"Do you need something?" I ask between logs. "Or are you here to complain about a bunch of trees? Because, frankly, I don't want to hear it."

Drea is quiet, her presence heavy at my back.

All right then.

I grab the next log. There's space enough to fit three more before hitting the perpendicular wall and closing the final gap. Goran is on his way with the men and women now. Considering we spent the last week sending the healthiest soldiers on covert missions to rid Kisk of both Volks and Asgyans, they should have a relatively uneventful trip.

"She lied," Drea says.

Cassia's face flashes before me and I wince. "It seems to be an epidemic these days." I slam another post into place. "Want to narrow down which *she* you're referring to?"

"Brisa."

I swivel to stare at my oldest sister. Drea's arms are folded over a plain white T-shirt, her dark hair braided loosely down her back. She watches me carefully with naturally wide eyes. Brisa is the only one that's told me the truth. The only sibling I trust. "Brisa lied?" My voice rises in disbelief.

Drea inhales, eying the pile of branches I stripped from the trees. "I never agreed to stand with her against Ebris. She never even broached the subject with me."

Her words are a punch to the gut. A fist flying in from a blind spot. It was surprising when Brisa told Ebris they agreed, but she said it with such authority. With such confidence. I should have questioned it after Ebris left, but I wasn't in the right frame of mind to think. If Ebris finds out, Brisa will be the next one on the chopping block. I rub my palms together to calm the tingling sensation.

"I didn't." Drea's arms drop to her sides. "But I would have."

The bubble of nerves pops, my mind temporarily blank. "I'm grateful," I manage.

"And shocked." A thin smile grazes her lips. "We've never quite seen eye-to-eye, but you're still my brother, and I'm not blind to Ebris' faults. Our time is coming to an end. He's worried."

"We won't disappear if no one believes in us," I say. "Most of them already don't."

"It would be rather lonely though, don't you think?" She sighs. "Anyway, I came to assure you we'll all work together keeping an eye on Ebris and do what needs to be done. *If* anything needs to be done. And I'm going to end the famine in Asgya."

My jaw drops. That will only cement her side of our last argument. "Why?"

The purr of engines drones in the distance—Goran with the Kiskens. I turn and slam the last two posts in place as the commandeered trucks from enemy bases around Kisk roll toward the open gate. Drea is gone, vanished without a goodbye, but it's just as well. I wouldn't know what to say to her, and her reasons don't matter as much as the end of the famine does.

Goran is the first to climb out of a green Humvee, followed by the weakest Kiskens. A handful of Kisken militia we tracked down help their wounded comrades before unloading a transport truck filled with tents and supplies. I watch from a distance while they move together, working as a unit. None of them can see me, including Goran. I needed my ring to have the strength to build the fence, but he knows I'm here. After Hex was true to her word and left, he conveniently fit the part of a blond liaison. They trust him because they trusted her.

Goran studies the fort until a woman pulls his attention away. I weave between soldiers and raw wooden crates until I'm beside them. Goran nods and smiles. The woman walks away, directing a small group to move things to the far end. They struggle to do as they're told but work as fast as their worn bodies allow. Goran hesitates at the truck door, casting another glance around the fort. When he climbs into the cab, I hop into the passenger seat and shove my ring onto his finger. He jerks to the side, smacking his head on the window.

I grin. "Things going well?"

"Better than expected." He rubs at the side of his head and someone calls to him from outside. He lowers the glass. "Yeah?"

A man calls up, "We'll be ready to go back for the second group in five."

"Got it." Goran puts the window up again. He talks down at his lap, barely moving his lips. "The Committee arrived in Volkana last night. The Volks are being charged with war crimes and every sanction in the book is being thrown at them."

I sit back against the cushioned seat. "Good. A cease-fire should be easy enough after that. Asgya should be amicable to the idea."

"We don't have to worry about that." Goran laughs, unsure. "They've agreed to a treaty in exchange for a crumb of leniency. The Committee has representatives from both Asgya and Volkana on their barge now. As soon as they sign the papers, the war is over."

I narrow my eyes. "That's too easy."

"Easy?" Stubble coats his chin, too light to notice without the glare from the sun. "What part of this was easy?"

Starting the war was easy. Angering my siblings was easier.

The man from before raps on the door, then hops into one of the other vehicles. "Good luck," I mumble. I take my ring back and slip outside.

The convoy backs out of the enclosure and sputters out of sight. I continue to stand there, watching the place they disappeared. This is almost over. I shouldn't feel so unnerved, but when I turn and glance at each of the hollow, detached faces, I find myself reeling. My goal has been to regain my abilities for so long that I don't know what else to do. How else to live.

But, if by some miracle, Cassia agrees to give me another chance, I can live for her. At least for a while. Another war will come. They always do.

Sudden, crippling pain rips through me, sending me to my knees. My muscles seize. Fire turns my lungs to ash. My ribs threaten to crack and my skin strains against the swell of energy. *My* energy.

The longer it goes on, the more unbearable it becomes, but I'm unable to scream. I'm frozen in place as it tears at each cell of my body, twisting and bending me into something new. *Something old.* Until a ragged cry breaks free and I collapse into the dirt.

When I wake, lush Kisken grass tickles my cheek. I force myself to my knees and rub at the ache behind my forehead. Power courses through me. Strong, familiar, and overwhelming. My bones ache with the effort to contain it. My eyes flutter shut and I blow out a shaking breath. *This.* I've missed this sense of being indestructible. *Invincible.*

A deep laugh rolls from my chest. It's back. *I'm* back. But I can't test it yet. First I have to get used to my new sense of self, then practice somewhere no one can get hurt. A voice bounces through my head, telling me not to hold back, to let the power explode, but I push it away. I won't lose this again by being reckless.

My gaze wanders over the men and women settling in, catching on the Colonel, huddled and pale as he sits against a post. The wounded arm is gone; only five inches remain below his shoulder. Blood stains the white bandages around the stump. I step toward him and pause.

I should have saved him, either long before Cassia arrived or shortly after. I rub my ear as it burns with shame and change course to where the medical supplies are boxed. Easing the cardboard lid up, I grab fresh bandages, antiseptic, and a pair of rubber gloves. I'm no doctor, but neither is anyone else here. The only person with real medical training left on Hex's ship.

With a fast sigh, I drop my shields and stride up to him before I can change my mind. Sweat shimmers on his face, beading heavily along his upper lip. The dullness in his eyes punches my conscience.

"Do I know you?" he rasps.

"No." I kneel beside him and try not to see Cassia instead. "But it looks like you could use a fresh bandage."

He shrugs his good shoulder.

I hold up the fresh gauze. "Do you mind?"

"If you have to."

I snap on the translucent gloves and pick at the edge of the paper tape holding the gauze in place. "How does it feel?"

His laugh is short and low. "Like someone sawed my arm off."

I don't say anything else as I work, concentrating instead on unwrapping his arm. My power pulsates through me. I push against it. The time has come to finally help Cassia's brother; I can't accidently shred him to bits.

"Forgive me for saying so, but you're not one of us." He pauses to study me. "And you don't look like one of the pirates."

"You're right. I'm neither." I pull the last bit off his arm, exposing a red, angry line, stitched shut with black X's. "I heard…" I shouldn't say this. It will call attention to myself but he deserves to know. I think Cassia would like him to have closure. "I heard you have a sister."

His hand flies up and grabs my wrist. "Who are you?"

I let him hold me as I twist the cap off the antiseptic. "No one, really. I met Cassia here, or, in your hometown, that is. We played a game of Fate one night and she told me about you."

"Is she okay?" His voice is raw. "My parents?"

"Your parents died in the bombing."

His hand falls away and his head slumps forward. I take the moment to squeeze a healthy dose of gel on a strip of gauze and position it over the laceration. Holding it in place with one hand, I circle his arm with the rest.

"And Cassia?" he asks after a moment. "She's still alive? She wasn't killed when the bombs dropped?"

"Not then, no." Perhaps I should tell him a lie. That his whole family died together when the bombs hit and they never felt a thing. It would be the kind thing to do, but the truth would come out eventually. There are only so many survivors left, and Goran is bringing them here when he's finished with the soldiers. Someone will talk. Someone always talks. The truth now is better than the truth later. "The...the zealots," I force the words out, "were desperate. They took her, unwillingly, and sacrificed her to the God of War."

"They *what?*" he hisses with such malice I'm not sure it came from his lips. "But that—how could they? They *murdered* my sister? You're sure?"

"I'm sorry." I rip off a long piece of paper tape and wrap it around his arm in a messy band. "If I knew, I would have stopped it."

I would have but not for the reason he may think. While I am sorry for his loss, I can't be sorry she came to my temple. Not if that means I never would have gotten to know her. I can only hope this time, when she's offered a choice, she'll choose me.

"Thank you for telling me," the Colonel says quietly.

I look away as his tears brim, ready to spill, and nod.

"I'm going to kill everyone that had a part in it," he adds in a stronger voice.

I don't doubt he wants to; I want to for what they must have put her through. "Cassia believed in you. She loved you." *Believes*, I want to say. *Loves*. But to him, she's gone. "I don't think she would want you to kill anyone in her name."

His gaze fixes on distant nothingness. I recognize that expression; I've seen it a million times in my own mirror. The want, the need, for revenge. "No, I imagine not," he says after a long silence.

TWENTY SIX

CASSIA

My nails dig into Leander's sleeve as we cross the Black River again. I thought it would get easier the more I did it, but it's almost worse. Sure, the tiny whirlpools haven't sucked me down in the last ten days, but day eleven could be the day the invisible barrier beneath my feet shatters into a million pieces.

"I hate this," I mutter.

Leander laughs but the sound is far away, muted. I cling harder. "Keep holding onto me and you'll be fine," he says.

No matter how many times he says that or how badly I want to believe it, my prickling nerves refuse to let me. "Easy for you to say." I swallow the bile rising in the back of my throat. "If we fall, you'll pop back up like a whack-a-mole."

"We aren't going to fall," he says with a smirk.

I grind my teeth together and focus on the shore. Sparks flash in the distance, hints of waiting souls. They're too far away to make out faces, but nausea sweeps over me anyway. One of them could be Oren.

"You know, I'll come get you if your brother arrives," Leander offers. "You don't have to come every day. I won't let him cross until you say goodbye."

"I want to come," I say. When he raises an eyebrow and shoots me a sidelong glance, I shrug. "I don't mind listening to them while they wait their turn."

What I don't tell him is that what's happening here gives me a clue about what's going on with the war. So far, the few Kiskens I've seen were elderly. No one of fighting age and no one with solid spots, which I've learned is their fatal wound. They probably died of heart attacks or cancer. Something natural. I don't ask—the thought of talking to the Kiskens makes me itch all over. Memories of robana laced water being forced down my throat and a sacrificial sword ripping through my flesh scratch at the cage I locked them in. *Traitor, traitor, traitor* brushes against my ears, though they don't say a word.

"It seems like Theo's keeping his word," I say, pushing one painful memory away in exchange for another.

"Of course he is," Leander says. "Nothing is worth being sent to the Between. Not even a broken heart."

I roll my eyes, but his words tug on something deep inside me. I'm trying to ignore the fracture in my chest, not remember what I did to Theo's. Not that I'm doing a very good job of it. The look on his face when he begged me to deny the truth rakes through me every time I hear his name. But, if offering to come here didn't prove my feelings for him, nothing will. I need to forget. I grind my teeth together and slam the door shut on my emotions, twisting the key.

"Can we walk faster? I want to get off this thing." Leander picks up the pace without a word and the swirling water splashes under my feet. I squeeze back another wave of nausea. "Can I request a hovercraft for my birthday?"

His laugh draws the attention of the souls on the bank. They turn to watch our approach with quivering faces, and I scan the crowd. Oren isn't here again today, and an easy breath falls from my mouth. There are enough dead to keep us occupied until dinner, at least, and more always pop in throughout the day.

At the shoreline, a single step away from the safety of the river, Leander pauses like he's done every other day. I stifle a groan. "I'm not going to look at the arch again," I say before he can issue another warning.

"Are you sure?" He watches me warily. "If I lose you, Theo will murder me over and over for eternity. Plus, you know, you've sort of grown on me."

"Sort of?" I smirk. But I understand where his worry is coming from. Even if I don't look at the arch, it reaches for me, caressing my cheek, offering me peace. I feel the tug deep in my core. "And here I thought we were on our way to being friends."

The flicker of joy in his eyes is unmistakable, but, before he can say anything else, a high-pitched murmur flows through the crowd. I cringe as it grates against my eardrums like nails on a chalkboard. When the souls fall silent again, Leander steps into the fray, leaving wet, black footprints on the white rock. I don't let go of him until we're far from the river and any possibility of being knocked in. I shake my stiff fingers and eye the throng.

"The same as always," Leander murmurs.

Don't look at the arch, stay away from the river, talk only to the calmer souls, and, if I can't be within arm's reach, be within earshot. It took a lot to get him to agree to that last one. For the first week, he made sure I was glued to his side, but the idleness of it drove me over the edge. There were things I could be doing, people I could be talking to, while he worked.

Besides, one day, for whatever reason, I could be standing here as one of them. I'd appreciate it if someone sat with me for a few minutes without another person hanging over us. Leander doesn't mean to rush them, but I can see the strain on his face when things get backed up.

I nod and turn, looking for an elderly person. Maybe it's because they lived full lives or were expecting death, but they seem to deal with this better. If I want to keep my sliver of freedom, I can't take risks until I learn to recognize the disgruntled souls.

A wrinkled woman with long strings of crystalline hair shimmers toward the back of the crowd. *Perfect.* I step in her direction but another soul flashes in front of me. I lean back on my heels to avoid crashing into him. "Sorry," I breathe. "I didn't see you."

"You," he says. A large fracture splits his skull. Cracks web out and chips flake around the gaping hole. I step away and try not to stare at what must be a grisly wound to his actual body. "You're not supposed to be here."

My nerves fire warning zaps along my spine. "Excuse me?"

"You're not like us." He matches each of my backward steps with one forward. "You shouldn't be here."

My breath catches and I almost look for Leander, but I'm too afraid to look away. "It's okay." I hold my hands up.

"But you're here." He cocks his head.

"Temporarily." My voice shakes.

He blinks rapidly. "And I'm here."

"I see that." My skin tingles and I shove down my rising panic. Any fast movement might set him off, and I have no intention of finding out which of us is faster. "Leander?" I call.

The soul latches onto my arm. "It isn't fair," he shouts.

A million icy needles penetrate me at once. The pain blinds me, my muscles convulsing. "Leander!" His name rips from my throat.

An arm wraps around my waist, yanking me backward, but the soul doesn't surrender his grip. Another scream rips from my throat as the skin under his hand burns with frost. Then Leander is beside me, his hand around the soul's throat. He tears the man away with one stiff tug and slams him to the ground. The man hits the rock with a sickening crack. Fury lights Leander's eyes, an expression I never would have thought he could show, and he drags the soul toward the arch. He tosses him through the onyx columns while the others flee the vicinity.

"Sorry," he says, running back. "I turned around for a minute and… Murder victims are almost always vengeful." He looks over my shoulder and back. "Are you okay?"

I nod, a roar filling my ears. I'm far from okay; it feels as if any move I make will splinter my body. When I reach for him, for the comfort of feeling a living thing, the arm around my waist tightens. I can barely feel the touch around my frozen middle, but I tear myself away as panic seizes my chest. I trip and land hard on the ground at Leander's feet.

"What is she doing on this side of the Black River?" a voice growls.

I jerk to my knees. *Theo?*

Leander offers me his hand and helps me to my feet. "She's looking for her brother."

I stay close to Leander, fearing both the souls that watch us from a distance and Theo's purpose in visiting the Netherworld. Has Ebris changed his mind? Has the war gone off course? The arch aches at my back—either a warning or an invitation.

"It's fine. *I'm* fine. I wanted to be useful," I say, blinking back the panic.

"It's not fine," Theo says. "I could've lost you forever."

I shake my head to ease the ringing in my ears. I swear he said *he* would lose me forever. As if he hasn't already. "Isn't that what you want?" My voice is laced with pain, my vocal cords taut and weary. "To seek your revenge and never see me again?"

His face tightens and his gaze drops to my chin. The way his mouth twitches, it looks as if he's chewing the inside corner of his mouth. He steps forward with half of his body. "I didn't mean what I said." He speaks quietly, halting between words. "I wouldn't have been able to do it. To kill you. I didn't mean…" His voice cracks.

Another screeching murmur builds as the souls creep forward. I'm not sure if they're merely curious or angry about what happened, but the atmosphere is different, thicker. The hair on the back of my neck stands on end. "Can we get out of here?" I ask.

Leander turns so his back blocks me from most of the souls. "Theodric, take her."

Theo grabs my hand and I narrow my eyes at Leander. Knowing he has to deal with the souls doesn't stop me from feeling as if he tossed me to a wolf as Theo strides back onto the river. My stomach flops.

"Wait," I whimper, ashamed at the desperation in my voice. He pauses a few feet from shore and turns his head to the side, waiting for a reason. If walking across the river is bad, standing on it is worse. "Nevermind. Keep going. If you let go of me, I swear I'll haunt you for all eternity."

I catch the hint of a smile before he faces forward again. Walking with Leander was slow and sure. Nerve-wracking but not as terrifying as Theo's heavy footfalls slamming against the invisible barrier. I wipe away the water as it splashes my face and try not to dry heave. When we finally—*finally*—reach the other side, the force of hitting solid ground reverberates up my legs.

Theo leads me around the base of the mountain instead of up the stairs to Leander's back entrance. His steady pull is the only thing keeping me moving, and the warmth of his hand spreads throughout my body, chasing away the chill. Without the energy to pull away, I allow myself a moment to enjoy the familiarity of it.

It isn't something I ever expected to feel again—his hand in mind. His expression when he said he would lose me…That was real. There's no reason he should fake it after everything, but I clamp down on the thought. It's dangerous to let my mind wander in that direction. It will only hurt more when he leaves. I tug free from his grip and stop.

His shoulder blades shift under his cotton shirt. The soft blues and yellows of the Netherworld play against the deep tan on his arms. "Cassia—"

"No. You don't get to go first." A deep breath scratches at my raw throat, and I realize I don't actually have anything to say. No more explanations or apologies waiting to be heard. Instead, I ask, "What are you doing here?"

"I wanted to see you."

I open my mouth but say nothing. I'm not sure what to do with this version of Theo. I'm not even sure what version this is.

"We need to talk," he adds.

I hesitate. I don't think I can bare another angry tirade when the last one is engraved in my memory. But, against my will, a small kernel of hope forms in my chest. "About what?" I mumble.

"Your brother is still alive," he whispers.

I look toward the river, to where Oren hasn't been. "I know."

"He lost an arm."

"What?" I gasp. "How?"

"A wound became infected." Theo scratches the back of his neck. "I told him what happened to you. That you were taken to the temple and forced to become a sacrifice."

I step in front of him, everything else falling away. "You talked to him? What did he say? Where is he now?"

"He's safe in Kisk. Angry. Sad. But safe."

Safe in Kisk. Those words seem too good to be true. Nothing has been safe there in years, and now my brother, the last living person in my family, the last human I love, is back. A half-sigh, half-laugh squeezes from my lungs.

"The war is officially over." He inches closer and I notice how wrinkled his clothes are, how rumpled his hair is. There's a ring of dirt around his fingernails. Energy sparks between us as he lifts a hand toward mine. When it drops without touching me, I bite my lip.

"Good," I say, breathlessly.

He taps the toe of his boot on the ground. Small, hollow thuds echo around us with each one. "Ebris restored me."

I blink. That hadn't been part of the deal. My mind reels in an attempt to understand why Ebris would give Theo his power back after the way I left them. "I'm glad."

"Are you?" he asks.

"Of course." I lower my brows and force the cork tighter over my emotions. "Why wouldn't I be?"

"It's…" He reaches out again, this time toward my cheek, but decides against touching me a second time. "You don't look happy, is all."

A vice grip tightens around my center. Of course I'm happy. The war is over and Theo did something worthy of being restored. Despite everything, he won. It doesn't wipe the slate clean—not for us—but this is what he wanted most. I force a smile. "I *am* happy for you, Theo."

He exhales quickly. "Cassia, I…"

"What are you really doing here?" I demand. The more my body thaws, the looser the hold on my patience becomes. "If you hate me so much, why would you come all the way to the Netherworld to tell me this? Did you want to rub it in that you're back to normal while I'm forced to stay down here?"

It's a low blow; I offered to come but I refuse to take the words back.

"I don't hate you," he says, quickly.

I laugh miserably. "Theo, I saw the look on your face when I admitted knowing Oren was alive."

"Only because I didn't believe you hadn't used me," he says. "I thought you were working with Astra. I thought…I thought you were with me to gain something, not because you cared." His head falls, wisps of hair skimming his forehead. "I know it started that way for you, but it didn't for me. Ever since that night we played Fate, I've felt something. It took me so long to understand my feelings for you, and when I did…" He winces. "I've never felt such consuming pain before."

I cross my arms, rubbing my palms over them. "I'm not sure what you're trying to say."

"I was afraid of *this*. Of not being in control." Electricity races through me as he glides his fingertips up my forearm. "Of giving it to you."

I clasp my hands behind my back to break contact. Not because I don't want him to touch me, but because I want it too much. I need to be able to think. "I don't want to control anything. That's not how a relationship is supposed to be."

"Is that what you want?" His voice wavers as he inches closer. "A relationship?"

Do I? I did. I still love him but we both lied, both hurt the other. I'm not sure how to come back from that. "It's complicated."

"It doesn't have to be."

A groan builds inside me, a bubble of frustration and want and regret. I don't let it surface. "Theo…"

"Please," he pleads. "If you had feelings for me, with all my flaws and all the terrible things I've done, let me try to make it up to you. I want to be better. You make me want to be better."

"I—"

"I know I've been horrible," he says, rushing ahead before I have time to say no. "I've only ever been feared, and I think I felt like I had to live up to that. I was wrong. I know that now."

"You've scared me plenty of times," I grumble.

He winces again. "I'm sorry. For everything, I'm sorry."

My heart hammers, one painful throb after another, and I ball my hands to stop them from shaking. I want to give him another chance as much as he seems to want to give me one, but pretending none of what happened, happened isn't healthy. There's a lot we have to work out, but isn't that what a chance is for? To see if we can overcome everything? He isn't asking me to commit to forever—just to right now. The treacherous sense of hope tries to break its chains again.

"Here." He pulls the ring off his right, middle finger. "If I do anything wrong, or if I can't make you happy, use this. It will take you to any of the temples without me." He holds it between us. "Anywhere."

I fixate on the black stone and reach out slowly. Complete freedom is a tempting offer. I could go wherever, do anything. I could see Oren without letting him see me. I can't very well waltz up to his door now that he knows my fate. But, even if he didn't, it wouldn't be fair to keep disappearing on him. I could never explain any of this. And then there's Leander. He'll be alone again, but with the ring I can visit him any time I want.

I inhale. This decision can't be made for either of our brothers. Theo is asking me to give *us* a second chance. He and I—not us and everyone else. My hand drops, empty.

"I'm not sure this is a good idea," I say. My body shudders in revolt.

Theo's fingers shake so violently he has to try twice to push the ring onto the tip of his thumb. "Before you decide, there's something you should know."

It sounds like the words are being torn from him, and I nearly slap my hands over his mouth to stop more from following. I don't though. Whatever it is, I need to hear it.

"Astra." His shoulders slump and he covers his face. "She wanted to stop the war. She thought that if we cared for each other, the sacrifice would be accepted."

I suck in a breath. "Are you saying Astra made us…" *Love each other.* I don't say the words—he said *cared for,* and I'm too much of a coward to admit anything more. I'm not sure what exactly he felt, or feels. Is it even what I feel? Is any of this real or some expertly spun illusion? My head spins, my vision blurring. "I don't…" I'm not sure what I want to say. That I don't believe it, or that I'm about to throw up. Both are true. Everything I thought I knew scatters around me, falling, spinning, as if I'd suddenly found myself in a snow globe.

"It wasn't until after…" He drops his hands and winces. "After the temple. When she brought you a change of clothes. But by then I already…" He sighs, a rapid exhale. "It doesn't change how I feel about you. Does it change things for you?"

"Change what things?" I say in a high voice. "You changed things between us before I came to the Netherworld and now this? How am I supposed to feel? Do I even get a choice, or is Astra going to step in and conjure more magic to make me forget?"

"Astra's in the Between." He lifts his hands to the space between us. "For this."

Good! I want to shout. I should have listened to Cy; he warned me over and over. He knew and I didn't listen—didn't want to listen. Because I thought I knew what I was doing.

"She couldn't have done anything to us unless there was something there to start with. A bead for her to string her power through," he explains in a hushed voice. "This is real. Deep down I know it is."

I shake my head and feel pieces of my life rattle against each other.

"Just..." He takes a tentative step forward and places his hands on my upper arms. The touch is feather light, but I shiver from head to toe. "*Feel* for a moment. Just one. Please. Don't write us off because of my sister."

I squeeze my jaw shut to keep my teeth from clattering. I don't have to stop and feel because I already know. My body thrums in response to his hands on me and warmth builds in the pit of my stomach. My fingers itch to return his touch and my lips burn in their desire to kiss him. I remember the coarseness of his hair and the firmness of his muscle. The brilliance of his smile and the way his face lights up when he's happy.

"Another chance," he pleads. "That's all I'm asking for."

The familiar scent of steel, of him, finds its way to my nose. I breathe it in, letting it consume me. This is crazy—*I* must be crazy—but I think, somehow, someway, he's right. Deep down, this is real. "We're a mess." I lean forward to try catching his gaze, but it's stuck on the hollow of my throat. "You know that, right?"

A smile touches his lips. "I hear love can do that to people."

I blink. It feels as if my soul has detached, soaring away from my body and toward his. "Are you trying to tell me you love me?" I ask, low and uncertain. He's implied it, but I want the reassurance of the words. After everything, I need to hear it out loud if I'm going to take a chance on us.

The intensity of his blue eyes as they lift to mine steals my breath. "I am."

"Say it," I whisper.

"I love you."

I leap to my toes, taking his face in my hands, and press my mouth against his. There's no hesitation as he pulls me against him and slides his hands to the base of my neck. While we hold each other gently, our lips are frantic. Starved for each other. My head swims with anger and confusion, relief and joy.

Theo steps back, his fingers curling into my hair, and I groan at the distance between us. His lips are swollen, his breathing as ragged as mine. "Is that a yes?" he asks.

I step back so his hands fall away and pluck the ring from his finger. I slip the too-large band over my thumb and smile. "Yes."

ACKNOWLEDGMENTS

First, thank you to my family. To my husband for always pushing me forward. To Ian and Ryan – I love you ten. To Nonny and Poppy for raising me to be the person I am today. To my mother for making up bedtime stories like Princess Periwinkle and Goldie Finch, and for reading my drafts with unflinching honesty. To my father for always being there to talk(even about the bizarre stuff). To my aunt for fostering a love of fantasy. To my brothers and sisters for being such remarkablepeople. And to Lindsay and Judy because sometimes family isn't blood.

I'm incredibly lucky to work with Radiant Crown Publishing. I'm so honored that Olivia saw something special in Theo and Cassia and offered me this opportunity to share their story. The openness and dedication they've given are unparalleled. A million times, thank you! I couldn't have asked for more.

To my editor, Leah, thank you for all the hard work you poured into this project! You're awesome!

Endless appreciation goes out to my critique partners: Lauren – you'll always be Leander's first and biggest fan. JoAnna – you're one of the sweetest people I know. Vanessa – long live Bash! Amanda – your advice is beyond priceless. I never could have done this without you guys.

Stacy – I can't thank you enough for everything. When I moved to Maine, I knew no one and our weekly Panera write-ins gave me something to look forward to. You've listened to me talk out more plot problems than anyone and are always ready to help. Your advice, support, and friendship mean the world.

A special shout out to all the amazingly supportive folks on Twitter!

Finally, thank you for taking this journey with me!

ABOUT AMBER

 Amber R. Duell was born and raised in a small town in Central New York. While it will always be home, she's spent the last six years living in Germany and Maine as a military wife where the next step is always an adventure. When Amber isn't writing, she's wrangling her two young sons. She is a lover of history, a fan of snowboarding, and a travel enthusiast. In her downtime, she can be found curling up with a good book and a cat or two.

FOR MORE, VISIT:

WWW.AMBERRDUELL.COM

END OF THE OSTRAN WAR

YEAR 1202
THEODRIC

A glass pawn explodes in a shower of yellow dust, and I grip the scrolled edge of the war table. Beneath the new layer of powder, a kaleidoscope of color decorates the onyx tabletop. Orange, purple, white, blue, pink—every eastern country is in play, but gray pieces dominate the board.

The Ostran Emperor won't stop. Not until every man and woman bends the knee.

This... I never should have agreed to this. To the utter destruction of five prosperous countries in exchange for a few pretty brides and wagons full of gold. They aren't even *my* brides, *my* gold. Not that I want either, but they belong to Ebris. Or they used to before Ostra turned to me in gratitude of so many victories. Victories that should have ended last year when Ebris demanded I stop the war.

But it was one order too many, and I didn't listen.

Why didn't I listen?